Praise for *Christmas at the Chalet*

"A beautiful and authentically heartfelt tale—Anita Hughes reminds us of the true miracle of Christmas: love."

—Patti Callahan Henry, *New York Times* bestselling author of *Becoming Mrs. Lewis*

"A vivid picture of blossoming love . . . in the opulent setting of St. Moritz. This enchanting love story will leave you pining for the winter holidays. I loved every page."

—Tracey Garvis Graves, *New York Times* bestselling author of *The Girl He Used to Know*

"*Christmas at the Chalet* hits all the right notes—a beautiful backdrop, a budding romance, and a little Christmas magic to help it all come together. A wonderful holiday indulgence!"

—Liz Fenton and Lisa Steinke, bestselling authors of *The Good Widow*

"*Christmas at the Chalet* transports readers to a world of glamour and romance, and reminds us that a fairy-tale wedding isn't just about the dress. It's about making sure the right Prince Charming is waiting at the end of the aisle."

—Barbara Davis, bestselling author of *When Never Comes*

"*Christmas at the Chalet* reminds us of why we first fell in love with reading. Escaping in the pages of picturesque St. Moritz and the glamorous world of bridal fashion . . . A dazzling read."

—Rochelle B. Weinstein, *USA Today* bestselling author of *Somebody's Daughter*

"If you need to escape during the holidays, read this book. No, really. Read it. Your in-laws, your stress, and your to-do list will all go away as you head to St. Moritz for a sweet romance."

—Cathy Lamb, author of *The Man She Married*

Also by Anita Hughes

California Summer
Christmas in London
Emerald Coast
White Sand, Blue Sea
Christmas in Paris
Santorini Sunsets
Island in the Sea
Rome in Love
French Coast
Lake Como
Market Street
Monarch Beach

CHRISTMAS AT THE CHALET

ANITA HUGHES

St. Martin's Griffin ✹ New York

CHRISTMAS AT THE CHALET. Copyright © 2018 by Anita Hughes. All rights reserved. Printed in the United States of America. For information, address St. Martin's Press, 175 Fifth Avenue, New York, N.Y. 10010.

www.stmartins.com

The Library of Congress Cataloging-in-Publication Data is available upon request.

ISBN 978-1-250-16667-8 (trade paperback)
ISBN 978-1-250-16668-5 (ebook)

Our books may be purchased in bulk for promotional, educational, or business use. Please contact your local bookseller or the Macmillan Corporate and Premium Sales Department at 1-800-221-7945, extension 5442, or by email at MacmillanSpecialMarkets@macmillan.com.

First Edition: October 2018

10 9 8 7 6 5 4 3 2 1

To my mother

CHRISTMAS AT THE CHALET

One

Seven Days Before the Fashion Show
5:00 p.m.

Felicity

FELICITY STOOD ON THE ELEGANT terrace of Badrutt's Palace
Hotel and thought St. Moritz really was the perfect location for
the debut of her winter collection. The snow-covered mountain
at sunset was pink and ivory, like the inside of an oyster shell. If
she peered over the ledge she could see the village with its quaint
chalets, as well as the frozen lake, rimmed with fir trees and filled
with ice-skaters wearing bright parkas and fur hats.

When Raj first suggested holding the fashion show for Felicity
Grant Bridal in St. Moritz during the week between Christmas
and New Year's, Felicity had been hesitant. It seemed like a logis-
tical nightmare to transport the dresses from New York to Switzerland. And how would they keep an eye on half a dozen models in
one of the most hedonistic capitals in the world?

But Raj always thought bigger than she did, and that's one of
the reasons they were successful.

"We'll book a whole row on the plane for the dresses," he said one evening as they sat in the bridal atelier on Madison Avenue in New York.

"What about the cream tulle?" Felicity asked worriedly. "If anyone so much as breathes on it, it wrinkles. And think about the models. I'm afraid of being responsible for them in a foreign country. I know they have contracts, but what if one of them falls in love and runs off with an Austrian ski instructor and we never hear from her again?"

"I'll personally hold the tulle on the plane," Raj suggested. "And we'll insist that the girls be responsible for each other. All the cosmopolitan set who frequent Paris and London will be there. At night there will be sleigh rides, and during the day everyone will attend the snow polo matches. They'll practically be forced to watch the show if we use the famous catwalk at Badrutt's Palace Hotel as a runway."

Raj was right, and Felicity had given in. This was her eighth collection, and she needed a bigger stage than the usual shows in New York, held in downtown lofts littered with fake snow. The same tired press, squeezing in a viewing between Elie Saab's event in her private atelier and the new designers who were always popping up with outrageous designs: rhinestone-studded pantsuits for the bride, or leopard-skin bridesmaids' dresses.

Felicity wished she were relaxing in the Palace's lobby, with its massive stone fireplace and picture windows overlooking the ski runs. Instead she was shivering on the hotel terrace and waiting for Katie, the model, to arrive.

The sneak-peek photo shoot was scheduled to begin in thirty minutes, and the model was missing. If Katie didn't appear soon, the pink-edged snow would be replaced by pitch darkness, and the wedding blogs and online fashion magazines would go with their backup fluff pieces and probably wouldn't cover the collection at all.

And the dress! She stroked the crepe fabric and fell in love with it all over again. It had come to her as her best ideas always did, at completely inopportune times: when she and her boyfriend Adam were going to dinner with one of his important clients, or in the middle of a heated game of Scrabble, or even in the delicious afterglow of making love.

That was the wonderful thing about Adam. He didn't mind meeting the client for cocktails by himself, or setting the board game aside, or letting her peel herself away from his embrace and slip out of bed. How many nights had she sat at the oversized desk in Adam's bedroom, wrapped in his robe and sketching on her notepad? She mused at how lucky she was that he took her career as seriously as she did.

The crepe sheath wasn't the most elaborate wedding dress in the show. That was an organza gown with diamond buttons shaped like snowflakes, which no one had seen except Raj and herself. That gown was safely locked in the hotel's storeroom, and Nell, the show's most famous model, would wear it for the show's grand finale. Felicity could see it so clearly, it gave her goose bumps: Nell with her huge emerald eyes striding down the runway, while the orchestra played and fireworks exploded above the mountain.

This dress was simple and fluid, like a waterfall that had frozen midflight. She had specifically chosen Katie to wear it, because Katie's natural beauty wouldn't overpower the sweetheart neckline and illusion sleeves. But Katie had disappeared when all the other models went to watch the luge races, and no one had seen her since.

Felicity spotted Raj striding toward her and gulped. He was alone, his shoulders hunched the way they were whenever he had to deliver bad news: a bolt of fabric had been ruined in a warehouse flood, etc.

"You promised you wouldn't come back until you found Katie," Felicity said. "St. Moritz is a small village, and it's five o'clock in the evening. It's much too early to go dancing, and anyway, she must be exhausted. We only arrived this morning; I can barely keep my eyes open from jet lag."

"I did find her." Raj joined Felicity on the terrace. "She's buried in an eiderdown comforter with a hot compress on her forehead. Apparently Katie suffers from altitude sickness, and every time she stands up she passes out."

"You specifically requested models who were used to high altitudes." Felicity frowned. "It was one of the prerequisites of the job."

"Katie's from Kentucky. The highest thing she's ever climbed is the ladder in her parents' barn." Raj sighed. "She sent the money she made this fall to her mother to buy Christmas presents for her younger siblings, and she's going to be late on her January rent." Raj paused. "She lied to the agency."

"Oh, dear," Felicity commented. That was one of the pitfalls of working with high-fashion models. They seemed impossibly sophisticated, with their long eyelashes and wide red mouths, but many of them had arrived in Manhattan with nothing but overdue credit cards and a suitcase. They supported boyfriends or families back home, and spent the rest of their money on trendy restaurants and apartments in doorman buildings.

"We'll have to send her home and ask the agency to provide a replacement," Raj suggested.

"How could she! Everyone knows how important this show is," Felicity said angrily. But then she thought of the pictures Katie had shown her of her twelve-year-old twin siblings. They both had big brown eyes and freckles on their noses. "It would be awful to send her home. It's Christmas; what if her mother has to take back the presents? Perhaps we should give her another chance."

"Katie is scheduled to wear three dresses in the show. The A-line with the matching ermine cape, the hand-embroidered tulle, and that spectacular Grecian column with the twelve-foot silk train."

"Katie would look lovely in the Grecian gown," Felicity said longingly. "I sewed two dozen amethysts into the train to make her eyes look like tide pools. Why don't we give her one day to stay in bed? If she's still not better, we can get someone else to model the dresses." She surveyed the terrace, packed with men and women sipping après-ski cocktails. "A pretty Swiss girl who's a waitress or works in a boutique."

"*Modern Bride* and all the important magazines will be there." Raj shook his head. "We can't parade around some girl who's used to folding sweaters or carrying trays of peach Marnier."

Felicity thought how lucky she was to have Raj as her business partner. If it weren't for him, Felicity Grant Bridal would still be a collection of doodles that covered every surface of the apartment they'd shared seven years ago during college.

Raj's parents had sent him to America from India to attend NYU and study computer science. He'd lasted three semesters before he realized he wasn't cut out to sit in front of a screen all day and decipher code. Raj was a people person; everyone loved his good looks and warm smile.

Felicity used to laugh at how girls would stop by the flat with a warm paper bag and tall-sized cups from Starbucks. Raj had somehow gotten into a conversation with a girl standing in line, and they'd both agreed the pumpkin muffins were the best they'd ever tasted. They exchanged contacts, and he might have mentioned he could only afford Starbucks once a week, but he hadn't expected her to show up with a whole bag of muffins and two cinnamon lattes with extra foam.

The wonderful thing about Raj was that he never hurt anyone's feelings. If he had to break up with a girl, he sent her flowers and said she was beautiful but he wasn't ready for anything serious. His work was his passion, and he didn't want to shortchange her.

And Raj charmed everyone in business. Every editor and online blogger fell in love with his easygoing nature and enthusiasm. If Raj predicted that Felicity's newest line was going to rival anything by Monique Lhuillier or Reem Acra, they happily agreed. And when he'd promised one mother of the bride (referred to him by Manhattan's most exclusive planner) that Felicity would design a tiered lace gown with a headdress that would make her daughter resemble Grace Kelly, the woman couldn't hand him a deposit fast enough.

Few people besides Felicity knew that underneath Raj's casual image—the dark hair that was always in need of a cut, the loafers that had seen too many years of wear—he had the sharp focus of an attack dog. Felicity Grant Bridal had grown from a sewing machine wedged into the hall closet to showrooms on Madison Avenue and in the Hamptons.

"You don't want to only be known in Manhattan and Sag Harbor forever." Raj rubbed his leather gloves. "We want Felicity Grant to be the name on everyone's lips in Hong Kong and Milan and Dubai."

Felicity pictured the dresses draped over every surface in her hotel suite and sighed. She had been working on this collection for so long; she couldn't let anything spoil it now.

"Call the agency and ask them to put a model on the next plane," Felicity said, relenting. "We'll loan Katie the money out of petty cash until her next assignment."

"You do know that Felicity Grant isn't a charity or a bank, right?" Raj grunted. "But it *is* Christmas, and Katie *does* have the loveliest smile. I guess this time I can make an exception."

"We'll have to cancel today's photo shoot," Felicity said, remembering. "The photographer will be furious. He was already grumbling about missing happy hour at the Dracula Club. All the celebrities hang out there, and a quick photo of some actor drinking schnapps and yodeling can earn him a fortune."

"We can't cancel," Raj protested. "I told *Style Me Pretty* and *Martha Stewart Weddings* that they had the exclusive first look at your collection."

"You promised both of them an exclusive?" Felicity laughed.

"I can't help it if someone leaks a photo and it ends up on more than one site. We have to do the photo shoot." He shrugged.

"I don't see how," Felicity said. The sun was setting, and suddenly she was cold. She was wearing almost every warm item she owned—cashmere slacks and a turtleneck under a wool coat—but they were no match for the Alps. Now she understood why so many of the women she saw had swathed themselves in mink and fox. She'd never kill an animal, but it really was the only effective way to stay warm.

Raj was looking at her the way he examined yards of brocade from a new supplier for blemishes. "You'll have to wear it."

"Me!" Felicity choked out. "Katie is almost six feet tall; the dress would be much too long. And I don't have a big enough bust. I'd look like a pipe cleaner."

"You don't have to walk down a runway. These are mood shots. Lean against the balcony and gaze at the snow-capped mountains. Hold a champagne flute and wink enticingly at the camera," Raj said, waving his hands. "And you're the designer; you know how to make small-breasted women look like *Sports Illustrated* covers."

"I'd never encourage a bride to wear a dress that isn't a natural fit for her figure," Felicity replied.

"You did when she waved a big check and insisted on wearing a mermaid-style gown, even though it made her look like a baby hippo."

"That was only once," Felicity said, feeling slightly guilty. Felicity had tried to convince the bride that a classic ball gown would show off her small waist and slender calves, but she had her heart set on the form-fitting dress she'd seen in a magazine. It was just after they had moved into the showroom, and Raj was worried about making rent, so Felicity had swallowed her suggestions and designed a dress that could barely contain the bride's curves.

"I suppose I could pin the hem and stuff some tissues into the bodice," Felicity said uncertainly. "But what about my hair and makeup? And I'm wearing boots. If I go all the way back to my room to get a pair of shoes, we'll lose the light."

"Your hair looks fine—just add a little blush and lipstick and you'll be gorgeous. Leave the shoes to me." He propelled her toward the glass doors. "Take the dress into the nearest bathroom and I'll meet you here in ten minutes. And practice that pouty look you get when you're angry at me for not letting you tip the pizza guy ten dollars."

Felicity gazed into the full-length mirror in the powder room and sighed. It really was the most beautiful dress. The side panels were white satin, and the sweeping train was barely longer than the gown and made a rustling sound when the bride moved. Felicity believed the bride should be the center of attention, and everyone needed to know when she walked by.

If she and Adam got married, she wanted a gown just like it: perhaps accompanied by a bouquet of purple peonies for a summer wedding in the Hamptons, or red and white roses if they held a winter ceremony at his parents' club in Manhattan. But they had gotten into a silly fight the day she left, and now a wedding seemed as far off as the white-sand beaches of Tahiti.

She reapplied her lipstick and reminded herself she didn't have time to think about Adam. If she didn't hurry, Raj would come looking for her and make a scene in the powder room of Badrutt's Palace Hotel.

The lace train trailed behind her and she walked quickly through the Grand Hall. It was known as the meeting place of St. Moritz, and all around her people were embracing each other and kissing each other on the cheek. The parquet floor was covered with rich oriental rugs, the oversized armchairs were littered with velvet cushions, and lining the walls were marble columns and huge urns of flowers. It looked so inviting; she longed to sit by the fire and order an amaretto and cream and a crepe with powdered sugar.

The terrace was crowded with après-skiers, and Felicity was worried she wouldn't find Raj and the photographer.

"Why are you looking at me like that?" she said when she spotted Raj standing in the corner. "Putting on a wedding dress takes time. There are buttons and hooks, and you have to get the hem to sit just right."

"I was thinking how stunning you look," Raj said, and whistled. "If you and Adam weren't the best couple I know, and if I couldn't personally attest to the fact that he's a great guy, I would be jealous."

"It's only a dress. Adam and I aren't getting married any time soon." Felicity flushed. "Besides, there's no room in your brain for jealousy. It's too full of flight attendants' phone numbers."

"I never date flight attendants; they treat your apartment like their own storage space." Raj handed her a pair of heels. "Here, put these on."

"Where did you get them?" Felicity admired the pink satin toes and kitten heels.

"Let's just say there's a brunette at the bar wearing an evening gown and no shoes." Raj grinned. "We better hurry. I promised I'd return them before she finishes her Moscow Mule."

The photographer pointed his camera at Felicity and she suddenly froze. She never modeled her own designs. She was always the one standing backstage, praying that a dress made of the sheerest tulle wouldn't be see-through under the lights, or that no one would step on a princess-style gown embroidered with freshwater pearls.

At first all she could think about was the icy cold air on her neck. But then the touch of the fabric against her skin was intoxicating, and the click of the camera's flash was a warm flame. She leaned against the snow-covered railing. The diamond earrings that Raj had hastily clipped in her ears were glittering like fireflies, and her train was the most glorious puddle of silk.

"That was perfect," Raj said when the photographer had gotten his shots. "I'd stay and have a drink, but I just got a text from one of the models. Apparently Crystal is upset that the Cresta Run is only open to men. She's threatening to post her disappointment on Instagram."

"Why shouldn't Crystal do the Cresta Run if she's brave enough?" Felicity removed the earrings from her ears.

"I'm a big supporter of female equality, but if that rule stops her from getting on a toboggan and careening headfirst down a course at 165 miles an hour before she walks down the runway, I'm all for obeying the rules." Raj slipped the earrings in his pocket. "You must be freezing, get yourself a brandy or hot chocolate. Don't order from room service—I checked the prices, and they were so outrageous I almost needed a Xanax."

Felicity stood in front of the powder-room mirror and unhooked her dress. The magical feeling of sipping champagne with the mountain looming behind her dissolved, and she felt like one of the wooden dolls in the Nutcracker ballet after the prince disappeared. She looped the train over the hanger and suddenly missed Adam so much it was a physical ache.

Their fight had started innocently enough; Adam had urged her to spend the night at his apartment on Christmas Eve and insisted on serving her breakfast in bed. She couldn't help hoping there would be a velvet box nestled between the slices of toast and pots of jam. They had been talking about getting married all year. But instead there was a flat envelope tied with a gold ribbon.

"I wanted to give you my present before we meet my parents at the club." Adam perched on the side of the bed. His light brown hair stuck

up straight, the way it did first thing in the morning, but he was boy-
ishly handsome in an old NYU T-shirt and sweats.

Felicity untied the ribbon and opened the envelope. "A day at Eliz-
abeth Arden's spa." Felicity looked up and gulped.

"You never give yourself time off." Adam kissed her. "And we both
don't have time for a vacation. I figure it was this, or post bodyguards
at your apartment and keep you under house arrest until you get some
rest."

"A spa day is very thoughtful. But . . ." Felicity's voice trailed off.

"St. Moritz might be one of the most glamorous playgrounds in the
world, but I know Raj." Adam chuckled. "Personal massages won't be
in the budget. You'll be lucky if he pays for your meal on the plane."

Felicity put the envelope on the breakfast tray and took a deep
breath. She and Adam had been dating for six years, and they told each
other everything. She couldn't hide her feelings about the most impor-
tant aspect of their lives just because she was afraid of his reaction.

"You wanted to wait to get married until your management firm
was established and Felicity Grant Bridal wasn't mired in debt," Fe-
licity said. "Raj thinks we're going to turn a profit next year, and you're
signing clients faster than you can print contracts." Her voice wobbled.
"An engagement is supposed to be a surprise, but we've been talking
about it for months. I was hoping you might give me a ring."

"You know how it is starting your own company." He paced around
the room. "I wanted to come to St. Moritz, but the quarterback for the
LA Rams is in town and begged me to show him around. It's like that
all the time: an NBA basketball player who's looking for new manage-
ment, and has always wanted to climb the Empire State Building. A
hockey player from Toronto who wants to see a hockey match at
Madison Square Garden."

"It wouldn't be any different if we were married," Felicity said uncertainly.

"Why are we in a hurry to get married?" He approached the bed and caressed her cheek. "We love each other and always want to be together."

They were much happier than many of their newly married friends. They didn't fight over closet space, or feel guilty if they worked late, or wonder if it was good for their relationship to keep separate bank accounts.

But Felicity saw the brides when they emerged from the dressing room in her showroom. They studied their reflections in the three-way mirror, and suddenly were transformed from girls with frizzy hair and pale winter skin into gorgeous women with peaches-and-cream complexions.

"Can we talk about it later?" Adam stripped off his T-shirt and walked to the closet. "We'll be late for Christmas brunch."

"I'm afraid I won't be able to stay for the whole brunch." Felicity clutched the envelope. "My flight leaves this evening. I have to finish packing and make sure Raj brings all the veils and stockings."

"What do you mean, you're not staying?" Adam turned around. "It's Christmas brunch with my parents; they expect us both to be there."

Every year she and Adam traded off celebrating Christmas with his parents in Manhattan and her family in Michigan. But she had to keep it short. She couldn't bear for Adam's mother, Delilah, to stare at her naked ring finger as if she were examining a turkey to see if it needed more time in the oven.

At Thanksgiving Delilah had asked for Felicity's help with the pumpkin pie, and ushered her into the kitchen.

"I love my son, but he's a lot like his father." Delilah took the dessert *plates from the cabinet. "When John and I were dating, all my friends were picking out their wedding china, and I was still getting my hair styled for our Saturday nights." She took a bowl of whipped cream out of the fridge. "John has always been a terrible hypochondriac. One night I invited a few couples for dinner, and one of the men was a medical student. He said studies have shown that men who marry later in life are more likely to die from a heart attack." She chuckled. "I had a ring on my finger within a month."*

"I've never heard that before." Felicity cut slices of pumpkin pie.

"The point is, every man has a weak spot—you just have to find it," Delilah replied. "I'd love to throw you a beautiful wedding, but mostly I want you both to be happy."

"We are happy," Felicity assured her. "We have the same goals and good careers and fun social lives."

"Life is about building something together. Sometimes John is so irritating, I want to stab him with a martini olive, but marrying him is the best thing I've ever done," Delilah answered knowingly. "Talk to Adam about the next steps in your relationship. You'll both thank me."

Felicity studied herself in the powder-room mirror at Badrutt's Palace and remembered the rest of Christmas Day, which had gone miserably. The distance between her and Adam at brunch had been as wide as the Gulf of Mexico. When she had stood up at the table and said she had to pack, she could tell that he was angry.

Later, on the drive to JFK, she and Adam were silent. At any other time he would rest his hand on her knee and she'd talk excitedly about bringing Adam his favorite Swiss chocolates. Even when they reached the departure terminal, and the sidewalk overflowed with couples hugging goodbye, she couldn't think of anything to say. She pecked Adam on the cheek and mumbled that the next time they saw each other it would be the new year.

Perhaps Adam was right. Maybe she could wait a little longer to get married. Even if she hired a wedding planner, she'd have to make so many decisions. As soon as she returned from St. Moritz, she had to start designing the summer collection. Wasn't the important thing that they loved each other, and wanted to be together? They shared so many things in common. They both planned on donating a percentage of their profits to charity, and their dream was to work hard and retire when they were sixty so they could travel the world.

She had been so upset yesterday that she hadn't even given Adam his Christmas present. It was sitting in her apartment in New York, and he wouldn't get it until after New Year's. What if she picked up something in the village and asked the concierge to overnight it to him? After all, she was in St. Moritz, and the guidebook said it boasted some of the best shopping in Europe.

She left the gown with the concierge and walked the few blocks into the village. It was even prettier than it had looked from the balcony. Christmas lights were wrapped around lampposts, and shop windows were decorated with gold and silver snowflakes. Carriages were outfitted with thick blankets and sleigh bells. A mannequin at Prada wore head-to-toe cashmere, and Tiffany's had a blue Christmas tree festooned with diamond ornaments.

It was almost seven p.m. and she realized she was starving. The food in the shop windows all looked so tempting. Thick sausages hung in the delicatessen, patisseries held trays of cakes with raspberry fillings, and there were boxes of pralines coated with white chocolate at Godiva Chocolatier. First she would buy the present for Adam, and then she would treat herself to a Swiss delicacy.

She entered a men's store and eyed the stacks of wool scarves.

"Can I help you?" A saleswoman approached her.

"I'm looking for a present for my boyfriend," Felicity replied. "He's in New York, and I want to buy something very special."

"I have just the thing." The saleswoman walked to the back. She returned with the softest cashmere sweater Felicity had ever felt.

"This was handmade in St. Moritz." The woman handed it to her. "You won't find anything like it in America."

Felicity glanced at the price tag and gulped. It didn't matter if it did serious damage to her credit card. The important thing was that she sent Adam something to show how much she missed him.

"I'll take it." Felicity handed her the card. "Could you please wrap it up?"

The saleswoman handed her the wrapped box and Felicity walked back onto the street. A soft snow was falling, and the sidewalk was slick with snowflakes. Suddenly her heel slipped, and the package flew in the air. She reached for it and landed on her back on the pavement. The pain in her ankle was so sharp she couldn't catch her breath.

"Are you all right?" A man crouched beside her. "You took a bad fall."

"Thank you, I'm fine," she said, rubbing her ankle. "It's nothing."

"You're not fine. That's a nasty bump. I'm a doctor—can I take a look?" he asked. "You shouldn't move until we see if it's sprained or broken."

Felicity glanced at her borrowed heels and realized she had forgotten to change into her boots. "That's very kind, but I really have to go." She gathered her purse. "I have an important package to mail."

She tried to stand up, but the pain was so fierce that her cheeks paled and she gasped.

"I told you not to move—you could do more damage," he said with a smile. "My name is Dr. Gabriel Innes. Let me help you inside, and I'll take a look where it's warm."

"I appreciate the offer, but I don't have time." Felicity looked at him properly. He was in his early thirties, with dark hair and brown eyes. He was wearing a sweater with a snowflake pattern and corduroy slacks. "I have to mail this package tonight. I promise I'll see the doctor at the hotel, you don't have to worry."

"If you try to limp up the hill to wherever you're staying, your ankle will be the size of a baby calf's," he said, concerned. "Put your arms around my neck and I'll carry you."

Before she could protest, he picked her up in his arms. He carried her across the street and into a brick building with plate glass windows.

"This is Hotel Hauser," he said, as they entered a lobby with a stone fireplace. "It's a St. Moritz institution."

"Oh, it's lovely!" Felicity inhaled the scent of logs burning. Stockings hung from the mantle, and there was a giant Christmas tree with red and green ornaments.

"We'll sit in the restaurant and the hostess will get us a cold compress. The concierge is my friend, and I'll ask him to mail your package. You can relax and have a glass of elderberry punch with vodka." Gabriel carried her into a wide room with a beamed ceiling.

Felicity sank into a booth and admired the blond wood floors and velvet wallpaper. The walls were covered with posters of movie stars, and she noticed a glass case filled with tarts and strudels that made her mouth water.

Gabriel spoke to the waitress in German, and she brought plates of veal sausage and rösti potatoes and homemade ravioli. There was a wedge of semi-hard cheese with a thick orange rind and crusty bread.

"God, I forgot I was so hungry," Felicity said when Gabriel had wrapped her ankle in an ice pack and propped it on a chair. "You don't even know me, and you're being so kind. This all looks delicious."

"It's my pleasure. I forget to eat all the time when I'm working," he said, scooping up ravioli. "You can't miss out on the Hauser's Emmental cheese, it's the best in the Engadin valley." He leaned back and studied Felicity's pale cheeks. "Sip your drink and you'll feel better."

The ice pack did feel heavenly; the throbbing in her ankle was reduced to a dull ache.

"I really shouldn't." She shook her head. "If I drink alcohol after an international flight I get dizzy. And it's terrible for jet lag; I won't get anything done."

"Doctor's orders," he said jovially. "You've had a nasty fall, and it will make you feel much better." He placed the glass in front of her. "If you don't, you'll be knocking at my door at midnight pleading for a Vicodin." He offered a smile. "I'm afraid my bedside manner won't be very good. I'm prone to insomnia, and I get cranky if anyone disturbs my sleep."

"You've done so much, I wouldn't dream of disturbing you. Anyway, I'm good at handling pain, and I have to stay awake." She pushed the glass away. "I've got to make sure six models are in their beds by eleven p.m., or they'll never wake up for their morning photo shoot."

"That doesn't sound like someone on holiday," Gabriel said.

"I'm a wedding dress designer," Felicity explained. "I'm debuting my winter collection at Badrutt's Palace Hotel on New Year's Eve. Raj had the idea to take photos all week and post them on social media. We're going to show the girls at snow polo matches, and playing blackjack at the casino, and catching the sun at those wonderful huts on top of the mountain."

"Who's Raj?" Gabriel asked.

"He's my business partner," she answered. She had forgotten about Raj! She grabbed her phone and sent a text explaining that she'd forgotten to give him the shoes, but she'd be back at the hotel shortly.

"I'm so lucky to have him. He's a marketing genius." She looked up from her phone. "While other people count sheep to go to sleep, Raj thinks of ways to make Felicity Grant Bridal one of the premier bridal shops in the world." She paused. "I can't remember the last time I had a vacation, and sometimes my back aches from sitting all day in front of a sewing machine. But I've wanted to design wedding gowns since I dressed my dolls as a girl."

"Is that for Raj?" Gabriel pointed to the box tied with a green ribbon.

Felicity thought about Adam, and tears formed in her eyes. "It's a gift for my boyfriend in New York. We got into a fight on Christmas yesterday, and I forgot to give him his present. That's why I have to get back to the hotel. I'm going to ask the concierge to overnight it to him. Do you think you could ask your friend to ship it urgently?"

"It sounds serious." Gabriel frowned. "I'm used to listening to my patients' problems, if you want to talk about it."

Felicity hastily wiped her eyes and ate a small bite of potato.

"You fixed my ankle; I can't expect you to help with my love life, too," she said weakly. "It's just that Adam and I have been together for six years. I'm worried that I said the wrong thing and spoiled everything."

"I promise I don't mind," he urged. "We're going to be here for a while. You aren't moving until the swelling goes down."

Felicity remembered Adam driving away from the terminal at JFK, and a lump formed in her throat.

"I was hoping Adam would ask me to marry him at Christmas," she began. "We're both almost thirty, and we've talked about getting married for ages. He said it wasn't the right time because he just started his own company." She paused. "I bought him this sweater, and I'm going to send it to him. Then I'll call and apologize. I've been here less than a day, and I already miss him."

Gabriel ran his fingers over the glass.

"So you don't want to get married?"

"Of course I do." She nodded. "I love my career, but I want children and a family. And I love Adam. He's everything I dreamed of."

"Tell him how you feel." He looked up from his plate. "If he loves you enough to want to spend the rest of his life with you, he'll propose."

"Do you really think so?" she wondered. "We want the same things, and I know he loves me."

"Then you have nothing to worry about," Gabriel said confidently. "Have a shot of vodka and I'll order some dessert."

"The first thing you'll learn about the Swiss is, we are passionate about our chocolate," he said when the waitress set down a plate of chocolate cracknel with honey, and nut cake dipped in milk chocolate. "This is called a 'non torte,'" he said, handing her a sliver of nut cake. "It's one of our most beloved treats."

"It's the best thing I've ever tasted." Felicity bit into walnuts and brown sugar and chocolate. "What's it like being a doctor in St. Moritz? You must meet all sorts of interesting people."

"It can be challenging," he admitted. "Yesterday I treated a sixty-year old tourist who attempted the piste at Corviglia and ended up with a fractured pelvis. It's hardly surprising; that's one of the steepest runs in the Alps. And then there was the young woman who went dancing in heels and broke her ankle. I spent the whole morning with a boy whose mother let him eat anything on the Christmas menu. He feasted on cheese fondue and chestnut puree and ended up with a terrible stomachache."

"I didn't realize St. Moritz was such a dangerous place," Felicity laughed.

"It isn't if you use common sense," he replied. "But most visitors leave theirs in the hotel safe, with their passports and Cartier watches."

"Then why are you here?" she asked.

"I studied medicine at the University of Zurich, with a specialty in pediatric allergies and immunology," he answered. "I had asthma as a child, and if someday I can help one child fall asleep without worrying if his inhaler is on his bedside table, I'll be happy. I worked at a clinic in Geneva, but my father had a mild heart attack and I had to come home." He paused. "He's had a practice in the village for over thirty years, and he's a terrible patient. If I hadn't taken over, he'd be braving the snow at all hours to fix broken bones and prescribe altitude medicine. I'm stuck here until he recovers."

"I can't think of a place I'd rather be," Felicity said dreamily.

"The village square is like the Christmas window at Bloomingdale's, and the mountains are so peaceful. In New York, you can't move without cars honking and bicycle messengers yelling and the constant drone of construction." She ate another bite of torte. "Being in St. Moritz is like diving under a down comforter on Sunday morning and never having to get out of bed."

"St. Moritz is like a make-believe kingdom in a Brothers Grimm fairy tale," Gabriel reflected. "You begin to believe everyone travels by private jet and thinks nothing of flinging ten thousand Swiss francs on a roulette wheel, or staying up all night drinking champagne out of an après-ski boot. Then you leave and realize there are so many problems in the world: childhood diseases that need to be erased, and better nutrition for millions of people."

"There's nothing wrong with make-believe," Felicity said abruptly. "A bride could get married wearing a cotton dress, but the minute she buttons the hooks of a chenille gown with an oversized satin bow, she feels like a movie star. We need a little fantasy in our lives; it makes us happy."

"I suppose you have a point." He shrugged. "I'd just like the chance to help people who really need it."

Felicity suddenly remembered she was sitting in a café with a complete stranger, when she should have been pressing the models' outfits for the morning shoot.

"You mean, instead of spending your time helping an American tourist who slips on the sidewalk because she's wearing heels." She looked at Gabriel. "I appreciate everything you've done, but I really should go. If you give me my part of the bill, I'll put it on my credit card."

"I apologize, I didn't mean it that way. You shouldn't move until we check that ankle." He touched her arm and smiled. "And you'll offend the waitress if you don't finish your non torte. No one sends back a half-eaten dessert."

Gabriel unwrapped the cold compress and examined her ankle. The swelling had gone down, and the throbbing was reduced to a mild ache. He offered to walk her home, but she shook her head.

"It's only a few blocks, and it all looks so magical," she said when they stood in front of the restaurant. Colored lights were strung across the cobblestones, and the air smelled of pine trees and cinnamon. "I've always believed in Christmas miracles; perhaps you are my guardian angel. Without your help, I might still be lying on the frozen sidewalk. And you gave me advice on my love life. I really should thank you."

"You can thank me by taking care of your ankle. Try not to put any weight on it, and keep it raised as much as possible," he offered. "I don't think you told me your name."

"It's Felicity, the same name as my company." She held out her hand. "Felicity Grant Bridal."

"It's nice to meet you, Felicity Grant." He shook her hand and gave her his card. "Take this. If it swells up again, give me a call."

"But not at midnight," she said, laughing, and tucked the card into her purse.

"Definitely not at midnight," he said, buttoning up his coat. "It's a small village. I'll find out if you don't follow my instructions."

Felicity left Gabriel and wrapped her arms around her chest to keep warm. It all looked so festive: shop windows filled with boxes wrapped in tissue paper, Christmas trees decorated with glittering ornaments, a reindeer pulling a sled overflowing with dolls and race cars and caramel apples. She wanted to come back in the morning and browse in the ski shop.

Gabriel was right; she had to tell Adam how she felt. They could have a long engagement; maybe they'd get married next Christmas in St. Moritz. The ceremony could be in the little church above the village, and a horse and carriage would whisk them to the reception at Badrutt's Palace. She pictured wearing a white cape over a satin gown, with Adam looking handsome in a dark cashmere overcoat and a yellow boutonniere.

The moon shimmered on the frozen lake, and Felicity noticed four stars shaped like a diamond. She remembered when she was a girl, and had wanted a bridal doll for Christmas. She had peered out her window to see if Santa Claus was climbing down the chimney, and instead she'd seen the same four stars. The next morning under the tree, there had been a doll wearing a white silk dress and diamond slippers.

Maybe these stars would prove just as magical. She was in St. Moritz for the week between Christmas and New Year's, and it all looked like a fairy tale. She had to make everything all right with Adam, and a Christmas miracle was just what she needed.

Two

Felicity

FELICITY PUT DOWN HER SKETCHPAD. It was hard to believe she had only been in St. Moritz for twenty-four hours. It had been the most spectacular morning. Felicity and Raj and the models had taken the funicular to the El Paradiso restaurant at the top of the mountain. Felicity had read in the guidebook that its nickname was "Close to Heaven," and as soon as they hopped off the chair-lift she understood why.

The restaurant was a long, low hut, like something out of *The Sound of Music*. An outdoor terrace was scattered with wooden tables, where skiers sipped steaming hot chocolate and ate muesli with nuts and sliced fruit. Metal racks were crammed with skis, and there was the sound of boots crunching on fresh snow.

And the view! The sky was the color of topaz, and the snow was so white, Felicity had to shield her eyes. Raj insisted they order breakfast, to stay on schedule, but Felicity wanted to stand forever and admire the swath of fir trees and valley that spread out far below.

Grudgingly she pulled herself away and joined the others at the table. They ate mountain cheese with homemade chutney, grilled sausage, and pear bread, spread thick with butter and jam. The coffee was served in mugs bigger than a cereal bowl, and the cream was so fresh, Felicity was certain the cows had been milked that morning.

The girls chatted about the movie star they'd spotted at the King's Club, as well as the Italian count who'd offered to fly them to Venice on his private jet, and the Arabian prince who'd invited them to a party at his chalet. Raj downed black coffee and insisted that no one think about getting on a private jet until after the fashion show, and warned them to stay away from private parties. He didn't need anyone drinking too much champagne and sleeping through a photo shoot.

Katie was still in bed, but the doctor had given her some Benadryl and predicted she'd be fine by the next day. Raj held off flying in a replacement, and Felicity said a quick prayer over breakfast that the doctor would be right.

After breakfast they took the chairlift back to the village, where the photographer captured the girls trying on ribbed sweaters at Bogner and suede jackets at Asprey. Raj persuaded the models to put on a little show for the tourists, and they happily obliged. Two models climbed into the window of Armani and planted lipstick kisses on a male mannequin in a tuxedo.

Even in the late morning, the village square was filled with elegant shoppers and skiers in bright ski clothes and woolen caps. There was that giddy sensation of being on vacation, and people were talking about stopping for lunch at La Marmite on top of the mountain, and meeting for whiskey sours later at the Kulm Hotel.

"I can't believe we're really in St. Moritz," Felicity sighed, watching the models posing in the window of Hermès. "It's all so perfect," she said, turning to Raj. "You really are a genius."

"You're the genius." Raj was in a particularly good mood. He'd had a drinks date with the blonde concierge, and had received an RSVP from the crown princess of Sweden. "You create the gowns the most sophisticated brides want to wear; I just get the right people to see them."

"It's because of you that we're here," she said warmly. "If we were showing the collection in New York, we'd be cramming gowns into a cab and trying to get through rush-hour traffic to some freezing loft in the Village."

"St. Moritz is fantastic, and the hotel is being so accommodating," Raj agreed. "You should go with the models to the Jacuzzi after this. They serve mulled cider with nutmeg, and it's all complimentary."

"I can't." Felicity thought about Adam, and her chest tightened. "I have to make an important phone call."

After they left the village, the girls went to put on bathing suits and Raj disappeared to post photos on Instagram, while Felicity returned to her suite. Just entering the living room made her happier. The parquet floors were covered with blue-and-gold oriental rugs, and there was a balcony with a view of the lake. The bedroom had a king-sized bed with a quilted headboard, and last night the maids had left a complimentary hot water bottle and a tray of mini cheesecakes.

Originally Raj had said it was out of the question that she stay in a suite, but Felicity had begged him to reconsider. It wasn't for herself. She could sleep curled up in an armchair, or on an otto-man. But the wedding gowns couldn't be scrunched together on the bed or jammed into a closet; they needed space to breathe.

Raj had reluctantly agreed, and somehow convinced Badrutt's Palace to give them a discount. Felicity didn't know how. It was already one of the most famous resorts in the world; it didn't need to be promoted on social media. That was the thing about Raj; he could charm anyone into doing what he asked.

He'd once convinced Donna Karan's assistant to let them hold a fashion show at Donna's estate in the Hamptons, when the only press Felicity had received was one line in Page Six of the *New York Post*. Felicity had noticed when she met the assistant that she was a pretty brunette, and there had been a charge on the company credit card for two dozen yellow roses and a tin of Momofuku cookies delivered to the assistant's address, but she couldn't com-plain. The fashion show had been covered in *Town & Country Weddings*, and helped make Felicity Grant Bridal one of the most talked-about new names in the industry.

She studied a sketch of a pewter-colored princess gown and wondered if it would be good enough. It had to be the most amaz-ing wedding dress she had ever drawn: better than Armani's last collection, where the bridesmaids' dresses had been the most spec-tacular iridescent gold, and more stunning than the wedding dress Naeem Khan had showcased at his fall show, with a silk train as long as the runway and a bodice stitched with sapphires like birds' eggs.

Ten days ago, Felicity had been sitting in her studio working on a dress for the winter collection. The bell had tinkled, and a woman in her thirties entered the atelier. She had blond hair and wore a long wool coat and many-colored scarf.

"Can I help you?" Felicity asked.

"You have some beautiful designs," the woman said, fingering a lace dress that Felicity was particularly proud of. The neckline was stitched with pearls, and it was the most unusual color; it changed from pale pink to ivory depending on the light.

"Thank you. Are you having a spring wedding?" Felicity asked. "The spring fabrics are going to be fabulous: plenty of organza and tulle."

"I'm not engaged," she said, waving her hand at Felicity. "I don't even have time for a boyfriend." She took a card out of her purse and handed it to Felicity. "I'm Camilla Barnes, and you must be Felicity Grant."

Felicity didn't have to look at the card to know who Camilla Barnes was. Camilla was the head of Bergdorf Goodman's bridal salon, and one of the most important people in the wedding industry in New York. Bergdorf's only carried a handful of designers, and being given space in their bridal salon was like being anointed by the Queen of England.

"It's a pleasure to meet you," Felicity said. She wondered if her lipstick was smudged and if she had remembered to put on mascara that morning.

"I attended a friend's wedding at the Knickerbocker Club a few weeks ago, and the bride wore the most unusual dress; it had a purple-and-silver brocade bodice and a see-through violet-colored veil."

The dress had been one of Felicity's most ambitious designs, and she'd wondered if the purple would work. But the bride was a young digital media entrepreneur, and she'd wanted her gown to stand out on Instagram.

"Then I was flipping through *Hamptons Magazine* and there

was a two-page spread on a wedding in Montauk. The brides-maids' dresses had a sailor theme, and they were so smart and witty." Camilla smiled at Felicity. "The credit on the page was Felicity Grant."

"Those were fun dresses to make," Felicity acknowledged. "The wedding party arrived at the reception by sailboat."

"How would you like to have a couple of dresses in Bergdorf's spring bridal show?" Camilla asked.

"But the show is only for designers featured in your salon," Felicity gasped.

"Send me sketches for two gowns, and I'll see if they work for the fashion show," Camilla said, and smiled. "Then we can talk about adding Felicity Grant designs to the salon."

"Thank you so much, I'll get right to work!" Felicity said excitedly. "When would you like the sketches?"

"It *is* the spring collection, so we *are* a bit short on time." Camilla walked to the door and turned around. "Can you email them to me by New Year's Day?"

Felicity had spent the rest of the day after Camilla left in a state of shock. How many hours had she spent admiring the wedding dresses in the famous seventh-floor salon? Now she had the chance to have her designs share space with dresses by J. Mendel and Oscar de la Renta. It took all of her willpower not to tell Raj. It would only have caused him more stress before the winter collection in St. Moritz, and he wouldn't have given her a minute's peace. After she submitted the sketches and Camilla said yes, she would tell him all about it.

But now she put the sketchpad on the coffee table and picked up her laptop. She couldn't concentrate on her sketches when all she could think about was the fight with Adam. It was eight a.m.

in New York and she wanted to catch Adam before his client breakfast. Gabriel was right. She had to tell him her feelings; she couldn't let them simmer like a pot of oatmeal on the stove.

The FaceTime icon glowed, and she saw Adam standing at the desk in his bedroom. He was wearing a white button-down shirt, and Felicity was reminded of how handsome he was. His light brown hair was combed to the side, and he fiddled with his tie.

"This is a pleasant surprise," Adam said into the camera. "I thought Raj would keep you so busy, I wouldn't hear from you all week. I know what he thinks about downtime—if you aren't earning money, you may as well not be breathing."

"He's not that bad," Felicity laughed. "Though he did warn the girls that if anyone sends their underwear to be laundered, he'd make them go down to the laundry and wash their own bras. And he almost had a panic attack when he got our bill at El Paradiso; I thought the paramedics would have to carry him down the mountain on a stretcher." She pushed her brown hair behind her ears. "He was right; St. Moritz is the perfect setting for the fashion show. Everyone tosses Swiss francs around like Monopoly money, and I've never seen so much Louis Vuitton luggage. I wish you were here. There are marvelous wooden huts at the top of the mountain where couples can order breakfast and turn their faces up to the sun."

"All the glamour must be rubbing off on you. You've never looked so beautiful," Adam said. "If I could postpone these meetings, I would be on the next plane."

"You would?" Her voice wavered. "You were so distant at Christmas. I thought . . ."

"That I was still upset? You know what it's like having Christmas brunch with my parents," he answered. "My mother asks too many questions about the menu, and my father points out that at my age, he owned two insurance agencies."

"We were going to talk about getting married, but we never got back to it." Felicity ran her finger over her teacup. "I know we're busy, but we've always supported each other. Being married wouldn't change anything."

"Of course it would," Adam replied. "I had dinner last night with Doug, the quarterback for the Rams, and it's one of the reasons he's going to sign with the agency. He was so relieved he didn't have to worry about me running home to dinner or not being available on weekends."

"We're both turning thirty next year," Felicity tried again. "We want to start a family."

"There's no hurry." Adam shrugged. "All the studies show that older parents are more relaxed and can spend quality time with their children."

Adam was talking like some relationship guru on cable television. She noticed Gabriel's card on the coffee table and took a deep breath.

"I want to have children when we're young and can go days without sleep. There's no reason we can't build businesses and be married at the same time. We could have the wedding in St. Moritz next Christmas." Her face broke into a smile. "There's something magical about the mountains. The valley is studded with forests and wooden chalets, like an illustration in a fairy tale. Everyone clumps around in ski boots, and at night the ski slopes are lit up brighter than the most magnificent Christmas tree."

"I'm sorry, but it's not going to happen." Adam drummed his fingers on the desk. "I can't even think about getting married until the firm is well established."

"I'm afraid you're going to keep putting it off for years," Felicity said, and the tears threatened to return. "Would it be so terrible to get engaged?"

"I've always thought we were great together because we share the same goals," Adam said slowly. "We want to be the best at what we do, and we don't mind putting in the hours. But if that's not enough for you, maybe we should take some time to think. Maybe even see other people."

"What do you mean, take time to think?" Felicity's heart was suddenly beating so fast she put her hand over her chest. "And why would we see other people? We love each other!"

"I think we should take a break and figure out why we're together." He looked into the camera. "I do love you, but maybe our relationship means something else to you. You believe the women who come into your bridal salon and drool over three-quarter veils have something you don't."

"Of course I believe in marriage!" Felicity was suddenly angry. "I want the honeymoon where the bellboy calls us Mr. and Mrs. Adam Burton, and the first house with the living-room floor that we don't notice is sloped until we sign the papers, and the two children who make us so exhausted we long for the nights when we flopped into bed with a carton of takeout and the remote control. Marriage is about moving forward together, and it's the best thing in the world. But that doesn't mean I don't love you. I don't want to see other people." Her anger dissolved and she became frantic. "There's no one in the world I'd want to be with besides you."

Adam reached for his jacket. "We don't have to make any decisions, so why don't we talk about it later? I have to go—I'm meeting Doug for breakfast, and tonight we're going to a Knicks game.

You know I love you, Felicity, I just think we both have some thinking to do."

The screen went dark and Felicity slammed the laptop shut as if she could erase their whole conversation. How could Adam accuse her of caring more about marriage than she did about his feelings? What if he'd met someone? That wasn't likely; there wasn't time for anything besides work.

She remembered when she and Adam had met, just after she'd graduated from college. Adam was a friend of Raj's, and had come to the apartment. It was pouring rain, and Raj had texted that he was stuck at the laundromat. Felicity was making dinner, and offered Adam a bowl of soup and half a lamb chop.

They talked about the impossibility of making ends meet in Manhattan, and how lucky Felicity was to have Raj as a roommate. He was incredibly neat, and kept them on a strict household budget. And whenever a girl brought him homemade brownies, he left them on the counter to share.

It was when she was clearing the dishes that she thought Adam might be someone special. He came into the kitchen carrying two empty soup bowls.

"Did you know you have a leak in your bathroom ceiling?" he asked. "If you give me a bucket, I can put it on the floor."

"A leak in the bathroom?" Felicity's eyes widened. The first wedding gown she had ever sold was hanging on the shower-curtain railing. It was a white charmeuse gown with lace sleeves. She'd spent every penny she received from graduation on the fabric, and was supposed to deliver it to the bride in the morning.

She dropped the dish towel and raced down the hall. There was a water stain on the skirt, and the veil was a sodden ball.

"Oh, it can't be," she cried. Adam stood behind her, and she was afraid she was going to burst into tears in front of one of the most attractive men she had ever met.

"Are you getting married?" he asked. "We've been talking for an hour and you didn't mention anything about a boyfriend."

"Of course I'm not getting married." She stroked the fabric. "I'm a wedding dress designer. It's my first sale, and I've been working on this dress for months. I'm supposed to deliver it to the bride's hotel tomorrow, but now it's ruined."

Adam unhooked the dress and gathered it in his arms. "Wait here," he said, and walked to the door. "I'll be right back."

"You can't just take my dress!" She ran after him. "I don't even know your last name. And it's pouring rain—if you take it outside, it will get drenched."

Adam was already clattering down the staircase and into the street. Felicity peered out the window and saw him standing under the awning. She was about to run after him, but he hopped into a taxi and disappeared.

She paced around the room and tried to stay calm. Twenty-something men in New York didn't steal wedding dresses. But what could he possibly be doing with it? She'd finally opened the emergency bottle of brandy Raj kept under the sink when she heard a knock at the door.

Adam was standing in the hallway carrying a dress wrapped in plastic. His wet hair was plastered to his head, and his leather jacket was spattered with raindrops.

"Where did you go?" Felicity demanded, cradling a shot of brandy. "I was about to call NYPD and report a stolen wedding dress."

He unwrapped the plastic and Felicity gasped. The wet spot was gone, and the veil was perfectly pressed.

"My parents live uptown, and my mother has a steam room," he said, and grinned. "She can get the wrinkles out of anything. She even gave me the sheet of plastic so it wouldn't get wet."

"You did that for me?" Felicity's cheeks colored. "We don't know each other."

"At first she was worried I was getting married and didn't tell her," he said. She noticed his eyes were very blue. "When I explained you designed the dress, she was impressed. She asked for your card, and said she'd recommend you to her friends whose daughters were engaged."

"I'm so glad it's back." Felicity sighed as if a beloved pet had gone missing and been returned to her. "Do you see these pearls?" She pointed to the sleeve. "I sold my grandmother's ruby earrings to pay for them. And it was either go on a post-graduation weekend to the Berkshires or buy the appliqués for the train. I couldn't pass on the appliqués. When the bride walks down the aisle, the train is what the guests remember." She looked up. "That was so kind—how can I repay you?"

"A shot of that brandy would be nice." He brushed the rain from his hair. "I managed to keep the dress dry, but my jacket is soaked."

They sat in the cramped living room and sipped brandy and shared a slice of pumpkin pie. By the time Raj came home, Felicity knew that Adam loved deep-dish pizza, volunteered on weekends at the animal shelter, and was crazy about the Knicks and basketball. He'd just started in the mailroom at CAA, and hoped one day to open his own sports management firm.

"Thank you for the brandy," he said after Raj had gone to bed. It was almost midnight.

"If it wasn't for you, my career would be over before it began,"

Felicity said, smiling. "The wedding industry is word-of-mouth, and everyone would know I ruined the bride's dress."

"There is something you can do for me," he said as he walked to the door. "Next Friday is the company Christmas party. Would you like to come? It would look much better if I had a pretty girl on my arm."

Felicity flinched and thought maybe Adam wasn't special after all. He was like most of the men she knew, who were always after something.

"You want me to come to the Christmas party to impress your boss?" she asked.

"No, I want you to come because you're the most interesting girl I've met in ages, and you have beautiful brown eyes." He paused. "I'd like to see you again."

She reached forward and kissed him on the cheek. "In that case, I say yes."

Now Felicity gazed around the hotel suite of the Badrutt's Palace and thought of everything they'd done together. Adam had driven her to Michigan in a snowstorm for her grandmother's eightieth birthday party because all the flights were cancelled. Then there was the vacation in Mexico when they'd both been so sick they took turns rubbing ice on each other's foreheads. Just last month Adam had found a lost dog, and they'd both spent an entire Sunday plastering posters around the neighborhood.

Tears filled her eyes and she resolved not to cry. They couldn't break up over a silly argument on FaceTime while they were five thousand miles apart. But Adam was stubborn; it was one of the reasons he was successful. If a potential client wavered, Adam created a whole spreadsheet of reasons why the client should hire him.

The suite felt stifling, and she took the elevator to the lobby. She had spent so long just sitting in her suite after talking to Adam that now it was early afternoon; the models were probably soaking in the Jacuzzi. Raj would be calling her soon to go over the plans for the evening. All the models were going to take the train to Alp Grüm to see the winter sunset. It was the highest elevation in Europe, and the views were supposed to be spectacular.

Felicity entered the Grand Hall and inhaled the scent of pine needles. The winter light streamed through the floor-to-ceiling windows; men and women were wearing cashmere sweaters and après-ski boots. Waiters in white dinner jackets carried trays of cream-filled cakes, and a pianist was playing the baby-grand piano. Huge vases held purple orchids, and there was a Christmas tree decorated with miniature skis and sleds.

A young woman wearing an orange sweater and navy leggings sat on a velvet sofa. Felicity recognized the jet-black hair of Nell, her star model. Three waiters were hovering around her, and Felicity had to laugh. Nell was like honey to men: no matter that she wore a two-carat diamond ring on her left hand and never flirted. They couldn't stay away from her almond-shaped green eyes and legs that went on forever.

"There you are." Felicity approached her. "I thought you'd be in the Jacuzzi with the other models."

The first time Nell had modeled one of Felicity's designs—a satin A-line with a strapless embroidered bodice—Felicity knew she would be one of the hottest models in the industry. Nell's high waist and narrow hips could carry off anything. And she wasn't just in demand on the runway; her round mouth and fine cheekbones had graced the cover of *Vogue* and *Bazaar*.

"I ordered one of these—it's called a green spider." Nell waved at her cocktail. "My mother arrived and I'm going to need it. She's joining me for afternoon tea in half an hour."

"You invited your mother to St. Moritz." Felicity sat across from Nell and surveyed the coffee table. There were platters of roast beef on rye bread and cucumber sandwiches with sour cream and chives. A silver tray held pastries, and there were plates of custards and scones with jam and clotted cream. "You wanted to spend a whole week with her."

"I'm thrilled that she's here." Nell nodded. "Ever since the divorce, her world gets smaller and smaller. She says she loves puttering around the house in Beverly Hills and managing the bookstore. But she's forty-eight—why did she have to open an antiquarian bookshop? The only customers are dusty old professors looking for outdated texts; she'll never find someone new." Nell stirred her drink.

"Did you know my parents met in St. Moritz twenty-eight years ago? My mother was one of those chalet girls who get paid for doing practically nothing except looking pretty, and my father was a hotel waiter," Nell continued, laughing. "He pretended to be rich to impress her, and she saw right through him. Now I can't imagine her putting on a pair of skis and schussing down a mountain. The only way I convinced her to come was by promising better shopping than Rodeo Drive, and the finest dark-roast coffee." Nell paused. "And she couldn't resist spending a week with her only daughter. I am glad she's here; it's the perfect opportunity to insist she come to the wedding."

"She isn't really going to miss your wedding?" Felicity scooped up a handful of pistachio nuts. Nell and her fiancé, Eliot, were having a June wedding on Nantucket. Nell had planned an intimate ceremony in a stone church followed by a reception at the yacht club. She'd told Felicity that they would serve lobster and oysters, and the wedding cake would be a tree of pink and yellow cake pops.

"She said being in the same place as my father gives her heart palpitations," Nell sighed. "I tried to appeal to my father, but he claimed being around my mother raises his blood pressure to dangerous levels. He offered to pay for two weddings, but I don't want to get married twice. I want both my parents there when I walk down the aisle."

"Of course you do. Having both parents present is the number-two item on every bride's dream wedding list. I read it on the wedding blogs," Felicity agreed. "Followed by a honeymoon trousseau of string bikinis and one good black dress to wear at night."

"Speaking of wedding blogs," Nell said, "I saw the gorgeous photo of you in the wedding dress. We've both been busy since we arrived, but how could you not tell me that Adam proposed? I want all the details."

"What are you talking about?" Felicity looked up.

Nell clicked on her phone and read, "Felicity Grant, whose bridal salon of the same name is one of the most renowned in New York, might just be in the market for a wedding dress. She was spotted at the glamorous Badrutt's Palace Hotel in St. Moritz wearing one of her own designs. Is she planning her nuptials to sports-star-manager boyfriend Adam Burton? And if so, will she go with a traditional gown, or will she create a new style that will become the most wanted dress of the season? Stay tuned! Our spies on the ground will keep you posted."

"Where did you get that?" Felicity gasped.

"It's everywhere: the *Post, Elle*." Nell handed her the phone. "You look stunning. I want to know everything: how did Adam propose, and where's the ring? Eliot didn't want me to wear mine when I was traveling, but I couldn't take it off." She gazed at the pear-shaped diamond on its platinum band. "Just looking at it makes me smile."

"There's no ring and no engagement." Felicity gave the phone to Nell. "Adam and I sort of broke up."

"What did you say?" Nell downed her cocktail.

"I hoped Adam was going to propose at Christmas, but he said he wasn't ready," Felicity began. "Yesterday I went to the village to buy him a present, and I slipped and fell. A doctor helped me up and wrapped my ankle in a cold compress. Somehow I told him the whole story, and he said I had to tell Adam how I felt." She looked at Nell. "Adam accused me of only caring about the dress and the wedding and said we should take a break. He even suggested we see other people."

"You need one of these," Nell said, pointing at her drink, and waved to the waiter. "Let's start at the beginning. You let an old Swiss doctor give you advice on your love life."

"He wasn't old, and he was very kind. He carried me inside and wrapped my foot in a bandage," Felicity defended herself. "And it made sense: I can't be in a relationship if we're not honest with each other."

"All couples tell little white lies." Nell shrugged. "Eliot can't make waffles without burning them, but I say they're delicious and eat them anyway. You have to ignore the small stuff, or it'll never work."

The waiter set a glass in front of her and Felicity swallowed the sweet liqueur. "Wanting to wait years to get married and have children isn't small stuff! Adam may not talk to me again."

"Of course he'll talk to you." Nell ran her fingers over the menu.

"You just have to make him think getting married is his idea. Pretend there's a fabulous apartment in a co-op building that only accepts married residents, or make up some tax loophole that applies to married couples."

"I don't think that would work with Adam," Felicity sighed. "Anyway, I would never trick him into getting married."

"What are you going to do?" Nell wondered.

"I don't even have time to think about it. I have to go into the village to buy some colored pens." Felicity thought about the sketches she had to send to Camilla Barnes by New Year's Day. "Then I have to work on some designs and make sure none of the veils got wrinkled on the flight. After that I'll think about what to do about Adam." She sank back on the cushions and groaned. "Maybe I'll crawl into one of those huts at the top of the mountain and hope there's an avalanche."

"An avalanche won't do you any good if you're at the top of the mountain," Nell said, and laughed. "You're beautiful and smart and talented. Adam would be a fool to let you go."

"Adam doesn't seem to think so," Felicity said gloomily. "Maybe he's already planning who to take to see the ball drop on New Year's Eve."

"He was just upset, he'll call or text and apologize." Nell glanced at her watch. "Speaking of texts, you'll never guess who texted me an hour ago. My father! The company jet arrives this evening, and he asked if I could pick him up at the airport."

"Your father is in St. Moritz!" Felicity exclaimed. "You didn't say he was coming."

Felicity had met Nell's father, Todd, a few times when he'd visited Nell in New York. He was the head of an independent movie studio, and lived in a beach house in Malibu. He was ridiculously handsome for a father, and loved to spoil Nell when he was in town.

Even after Nell became a supermodel and could afford a car service and a table at the Four Seasons, he insisted on picking her and Felicity up in a town car and taking them to the hottest restaurants in Manhattan. He often brought them small gifts: a pair of earrings, or a bottle of California wine.

"Shooting for the movie wrapped early, and he doesn't have to be in LA until January." Nell reclined on the love seat. "I couldn't say no, and I would love to see him. Ever since the divorce, he never stays in one place." She paused. "He says he feels twenty years younger. Honestly, I don't know how my parents were married in the first place. They could fight about anything: whether brussels sprouts had any nutritional value if they were baked with sugar, and if the environmental benefits of putting in a fake lawn outweighed the disadvantages of taking away jobs from the gardener." She sipped her drink. "It was like living at the United Nations when everyone argues their point at the same time."

"Your mother must be furious." Felicity's eyes were wide. "If she can't bear seeing your father at your wedding, how is she going to handle a week together in a tiny ski resort?"

"I didn't tell her," Nell admitted. "She'd pack her bags and take the first taxi to the train station."

"What about your father?" Felicity wondered. "He's not going to be happy when he spots her at breakfast over his bowl of muesli."

"I didn't tell him either," Nell said guiltily.

"You're not serious! You're going to cause an international incident," Felicity said, horrified. "They'll run into each other in line at the chair lift and poke each other's eyes out with ski poles."

"If he had given me some advance warning, I would have said something," Nell agreed. "But the pilot had already logged the flight plan. Anyway, it might be a good opportunity."

"For what?" Felicity inquired. "You said the sight of each other could put either one of them in the hospital."

"I planned it out." Nell unfolded a piece of paper. "My father loves to get up early and ski the first run of the day. He takes a nap in the afternoon, and doesn't eat dinner until ten p.m." She stopped and smiled. "He says the best thing about being divorced is not being expected to eat at seven p.m. My mother always eats ridiculously early; she loves to spend the whole night curled up with a book. She sleeps until ten a.m. and enjoys a long walk in the afternoon."

Nell turned the paper over. "She loves to browse in the boutiques, and can't stand smoky nightclubs. If I can keep them apart all week and make them see how immature they're being, they might change their minds about attending the wedding."

"You would have made a great double agent in World War Two. I hope it works," Felicity said admiringly. "I should go. All the shops in the village are going to be crowded, and Raj wants us to meet to go to Alp Grüm at five o'clock."

Felicity walked through the lobby and thought that whoever had nicknamed the Grand Hall "The Catwalk" was right. She'd never imagined après-ski wear could be so fashionable. Women wore cigarette pants and ski parkas and knee-high boots. She would have to scribble down the designer names so Raj could mention them on Instagram.

Yesterday she'd believed that the mountains were magical, and that her collection was going to be a success. Now she couldn't think about anything but Adam telling her they should take a break. How could she spend all week working on her designs for

Bergdorf's and shuttling the models between carriage rides and toboggan races, when all she wanted to do was curl up in a ball?

Her eyes brimmed with tears, and she stumbled onto the terrace. She shouldn't be thinking about Adam at all. She should be drawing the sketches for Camilla and going over the itinerary for tonight's activities. But she was glad she had to run some errands in the village. Her head was blurry from the alcohol, and it felt good to get some fresh air. Seeing the icicles dangling on the fir trees and listening to the soft chatter in French and German was strangely soothing.

She let herself out the side gate and kept walking. The cocktails must have been stronger than she'd thought, or maybe it was just the high altitude. Her legs were wobbly, and her ears felt as if they were stuffed with cotton wool.

Suddenly there was a whizzing sound and she looked up. A sled was careening down the mountain toward her. The driver waved his hand and yelled in German for her to move. She tried to get out of the way, but he was coming too fast. At the last minute, she jumped out of the sled's path and slipped and fell backward onto the snow.

"Are you all right?" A man ran over to her. "Some of those tourists should be put in jail, they think they're behind the wheel of a race car. Thank God the sled didn't run you over."

Felicity blinked and opened her eyes. She looked up and recognized the doctor who'd bandaged her ankle.

"Oh, it's you!" she said, and wondered why he seemed so fuzzy. "I heard someone yelling, and suddenly the sled was practically on top of me." She tried to sit up and sank back onto the snow. "You must think I'm terribly stupid. I can't seem to stay out of trouble, even in the daytime."

"I'm glad I was here. I was on my way to the hotel to check on some patients." Gabriel crouched down beside her. "And I don't think you're stupid; it was the driver's fault. I'm just happy you're all right."

Felicity dusted snow from her turtleneck. There was a sharp pain between her shoulders, and her head felt like it was being pounded by a hammer.

"I'm fine." She tried to smile. "Though my clothes are soaked. I feel like I just took a bath in a tub of ice."

"Your cheeks are pale and you're shivering," he said. "Let's get you inside and you can get out of those wet clothes."

"I can't ask you to rescue me again," she said, and noticed the ground was spinning. "I'll sit here for a moment and then I'll go back to the hotel."

"You can't be too careful with a bump to the head. You might have a concussion." He studied her carefully. "Why don't I walk with you to your room, and you can warm up?"

"I suppose that wouldn't hurt," Felicity murmured. "I do feel a little odd."

Suddenly the sun was too bright and there was a buzzing in her ears. She tried to sit up again, but the mountain seemed to curve in a strange shape, and it felt like she was moving away from Gabriel. She put out her arms and then everything went black.

"Where am I?" Felicity asked, wincing at the pain in her neck. She was lying on a sofa, covered by a thick blanket. Her eyes adjusted to the dim light and she recognized Gabriel hovering above her. His stethoscope was around his neck and his brow was furrowed.

"You're awake! You gave me quite a scare." He let out his breath. "You blacked out and I carried you to your suite. Thankfully the concierge is a friend and told me your room number. Your blood pressure is normal, but you have a nasty bump on your head."

"It did hurt quite a lot," Felicity admitted grudgingly. "Thank you for taking care of me. I'm feeling much better."

"You have to be careful with head injuries. You might feel all right now, but it can turn into a concussion." He stood up and walked to the minibar. "Why don't I make some coffee and rustle up something to eat? Nausea is a common side effect of a head injury, and it would be good to eat some cheese and crackers."

"Please don't touch the minibar," Felicity said weakly. "Raj doesn't want any personal charges on the bill. One package of Toblerone chocolate cost more than extra baggage on the plane. I'm not really hungry, and my head feels fine. I'm sure I'll be perfectly okay."

"Raj won't mind if I heat up hot water and make tea. And there have to be some pastries around here somewhere. It's Badrutt's Palace; the maids always leave baskets of fresh fruit and nut tortes."

"A cup of tea sounds lovely," she said gratefully. "But then I have to get up and get dressed. Raj scheduled a photo-op trip on the Rhaetian Railway to Alp Grüm, and I have to be at the train station in an hour."

She accepted the cup of tea and took a long gulp. The fog in her brain cleared, and it all came back to her: telling Adam that she wanted to get engaged, and Adam saying they should take a break. "I told Adam I want to get married, and he didn't take it well. He said we should take a break and maybe see other people."

"You can't be serious?" Gabriel said in surprise. "You told me you were practically engaged."

"That's what I thought," Felicity said. "He was terribly hurtful. He said I cared more about the wedding than I do about him."

"Here." Gabriel opened his doctor's kit and took out a bar of chocolate wrapped in red-and-gold paper. "This is a Côte d'Or: milk chocolate and pralines and nougat. It's the best chocolate in the world; it can make anyone feel better."

Felicity ate it tentatively and wiped chocolate flakes from her mouth. "It's delicious, but one piece of chocolate can't fix everything. Do you believe in Christmas miracles?"

"I don't know; I hadn't thought about it." He shrugged.

"Well, I do. It's the most magical time of the year," she answered. "I was so upset yesterday, and then you rescued me and gave me advice. I thought you were my guardian angel."

"No one has called me a guardian angel before." He grinned. "I'm just a doctor with a slightly grumpy bedside manner."

"You were wonderful. And everyone has a guardian angel," she commented. Suddenly her head felt heavy. "They just don't appear until you really need them. I still don't know what to do about Adam." She looked at Gabriel thoughtfully. "You gave me good advice yesterday. What do you think I should say to him?"

"You're in no condition to worry about that now," Gabriel answered. "You need to keep warm and get some sleep. I suggest you tell Raj that you're going to skip the train to Alp Grüm and take a nap."

"The train *did* look as flimsy as those toy trains in the Christmas display at Bloomingdale's," she said, wavering. "And I *am* terribly tired. Maybe I'll sit here for a while and close my eyes."

"That's a much better idea." Gabriel stood up. "It's important to monitor your progress and make sure you don't get any headaches. I want you to lie here and get plenty of rest. I'll check on you tomorrow and see how you are."

"Thank you," she said drowsily. "You really are kind. But I don't have time to rest. I have to finish some sketches and finalize details for the fashion show."

"None of that's going to mean anything if this turns into a real concussion," he countered. "The important thing is to empty your brain, try not to think about anything."

Images of Adam snapping at her on FaceTime blended with Camilla Barnes standing in her studio, and her heart started racing. How could she clear her mind when there were so many things to worry about?

"Maybe you can help," she suggested. "I read in the guidebook that the Swiss have lots of wonderful folktales. Could you tell me one?"

"You want me to tell you a folktale?" he asked.

"When I was a child, my mother used to read me fairy tales when I was sick." She nodded. "It always put me to sleep."

"I suppose I could; I do know a lot of Swiss folktales. My mother used to tell me one called 'The Haldenstein Maiden's Tale.'" Gabriel sat beside her. "A beautiful maiden wearing a white gown sits by a lake near Haldenstein castle, dangling her hands in the water. A handsome young hunter approaches and sees that she is crying. He asks what is wrong, and she replies: 'If you will hold my hand and not let go until I tell you, it will break the spell that was cast on me by a witch.'

"The young man takes her hand and holds it in his own. At the same time, a little old man emerges from the castle and offers the hunter a jeweled basket full of gold. If he is to accept the gold, he will have to let go of the maiden's hand. He turns down the gold, and the maiden beams with pleasure. 'You have shown that you can be trusted! You can now let go of my hand and accept the gold as a symbol of my appreciation.'

"The hunter turns to accept the basket, but when he turns around the maiden has vanished. All that is left is the daisy chain she was making and the white veil that had been on her head."

"What happened to the maiden?" Felicity asked. "Fairy tales are supposed to have happy endings. The maiden and the hunter kiss and ride off into the sunset on a white horse or something like that."

"I don't know." Gabriel shrugged. "My mother always closed the book there and insisted I go to bed."

"It was a nice story anyway." Suddenly her eyes were heavy and she could barely stay awake.

"You'd better get some rest." Gabriel stood up and walked to the door. "I'll leave a message with the concierge to tell Raj that you're all right."

"Thank you," Felicity said drowsily. "Could you do one more thing for me?"

"What is it?"

"Could you turn off the light?" she asked. "I can't sleep when the room is so bright."

The door closed and Felicity ate the last bite of chocolate. It really was delicious, but it didn't stop the ache in her heart and the feeling of emptiness that washed over her. She closed her eyes and pulled the blanket over her shoulders.

Three

Nell

NELL SAT IN THE BAR at the Carlton Hotel nibbling Brazil nuts and waited for her father. The hotel was perched above the lake, and French doors overlooked skaters bundled against the evening air. A white Christmas tree stood near the fireplace, and the lights of snow-covered chalets twinkled in the distance.

She had picked her father up at the airport and dropped him off at his suite at the Kempinski Hotel. There had been a moment of panic when he suggested he stay at Badrutt's Palace, and she worried about him running into her mother in the lobby. She quickly explained that the Palace was fully booked, and the Kempinski was better anyway: it was the closest hotel to the ski gondola, and served the most delicious breakfast buffet in St. Moritz. The spa was world-class, and there was an indoor swimming pool and Finnish sauna.

She knew the indoor swimming pool would convince him; her father was passionate about exercise. Her earliest memories of him were with wet hair and a towel draped over his shoulders after swimming fifty laps in the pool. He maintained that you couldn't think clearly unless you kept your body as well-tuned as a sports car. He rarely ate rich desserts, and the few times she'd visited his new house in Malibu, his pantry had been stocked with brown rice and quinoa.

The real reason she'd chosen the Kempinski was that it was on the far side of St. Moritz. She guessed her mother wouldn't go near the ski gondola, and she had never been fond of swimming. For Nell's whole childhood, she'd sat on a longue by the pool and barely dipped her toes in the shallow end.

Really, her parents were acting like children squabbling over a toy in the playground. How difficult could it be for them to sit in adjoining church pews at her wedding, when they'd shared a bedroom for twenty-eight years? Then she remembered the nights when her mother would toss her father's pillow down the staircase and her father would retreat into the den. Or the mornings when the chill in the air at breakfast was so icy, a pot of Jamaican coffee couldn't thaw it.

A man stood at the entrance, and Nell recognized her father's dark hair. He had always been handsome. It wasn't just his green eyes, or the long eyelashes that he had passed on to her. It was the way he gave her his full attention. After the divorce, women hovered around them wherever they went: at an outdoor café in Malibu, or at a diner on the Lower East Side. He'd give them a quick smile, and then turn back to Nell and want to know everything: was she getting enough sleep, did she spend too much time on airplanes, and were she and Eliot happy and in love.

"Nell!" Todd squeezed between the tables. He was wearing a wool overcoat, and held a gold box. "I'm sorry I'm late. I picked up something for you in the village."

"You gave me a Christmas present when you arrived." Nell pushed her hair from her ears. "The earrings are gorgeous; I'm wearing them."

"I did choose well. The emeralds match your eyes." He beamed. "I had to buy this for you, it's from the House of Lamm. I haven't been there in twenty-eight years. They sell the finest après-ski couture in the world."

Nell unwrapped the tissue paper and took out a magenta scarf.

"It's lovely." She looked up and smiled. "You can't give me a present every time we meet. I won't have room in my closet."

"You wrap it around your neck; it doesn't take up any room at all." Todd picked up the menu. "You're not used to the cold in the Alps. It makes winter temperatures in New York seem mild in comparison."

Nell placed the scarf in the box. "Thank you. It's beautiful, and Raj will be thrilled that I'll stay warm. He's terrified of anyone getting sick before the fashion show."

"I'm glad you like it," Todd said, and waved to the bartender. "We'll have two glasses of Martell Cognac and a plate of Pasta Nicolai." He turned to Nell. "It's one of the Carlton's specials. Fusilli pasta with vodka and tomato paste."

"The cognac sounds wonderful, but I really shouldn't drink," Nell said, wavering. "We have an early-morning photo shoot."

"I can't drink alone, and we're celebrating." Todd closed the menu. "We finished filming ahead of schedule, and I get to spend six days with my daughter. The best part is I don't have to worry about your mother calling to ask if I have her favorite Christmas ornament. Last year she accused me of stealing the papier-mâché angel you made when you were six. I told her she can come and inspect my tree herself." He grinned like a boy who'd pulled a practical joke on his teacher. "She'd rather walk into the ocean than set foot in my new house."

"I'm sure the ornaments are in a box in her attic," Nell said. "She must have forgotten."

"Your mother has an excellent memory. She can tell you the hour and minute you were born," Todd scoffed. "She just doesn't know how to throw things out. One of the greatest things about the divorce is starting fresh. My house is three thousand square feet of tile floors and floor-to-ceiling windows, and it will never overflow with books and knickknacks like some overpriced thrift store."

Nell thought fondly of the house where she'd grown up. It was different than her friends' houses, which had looked like they belonged in a magazine spread. Her mother had designed their home to be elegant and lived-in at the same time: a living room with high ceilings, and glass coffee tables scattered with books. Pots and pans hung from the ceiling in the kitchen, and the walls in the foyer were lined with original art.

"I love her decor," Nell said, defending her. "Most of my friends weren't even allowed in their living rooms. I was never bored. There were books everywhere."

"There's nothing wrong with books, unless you use them to avoid facing the problems in your marriage." His eyes clouded over. "Every night she was glued to some paperback and barely looked up when I climbed into bed." He sighed. "When she did say something, it was to ask me not to set my alarm too early, or to change my brand of toothpaste. She couldn't stand the scent of mint."

Nell stabbed the olive in her martini. This wasn't going well. She had to change the subject, or her father would get so upset, he'd never agree to attend the wedding.

"Speaking of ornaments, one of my favorites is the snow globe of St. Moritz," she began. "You bought it one year when you were filming a movie in Zurich."

"That was years ago, when your mother and I were still getting along." Her father nodded. "Filming ran over, and I completely missed Christmas. I stopped in St. Moritz long enough to grab a snow globe and a pair of leather gloves at the hotel gift shop. I wanted to give your mother something to remind her of where we met." He glanced around at the paneled walls and art-deco mirrors. "It was right here in this bar. I was a waiter, and she came in with a group of friends. God, she was beautiful. Twenty years old with blond hair and blue eyes."

Todd swirled his glass the way he did when he told a story. Nell enjoyed hearing his memories: How his first job was washing his father's car, and he saved every dollar to buy flowers for the girl who lived across the street. How he could never afford to see movies as a teenager, and snuck into the cinema to watch the final scene and the credits. How having Nell and her brother, Pete, was better than all the gold watches and ties money could buy.

St. Moritz
Twenty-Eight Years Ago

Todd

Todd wiped down the glass and sighed with pleasure. Yesterday had been his twenty-second birthday, and he had accomplished three things he had always dreamed of: he'd traveled outside of America for the first time, he was wearing a tuxedo, and he was mixing his first proper cocktail other than a rum and Coke hastily stirred at a party.

The other bartender signaled for him to collect his tray, and Todd thought he would have to thank him. Christopher was his best friend; it was because of him that Todd was a waiter at the Carlton Hotel in St. Moritz, instead of working part-time at a record store in Cleveland.

After high school, Todd had attended Ohio State, and Christopher had received a scholarship to Yale. Along with learning political science, Christopher had acquired a new group of wealthy friends. He'd arrive home at the holidays and tell Todd about cruising on a yacht in the Mediterranean, or staying at someone's villa in the Bahamas. This winter he had been invited to spend a month at a chalet in St. Moritz, and had invited Todd to join him.

The airfare used up most of Todd's savings, but when would he get the chance to ski at places he'd only read about? Zuoz and Diavolezza, with its stunning backdrops and runs so wide they were as big as a whole country. The nightclubs had exotic names like Romanoff and Hemingway's Club, and there was a casino. Passing up the trip would be like turning down a lifetime supply of cheeseburgers.

He and Christopher worked at the Carlton to pay for their lift tickets, but there was plenty of time to experience everything St. Moritz had to offer: taking the Glacier Express to Zermatt, and riding the gondola to the summit of Muottas Muragl. When he stood at the top and adjusted his goggles, he wasn't a kid who had worked every day after school since he was fourteen. He was a young American who could navigate around the steep moguls and ski downhill straight to the bottom of the slopes.

"Stop staring at the girls and serve these whiskeys, or those guys are going to plant their fists in our faces," Christopher said to Todd, waving at three men with thick necks and bulging shoulders.

Todd tried to pull his eyes away from the girls sitting by the fireplace. They looked different than the other women, who were all wearing fur jackets and diamond earrings. These girls wore jeans with patches and hand-knitted ski caps, and their faces were free of makeup.

"See the girl with the blond hair and blue eyes? I swear she winked at me," Todd hissed.

"They're chalet girls," Christopher said dismissively. "They're hired by the chalets to cook breakfast for the guests. They are in St. Moritz for one reason, and it's not to ski the piste. It's to make some Italian race-car driver or Russian businessman fall in love with them over eggs benedict. We have as much chance with them as we do with the Swedes we met at the Altitude Bar."

Todd recalled the two girls they'd had drinks with last night. They'd all had a great time dancing, until the girls suggested going on to the casino. It was out of the question. One bad hand in blackjack, one cruel spin of the roulette wheel, and they'd lose all the money they'd earned.

The girl with blond hair caught his eye, and there was an odd feeling in his stomach. He straightened his bow tie and walked to the table.

"Can I join you?" Todd asked. "All the other tables are full."

"That one is empty." She pointed to a table by the window. She had an American accent, and even without lipstick, her mouth was the color of cherries.

"I got a little chilly this afternoon, and the fireplace looks so inviting." Todd pointed to the flames flickering in the wood-burning fireplace.

"Don't tell me you went on the mountain in this blizzard!" another girl exclaimed. She had a British accent and wore a pink sweater. "The snow is so thick, it's like a bowl of oatmeal out there. All the chalet guests gave up after the morning run." She groaned. "We had to make breakfast twice, and spend the afternoon drying ski socks."

Todd had never told a lie in his life. He had been a Boy Scout until the sixth grade, and in high school he'd been a member of the National Honor Society. But he couldn't impress these girls by pulling out a credit card from Bank Suisse. If he didn't say something, he wouldn't get another chance.

"That's the best time to ski. You have the whole mountain to yourself, and it's just you against the elements," Todd said knowingly. "I started above the tree line and skied the Fuorcla Grischa-Celerina. It's the longest run in St. Moritz. The black ice was a little sketchy, but I was rewarded by miles of fresh powder."

Todd would never have attempted the Fuorcla Grischa-Celerina in this weather, and he avoided black ice like the plague. But the girl with blond hair stopped sipping her cocktail and looked at him.

"That's a fun run, but it's nothing like the Selin." She flicked her hair behind her ears. "It has a 477-meter vertical drop, and when you attempt the last jump you feel like you're going to come."

Todd gulped and wished he had a drink. Had she really just compared skiing to sex, or was it too noisy to hear her correctly? At least she was talking to him. He sat down and picked up a menu.

"You should try the White Russian." The British girl held up her drink. "It's the best thing on the menu."

The other girls nodded in agreement, and Todd fiddled with his bow tie. If he ordered a drink, he could get fired. But the girl with blue eyes looked at him expectantly, and he felt like he was being sucked into a whirlpool.

"Why not?" He closed the menu. "Anything you girls recommend sounds delicious."

The girl's name was Patty, and she was a theater major at UCLA. She talked about places she had skied that he had never heard of: Courchevel and Val d'Isère and Saint-Martin-de-Belleville, which used to be a cheese-making village. Todd mentioned skiing at Alpine Valley in Ohio, but didn't admit he had only been there three times.

Patty signaled for the check and Todd reached into his pocket.

"Where are your friends?" he asked, noticing that the other girls hadn't returned from the powder room.

"They went on to some party," she said, waving her hand. "I hate parties, because they are always the same. Just because we served omelets to the men in the morning, they think they can grope us at night. I'd rather sit in bed with a good book than make conversation with guys who are only interested in whether I wear stockings under my chalet uniform."

Todd wondered what she looked like in her chalet uniform. Now was not the time to think about that. He had to pay his portion of the bill before the manager returned from his dinner break and found him chatting with a guest.

"They didn't leave any money." He picked up the check. He hadn't quite figured out the exchange rate, but four White Russians cost more than he had in his wallet.

"They never leave money." She suppressed a smile. "They expect the handsome man in a tuxedo who wanted to join us to pay for them."

"I seem to have forgotten my credit card," he gulped, momentarily pleased that she thought he was handsome. "I'll run over to my room. Wait here, I'll be right back."

Patty opened her purse and took out a gold card. She placed it on the table and looked at Todd. "I'll take care of it. I'll come with you and you can pay me back."

They walked outside and wandered through the village. The snow had stopped and a thick white carpet covered the cobblestones. A couple drove by in a horse and buggy, and there was the sound of horse hooves clip-clopping on the pavement.

"Christopher said chalet girls are in St. Moritz to pick up wealthy men," Todd began. "Why do you put up with guys asking you to add sliced bananas to their porridge if you have a gold card?"

"It's my parents' gold card, and I don't feel comfortable using it. My father doesn't approve of girls going on vacation alone. My mother is the chairwoman of four charities; she doesn't believe in having fun."

"They both sound frightening." Todd shuddered.

"Tomorrow is my twenty-first birthday." She turned to Todd, and her eyes were luminous. "I deserve to have a good time."

She reached up and kissed him. He kissed her back, and tasted cream and chocolate.

"I have to tell you something," Todd said when they pulled away. He couldn't start a relationship by lying to her.

"The tuxedo doesn't belong to you, and the credit card in your room has a two-hundred Swiss franc limit and is already at its maximum," she interrupted.

"How did you know?" he asked. She looked even more beautiful away from the bar. Her hair was dusted with snow and her cheeks glowed in the lamplight.

"The jacket is too big around the shoulders. Anyone who buys an Italian tuxedo would make sure it fit correctly," she mused. "And you looked at the bill as if your pet just died." She stopped and laughed. "Plus, I saw you mixing drinks at the bar."

The tuxedo belonged to the guy he and Christopher were staying with; his credit card was in a drawer where he'd tossed it, along with the letter from the bank explaining why they couldn't raise his limit.

"You knew I was a waiter?" Todd raised one eyebrow.

"I thought if you were willing to risk getting fired, maybe you were worth talking to," Patty said.

"And what do you think now?"

Patty stood on tiptoe and kissed him. Her eyes danced and a smile played across her face.

"I think I was right."

"I can't believe that was almost thirty years ago. Holiday romances should be outlawed," Todd said to Nell, scooping up fusilli pasta with tomato sauce. "It all seems perfect with the snow falling softly on the rooftops and shop windows filled with ornaments. Then you strip away the glitter and you're left with two people who are wholly unsuited for each other."

"You and Mom must have loved each other." Nell sipped her cocktail. "You were married for twenty-eight years."

"I thought we loved each other, but too many things got in the way. Your mother never liked that I worked at the movie studio with her father," he ruminated. "In the beginning it made sense; he gave me a job before I even finished college. But it caused a lot of resentment. Apparently she wanted to run the studio herself one day. How was I to know that? I thought she wanted to be an actress!

"Besides, he would never have turned the studio over to Patty. He believed women should either be waiting at the front door with a martini, or up on the big screen where one could admire them." He sighed. "I tried to involve her, but whenever I mentioned what happened during the day, she closed up like an oyster protecting a pearl. I finally gave up. She had every reason to be happy." He sat up straight as if defending himself. "A house on the flats in Beverly Hills, two children, enough money for karate classes and piano lessons." He looked at Nell and suddenly seemed older. "It always seemed that she wanted something I couldn't give her. She wouldn't consider therapy, and refused to attend couples' retreats." He managed a smile. "I couldn't blame her. The idea of being stuck in a log cabin with someone you're not talking to could drive anyone to divorce court."

"What about the family holidays in Portugal and Spain?" Nell insisted. "You swam in the ocean and Mom played tennis, and in the evenings you danced in the moonlight."

Todd's eyes clouded over and he waved at the bartender.

"Some places are magical, but no matter how you try, you can't take that feeling with you." He reached into his pocket and took out an envelope. "That reminds me. This is for you and Eliot."

"You can't give us more presents. You already sent an electric coffee maker and a cashmere blanket," Nell reminded him.

"There's no quicker route to divorce than starting your day without a decent cup of coffee, and there's nothing better than snuggling under a blanket and watching a movie." Todd grinned. "This is special; I promise you'll like it."

Nell opened the envelope and looked at Todd.

"A four-night stay at the St. Helena Inn in Napa Valley?"

"Napa Valley is the perfect location for a destination wedding," he said eagerly. "We'll have a ceremony at the inn followed by a small reception. The weather is perfect in June, and the chef can use vegetables from his garden."

"I don't know what you're talking about." Nell shifted on her stool.

"Since I won't be at the wedding, I thought you could have a second ceremony in California," he offered. "The vineyards are gorgeous in the summer, and I've been saving a bottle of Cabernet."

"I don't want two weddings." Nell frowned. "I want both my parents there when I walk down the aisle."

"That's impossible. Just breathing the same air as your mother raises my heart rate." He looked at his glass. "By the time the minister pronounces you man and wife, I'll have to be hooked up to an IV and transported to the hospital."

Nell put down her fork and glanced around the bar. A pianist was playing in the corner, and the other diners were talking excitedly about tomorrow's weather conditions. The snow flurries were going to clear, and the Piz Nair was going to be perfectly groomed. This wasn't the time to press her father; she needed to talk to him alone.

"I should go." She stood up. "All the other models are at Hemingway's Club; I told Raj I had an important errand. But I can't be late to get back. At night he stands in the hallway with a watch. If we're not in bed by eleven p.m., he threatens to withhold our paychecks."

"The nightlife is the best part of St. Moritz. I want to take you for a whiskey at Devil's Place, and to play the slot machines at the casino." He stopped and smiled. "Or are you embarrassed to be seen with your old father?"

"Nonsense. You're the most handsome father I know, and you keep getting younger." She kissed him on the cheek.

"I *feel* younger. It's because I'm away from your mother. I'm like Dorian Gray in reverse." He chuckled. "I'll stay here and have another cognac. It's not every day a movie comes in under budget, and I get to spend time with my daughter."

Nell walked through the village toward Badrutt's Palace. The streets were strung with Christmas lights, and shop windows glittered with fake snow. A stuffed dog wore a plaid sweater in the window at Burberry's, and two male mannequins were outfitted in black tuxedos at Roberto Cavalli.

Christmas was all about family and togetherness; why couldn't her parents put away their differences and agree to attend Nell's wedding? Her mother could be as immovable as the statue in the village square. And her father meant well, but he was being just as stubborn.

She climbed the steps of the hotel and entered the lobby. The lobby was incredibly busy, and she had to maneuver between women in tight pants and fur boots and men juggling shot glasses and cigarettes.

An older woman stepped out of the elevator. She had blond hair and red lipstick. Her slacks were suede and she wore a brown sweater.

"Mom?" Nell approached her. "What are you doing in the lobby? I thought you'd gone up to bed."

"I did everything I usually do to get to sleep: I took a hot bath and drank a cup of warm milk with honey. I even started the book I gave myself for Christmas." Her mother stopped and smiled. "One of the best things about the divorce is I pick out my own presents. Your father never understood that I didn't want expensive jewelry. I'd much rather have a book or a set of serving bowls. I'm just not tired." She pulled on her gloves. "I thought I'd go for a walk. It's so pretty outside; I want to see the village lit up at night time."

Her mother couldn't go out now! What if she ran into her father when he was walking back from the Carlton? They would both be furious with her, and the whole plan would be over before it began.

"You can't go for a walk," she said hurriedly. "It's almost ten o'clock at night."

"That's one of the wonderful things about St. Moritz, you can walk any time you like," her mother scoffed. "There's no crime, and everyone is strolling around the village, peering into shop windows and admiring the Christmas ornaments."

Nell's mother didn't go to bars by herself. She wasn't interested in meeting men. She'd said one marriage was enough; she wasn't going to subject herself to that again.

"The valet said there was a bear sighting in the village," Nell said quickly. "Everyone is encouraged to stay indoors."

"A bear!" Her mother's eyes were wide. "I spent a month in St. Moritz, and the only bear I saw was above the fireplace mantel of the chalet."

"They *are* quite rare, but there's one particular bear that makes an appearance every Christmas. Why don't we go up to my suite?" Nell took her mother's arm and led her to the elevator. "You can help me choose the fabric for my wedding dress. Felicity brought tons of samples; she's going to design something unique."

"I'm so happy you and Eliot are having a proper wedding. There's nothing more beautiful than a bride in a white wedding dress," her mother said, nodding. "Your father and I were married by a justice of the peace. I should have known then that it would never work."

"I can't wait to show you the yacht club in Nantucket where we're having the reception," Nell gushed. "Eliot's family has been members for years. One of his uncles knows Dad. They met at the America's Cup race in New Zealand."

Her mother pressed the button on the elevator and stepped inside.

"We've talked about this before. I can't come if your father is there," she said, suddenly impatient. "Being at your wedding is the most important thing in the world, but it simply wouldn't work."

"I don't see why," Nell said stubbornly.

"I don't expect you to understand." Her mother's voice softened. "It's like getting on a plane when you're so terrified of flying you can't breathe. Just the thought of it gives me tremors."

Nell had to change her mother's mind. But she was suddenly tired from the afternoon excursion to Alp Grüm, as well as cocktails with her father, and worrying that her parents would run into each other. It would be better to bring it up after they'd both had a good night's sleep.

"I'm glad you're in St. Moritz." Nell kissed her mother on the cheek. "We're going to have so much fun."

"So am I." Her mother beamed. "There's no one I'd rather spend the holidays with."

Nell sipped a cup of coffee and sank onto the striped armchair. Her room really was lovely: the king-sized bed had a quilted bedspread, and there was a marble fireplace hung with stockings. A silver tea service sat on the sideboard, along with a fruit loaf and mixed nuts.

Her mother had gone to her own suite, and Nell was going to take a shower and wash her hair. How could her parents be so difficult? All she wanted was a photo album with pictures of her father giving the toast and her mother eating chocolate fondant cake. Her mother would wear a vintage designer dress, and her father would have a rose boutonniere in his buttonhole.

Had her mother ever been so young and adventurous to take a job as a chalet girl so she could ski the black diamond runs? She tried to picture her father at twenty-two, without any money and wearing his first tuxedo. Her diamond ring glinted under the Tiffany lamp, and suddenly she had an idea. She slipped off her sweater and pulled a robe around her waist. Maybe everything would work out after all.

Four

Five Days Before the Fashion Show
7:30 a.m.

Felicity

FELICITY STOOD AT THE BASE of the ski gondola and rubbed her hands. It was too early in the morning, and she was freezing. The pine trees were blanketed in last night's snow and a squirrel darted sleepily across her path.

Raj had insisted that everyone meet at the gondola to ski the famous white carpet. It was supposed to be the most glorious run of the day: miles of fresh powder, without a single imprint. The sky turned from purple to blue before your eyes, and the snow was as soft as a down comforter. It was important to be the first skiers on the mountain; if you waited until later, the fresh powder would disappear.

First you had to ride in the gondola, and then you transferred to a chairlift, when you reached the top, it was so cold you couldn't feel your nose. It had been too early when she left the hotel for a cup of coffee. No matter that the guidebook said it was the experience of a lifetime; snuggling under a down comforter in her pajamas seemed like a better idea.

Raj hadn't been happy that she'd missed the excursion to Alp Grüm, because it had been the perfect photo opportunity; she couldn't beg off again. A photographer was going to meet them for lunch and take photos of all the models. Her head felt perfectly fine, and she had gotten plenty of sleep; after Gabriel left, she'd spent the whole afternoon and night in bed. At first, her mind had been a jumble of thoughts. How could Adam suggest they see other people, and how could she change his mind? When she finally slept, she never wanted to get out of bed. The mattress was soft as butter, and the pillows were filled with feathers and fitted with silk pillowcases.

She had been tempted to call Adam and apologize. But she thought about waiting years to get married, and knew she couldn't do it. Then she imagined losing him completely, and her chest tightened and she felt sick.

At least Raj had promised her lunch at the Alpine Hut. It was where all the fashionable people ate when they skied the Corvatsch, and needed to refuel before returning to the slopes. That was one of the wonderful things about the Alps. The mountain cafés served bratwurst and lamb cutlets and soup so thick you could eat it with a fork. Felicity was going to order pizzoccheri with beef noodles and potatoes and crepes stuffed with walnuts and jam.

"Let's go." Raj motioned for her to climb into the gondola. "The models are all on the first gondola. If we don't hurry, other skiers will get there first, and the white carpet will disappear."

"The only carpet I want to see at this time of day is the one in my suite," Felicity grumbled. "Even the squirrels think it's too early. They gave up collecting nuts and went back to bed."

"Greta said it's the experience of a lifetime." Raj sat on the hard surface and made room for Felicity beside him.

"Who's Greta?" Felicity asked as the gondola lurched and they started up the mountain.

"I met her at the Polo Bar last night and we went on to the King's Club. She's from Zurich, and she knows everything about St. Moritz." Raj adjusted his gloves.

"You took a woman to the King's Club?" Felicity raised her eyebrow. "Wasn't that expensive? The dress code says 'dress to impress,' and you practically need to show the bouncer your bank balance to get inside."

Felicity had read about the King's Club in the hotel brochure. It was the oldest nightclub in Switzerland, and every celebrity who visited St. Moritz sipped White Ladies or Vodka Fizzes at the club's bar. Disco balls hung from the ceiling, and the dance floor was so packed it was like attending some terribly sophisticated high school prom.

"I ordered two glasses of Sambuca, and they lasted all night." He fished a piece of paper out of his pocket. "And she was a wealth of information: Bobby's Pub is where all the young people hang out, and the only place to be seen for après-ski drinks is the Roo Lounge. You may think the patrons of the Miles Davis Lounge are simply enjoying casual conversation with their cigars, but they're most likely conducting cutthroat business deals."

Felicity glanced at the paper and looked at Raj. "Her name and phone number are on the top, and my German isn't very good, but I think she left her room number."

"We're going to meet this afternoon to discuss where I can get the best deals on toboggan rentals for the next photo shoot." He snatched up the paper. "Anyway, you should talk. Nell told me you and Adam had a fight, but she didn't mention you already met someone new."

"What are you talking about?" Felicity asked.

"It was all over the blogs this morning." He took out his phone. "Pictures of you in the arms of some hunky, dark-haired doctor. To be honest, I was shocked—that isn't like you at all."

"Of course it isn't like me—it never happened." Felicity's heart pounded. "A sled almost knocked me over and I took a tumble in the snow. I blacked out for a minute and he carried me to my room."

"According to silverweddings.com, 'Felicity Grant continues to surprise us in St. Moritz days before the debut of her winter collection. We broke the news that she might be planning her own wedding, but now the identity of the groom is in question. Was she modeling her own design in anticipation of nuptials with her longtime sports manager boyfriend, or is her future husband a dark-haired man rumored to be St. Moritz's doctor? All we know is they looked very cozy when he was carrying her down the catwalk at Badrutt's Palace. If only we had followed them into the elevator, we might have learned the whole story.'"

"Let me see that." Felicity grabbed his phone. There was a photo of Gabriel carrying her through the hotel lobby. Her arms were around his neck, and he was wearing a blue ski sweater.

"It's wonderful publicity for the collection," Raj commented. "I couldn't have planned it better myself."

"You can't even see my face, and I don't care about the collection!" Felicity gulped the cold air. "If Adam sees this, he'll never speak to me again."

"Nell said you weren't speaking to each other anyway," Raj

reminded her. "Though I didn't believe her. Ever since I saw him in our apartment six years ago, I knew you'd end up together. What guy would iron a wedding dress for a girl he just met, unless he was falling in love?"

"His mother put the dress in her steam room," she corrected. "And we were so young. It's easy to be in love when you don't expect anything of each other except a slice of pie as a thank you. We got in an argument yesterday. I told Adam that I couldn't wait years to get married. He said I cared more about the wedding than him, and that we should take a break."

"All grooms are the same. They never understand the significance of the perfect diamond ring or the right gown," Raj said thoughtfully. "A fancy wedding isn't necessary, but neither are expensive cars or memberships to the gym. You can travel up Fifth Avenue on the bus, and if you want to stay fit you can jog around Central Park. But the grooms all come round the day of the wedding. They drink beers with their groomsmen and slip into their rented Armani tuxes and everyone is happy. The bride posts photos of the bridal party on Instagram, and her friends can't wait to buy a gown just like ours."

"Can we not talk about Felicity Grant Bridal for a moment!" Felicity's veins felt like ice. "Adam and I got in a huge fight, and now there are photos of me in the arms of another man."

"I was just trying to distract you," Raj said gently. "You and Adam have had disagreements before. Do you remember the summer he wanted to take you to Disneyland, but you were designing the gown for a wedding at the Plaza? The bride wasn't happy with the alterations, and you had to cancel the trip at the last minute."

It had been Felicity's first society wedding, and five hundred guests had watched the bride walk down the aisle. And that dress!

Yards of silk taffeta and two petticoats and a peau de soie bodice. The bride had worn her grandmother's diamond-and-ruby choker, and her undergarments were hand-sewn in Paris.

"How was I supposed to know he was going to surprise me with a holiday in California?" she fretted. "Anyway, no one in the wedding industry takes a vacation in July. It's like telling Adam to go to Bali during the NFL draft."

"You see, your career is important to you," Raj countered. "Adam loves you. He just wants to wait until his firm is established to get married."

"I love my career, but I want a family before I'm too old to enjoy it," she said slowly. "It doesn't matter. When Adam sees these photos, our relationship will be over."

"Adam hardly reads *Silver Weddings* with his morning coffee." Raj slipped the phone into his pocket. "We're about to ski the most exhilarating run in the Engadin valley. Stop worrying and enjoy yourself."

Raj skied off with the models and Felicity perched at the top. Raj was right; she couldn't call Adam from the slopes, and what did it matter? He'd said they should take a break and see other people; he probably didn't care if she was in the arms of some Swiss ski instructor.

But what about Gabriel's advice? He'd thought she had to tell Adam how she felt. If she kept it bottled up inside, it would be like ignoring snow on the roofs in the village after a heavy snowfall. You had to shovel the new snow, or the whole chalet could collapse.

The sun caught the tips of her skis and she pushed off down the mountain. The wind touched her cheeks, and she felt the delicious thrill of picking up speed. For the next few hours she wasn't going to think about anything except the trees flying by and her skis digging into wet powder.

Four hours later Felicity unbuckled her boots and pushed her goggles onto her forehead. She had skied all morning, and now she understood the magic of the white carpet. The sky was the color of topaz, and the runs were so wide she barely saw another person. At one point she stopped to watch a squirrel collecting nuts, and it was all so beautiful, she never wanted to be anywhere else.

It was noon and the sun was high above the mountain. Her cheeks were sunburned and she realized she was starving. Raj was already inside the Alpine Hut getting a table, and a photographer was taking photos of the models.

Her phone buzzed and she fished it out of her pocket. The screen lit up and Felicity counted five texts. She clicked on the messages and read:

> Just checking on you. I saw an odd posting on a blog.
> The blogs must be wrong but I thought you should see them. Give me a call and I'll explain.
> Felicity, what is going on? I need to hear from you. You are all over the internet.
> Felicity, I've been texting you all night. Where are you?
> For God's sake, call me. I just got home from dinner and you're not answering your phone.

How had she missed Adam's texts? Her phone had been buried in her parka, and she hadn't heard it beep. It was six a.m. in New York; what if she called and woke him? Adam was often irritable first thing in the morning. But if she waited, he might leave for a client breakfast and she wouldn't be able to speak to him all day.

She rushed inside and approached the hostess. "Excuse me," she said.

"Welcome to the Alpine Hut," the woman answered. "Will you be joining us for lunch?"

"I'm trying to make a call," Felicity said urgently. "My phone doesn't have any bars."

"There's no reception at this altitude." She handed Felicity a menu. "Would you like to see a menu? Today's specials are cheese raclette and apple strudel for dessert. The chef makes it with whole cream and cinnamon; it's the best in the Engadin valley."

"I don't have time for raclette; this is an emergency." Felicity turned back to the deck. Music blared from the loudspeakers, and the outdoor tables were filled with men and women eating bowls of soup and hunks of bread with cheese.

She searched for her skis and found them wedged behind a pair of Rossignols. A voice called her name, and Raj waved from a table by the window. Felicity didn't have time to explain. She buckled her boots and pushed off down the slope as if her life depended on it.

Felicity paced around the living room of her suite and stared at her phone. She had skied straight down the mountain and hurried back to the hotel. Now it was two p.m. and she still hadn't replied to his texts. Texting back was tricky; what if he interpreted what she wrote the wrong way? She tried to call him but his phone went straight to voicemail. Adam was probably taking Doug out for ham and cheese omelets at some trendy breakfast place in Manhattan.

How could the photos of her and Gabriel have ended up all over the internet? She was tempted to open a bottle of scotch from the minibar. Even Raj would agree that her boyfriend seeing photos of her with another man was a good reason to spend fifty Swiss francs on a shot of alcohol.

She wished she could talk to Nell, but she was still on the slopes. Suddenly she noticed Gabriel's card on the coffee table. She hadn't gone to the village yesterday to buy colored pens, and she didn't want to get behind on the sketches for Camilla. She'd go now and pay Gabriel a visit at the same time. Her ankle throbbed, and she winced. Gabriel had warned her to take it easy, but she had skied the white carpet anyway. There was nothing she could do about it; she gingerly slipped on her boots and walked to the door.

Felicity strolled through the village with her new pens and consulted the card that Gabriel had given her with his office address. She turned a corner and glanced up at a wooden building strung with Christmas lights. It was perched above the village square, and looked more like a chalet than a doctor's office. There were window boxes and a red front door with a pine wreath. She knocked and waited for someone to appear.

"Felicity! This is a surprise." Gabriel opened the door. A long white coat covered his shirt, and he held a clipboard. "What are you doing here?"

"I had an errand in the village, and thought I'd come see you. I hope that's all right," Felicity said, walking inside. The waiting room had a linoleum floor and paneled walls. There was a vinyl sofa and a coffee table covered with magazines. "I would have texted, but I didn't want to disturb you if you were with patients."

"It's quiet now." Gabriel followed her. "You missed the afternoon rush: a girl broke her wrist skating backward even though her mother warned her not to, and a man needed stitches from attempting the Cresta Run. He's lucky it isn't worse. How any sane adult can torpedo down the mountain on a board as flimsy as a waffle is beyond me."

"I'm afraid I didn't come to talk about ski injuries." Felicity grimaced. Her ankle had felt fine this morning, but now there was a slight twinge. "I wanted to ask for your help. I'm in even more trouble than before."

"Don't tell me you hurt yourself again." He glanced at her ankle. "I told you to keep your foot elevated as much as possible. And what about your head? You had a nasty bump. Please don't tell me you went skiing after almost getting a concussion!"

"When I woke up this morning, my head felt perfectly normal. And I've been trying to be good about my ankle, but Raj begged me to ski the white carpet," she admitted. "It was worth it in the beginning. I've never experienced such soft powder, and the runs were so vast, it was like performing a ballet."

"I can give you some pain medication for your ankle if you like." He rummaged through his doctor's bag. "But you have to be careful; it's easy to get addicted. I'd rather you just listen to me and keep the ankle up in the first place."

"It's not my ankle—I told you, I'm good at pain." She sat on the sofa. "It's Adam. He saw photos of us on a wedding blog and sent texts demanding to know what was going on."

"Photos of us doing what?" Gabriel asked, perplexed.

"You were carrying me into the hotel lobby. A photo of me with my arms around your neck ended up on social media."

"Your boyfriend is worried about a doctor helping you, after a sled almost ran you over?"

"He doesn't know about the sled." She gave him her phone. "Someone made up a silly story that you're the mystery man I'm going to marry. It's all over Instagram and on the wedding blogs."

"I don't see the problem." Gabriel glanced at the photos.

"His texts were livid," she said anxiously. "I can't get hold of him to explain."

Gabriel opened a cupboard and took out a bottle. He found two glasses and poured large shots.

"My father always keeps a bottle of schnapps around for emergencies." He handed her a glass. "Your boyfriend broke up with you because you wanted to get married, and suggested you both see other people. Now he's angry because you're involved with another man? That doesn't make much sense."

"I'm not involved with anyone," she corrected. "It just looked like it from the photos. I don't blame him for being mad. I'd be furious if I saw pictures of him on Facebook having dinner with another woman."

"You're not the one who told him you needed a break," he reminded her. "Did he expect you to wait patiently until he decides what he wants?"

"It's only been a day," she said, wavering. "Maybe he thought something was going on before he gave me the ultimatum."

"Still, it was his idea. I don't see why he's upset." Gabriel sipped the liqueur. "Unless there was a time stamp on the break. Like a carton of eggs with an expiration date."

"You know what it's like when couples argue," she sighed. "People say things they don't mean. It happens all the time."

"So you don't think he wanted to break up with you?"

"He thinks he does, but he can't be right," she said uncertainly. "We've been together for six years. We had decided everything about our future: we'd live in Manhattan until I got pregnant, and then we'd move to Connecticut. We'd have two children, and if they were boys we might try for a girl." She paused. "It would be lovely to design her wedding gown."

"You agreed on all these things, but you couldn't agree on a date to get married?" Gabriel wondered aloud.

"We talked about all those things," Felicity said slowly. Had Adam agreed to them, or had she made all the plans while he never said yes or no? "I always assumed he wanted the same things. That's what's wonderful about our relationship."

"You Americans are supposed to be good at communicating," Gabriel commented. "It seems neither of you were listening."

"We're in love." She looked at Gabriel. "That's the most important thing in the world: when you wake up in the morning and you're so happy because your favorite person is beside you. Or when you work all day and you can't wait to share everything that happened."

"I wouldn't know. I've never been in love," Gabriel said.

"You've never been in love?" Her eyes were wide. "That's impossible."

"There was a red-haired British girl when I was ten." He swirled his glass. "She didn't like Harry Potter, so that ended quickly. Then there was the dark-haired Italian girl I met when I was sixteen. We carved our initials in the pine tree near the gondola, and I thought we would last forever. The next day I saw her initials carved on the same tree beside the initials of Franz, the German ski instructor."

"What about when you were at college?" she asked.

"When you're a medical student, the only thing you long for is your bed," he offered. "It has a never-ending allure because you see it so infrequently. I was too busy learning how the human body functioned to think about love."

"You'll fall in love someday," she said knowingly. "And then you'll understand why you'd do almost anything to hang on to it. True love only happens once in a lifetime. If you let it go, you might never feel that way again."

"I suppose I will," he ruminated. He looked at her closely and sipped his schnapps. "I don't understand why you're here. What can I do to help?"

"I'm not sure exactly." She leaned against the cushions. "All I know is that yesterday I fell and twisted my ankle, and I'd never been in so much pain. You're a complete stranger, but you carried me inside and made me feel better."

"I'm a doctor; that's what I do," he reminded her. "But what does that have to do with Adam?"

"It always helps to get an objective opinion," she said carefully. "When you're in a relationship, it's hard to separate how you feel from the right thing to do. Haven't you ever read the advice columns in the newspaper? I used to love reading Dear Abby; my mother saved all her columns. I even wrote to the advice columnist in *Elle* when I was having trouble with a college boyfriend." Felicity smiled at the memory. "She replied that any boy who thinks a first date could include a stop at the laundromat to fold his socks isn't worth seeing again."

"I'm a medical doctor," Gabriel said, and chuckled. "I don't know anything about giving relationship advice."

"You suggested I tell Adam how I felt, and you were right," she continued. "I have to know if he's ever going to ask me to marry him."

"I'm not sure I'm following you." He looked puzzled. "You did tell Adam, and he said you should take a break. What are you going to do next?"

"That's why I'm here," she said finally. "I thought you could tell me what you'd do if you were in my situation. It will help me see more clearly how I should respond to Adam."

"I've never met Adam. I don't know anything about the two of you together." He pondered. "I'd like to try to help, but I'm not sure I'll say the right thing."

"You're right—I won't bother you again." She stood up gingerly. "Thank you for everything. I hope I didn't keep you from anything important."

"Look, why don't we take a walk through the village?" Gabriel ruffled his hair. "We'll get something to eat, and I can think of a way to help."

"Are you sure?" she asked.

"Positive." He took off his white coat and opened the door. "I've seen all the patients for the day, and I'd much rather sample bratwurst than write up a report on intestinal blockage due to eating too much Swiss cheese."

They strolled onto the Via Maistra and Felicity shielded her eyes from the afternoon sun. The snow on the rooftops was pearl white, and the village teemed with shoppers. A tall Christmas tree was decorated with silvery ornaments, and the lampposts were tied with red bows.

Felicity had never seen such vibrant skiwear: sweaters with geometric patterns, padded ski pants, brightly colored scarves. The shop windows reminded her of Dylan's Candy Bar in New York, and she was dying to go inside and buy a turtleneck or a pair of gloves.

They toured Heuberger Butcher, with its huge slabs of ham hanging from metal hooks. Felicity was grateful to Gabriel for showing her, but she confessed she'd rather see her sausage on a plate with a side of potato salad.

He took her inside Glattfelder's, and she admired glass cases filled with coffee beans and jars of caviar. They tasted dark-roast coffees with names like Verona and Sienna, and sampled imported caviar.

"During World War Two, they had to keep the sale of caviar secret." Gabriel spooned a drop of caviar onto melba toast. "If the Germans saw anyone leaving the shop with a jar, they knew they were rich, and confiscated all the money in their pockets."

"I could never spend two hundred dollars on fish eggs and salt." Felicity took a small bite and grimaced. "I'd much rather eat a bowl of soup or a lamb chop."

They walked back onto the pavement, and Felicity glanced around. A man pulled a child on a toboggan; a woman in fur boots was carrying bags from Bogner.

Gabriel noticed Felicity's expression and frowned. "Are you all right? You look pale. I shouldn't have suggested we go for a walk. You should be lying in bed with your foot up."

"I'm glad I came. I love seeing the shops, and if I was in my suite, I'd be checking my phone to see if Adam called," she responded. "I'm just not used to the cold; every part of me is shivering."

"Why don't we go to the Kulm Hotel?" he said. "It's the oldest hotel in St. Moritz, and they serve an excellent afternoon tea."

"Are you sure you don't mind?" Felicity asked, even though just the thought of hot tea made her feel warmer.

"Everyone who comes to St. Moritz should try their chestnut puree with fresh whipped cream." He took her arm. "It will be my treat. My last patient was a Dutch industrialist, and he tipped me one hundred Swiss francs."

The Kulm Hotel resembled a fairy-tale castle with stone turrets and flags flying from different countries. A giant Christmas tree stood in the driveway, and valets sprinted between Bentleys and Range Rovers, unpacking luggage and ski gear.

The lobby had crystal chandeliers and marble pillars and oriental rugs. There was a stone fireplace hung with stockings and gilt mirrors resting against the walls. Felicity rubbed her hands and couldn't wait for a cup of hot tea.

"The idea of winter holidays began in this lounge," Gabriel said when they were seated on velvet chairs. There was a tray of meringues and slices of tiramisu served in porcelain cups. Felicity ate smoked salmon on pumpernickel and had never tasted anything so delicious.

"The story goes that, in the summer of 1864, four Englishmen joined the owner of the Kulm Hotel for afternoon tea. He urged them to come back in December when the sun shone every day and snow covered the Alps. They were used to miserable British winters, and declined. The owner made a bet that if they didn't enjoy it, he would reimburse their travel expenses." Gabriel sipped Darjeeling tea. "They took him up on it and had such a good time, they stayed until April. That's how winter holidays were born."

Felicity looked at Gabriel with curiosity. "I've lived in New York for ten years, and I wouldn't know where to take tourists except the usual places like Rockefeller Center and the Met. How do you know so much about St. Moritz?"

"I was born and raised here, and its history is fascinating," he mused. "I enjoy showing it to someone new. It makes me appreciate the beauty."

"I thought you said St. Moritz was make-believe, and you'd rather live in the real world," she reminded him. Her throat was soothed by the sweet tea, and for the first time since Adam sent the texts she felt almost happy and relaxed. As soon as she got back to the Badrutt's Palace she would try to call him again or reply to his texts.

"I'm a doctor; I want to help people." Gabriel shrugged. "I didn't pore over cadavers for years so I could learn how to remove a diamond earring from a little girl's nose."

"Did that really happen?" Felicity burst out laughing.

"Her mother wasn't paying attention, so the girl plucked it out of her ear and stuck it up her nostril." He sighed. "I don't know who was more upset: the little girl because of the pain, the mother because she'd lost her favorite earring, or the father because he had to pay my fee and buy a new pair."

Felicity took a bite of chestnut puree and licked her spoon thoughtfully. She glanced at Gabriel and her face lit up in a smile.

"You look like you just tasted whipped cream for the first time." Gabriel buttered a scone.

"The hotel is gorgeous, and the tea is piping hot, and you know so many interesting things." She traced the rim of her cup. "For a moment I forgot everything that happened and was enjoying myself."

Gabriel leaned forward to refill her cup, and tea spilled on the tablecloth. They reached for a napkin at the same time and bumped their heads. Felicity sat back and rubbed her forehead. Suddenly she didn't want the afternoon to end. She didn't want to go back to the suite and worry about Adam, and if Camilla would accept her sketches for Bergdorf's fashion show.

"Could you do something for me?" she asked. "Could you tell me another folktale?"

"You want me to tell you a folktale in the middle of the afternoon?"

"It did such a good job of clearing my mind yesterday and not letting me worry about anything." She looked at Gabriel. "If you don't mind, I'd love to hear another one."

"I'll tell you 'How the Devil Crushed His Foot.'" He rubbed his chin. "It was one of my mother's favorites.

"An old and pious woman lived in the Verena Valley. She devoted her life to helping the poor, but as she reached her old age she could no longer deliver food or make clothing. She built a small hermitage and spent her days praying for the inhabitants' well being.

"The old woman's prayers worked, and the devil realized he wasn't capturing as many souls in the vicinity. He traveled to the hermitage to investigate and heard the old woman praying. When he saw what was going on, he decided to put a stop to it. He rolled a boulder from a cliff and positioned it over the woman's head.

"Just as he was about to deliver the fatal blow, the rock slipped and landed on the devil's foot. He howled with pain and ran away, leaving the boulder where it fell. The woman lived to be one hundred, and the rock is still there, where people visit it today. My mother used to fix a picnic and we would go and eat it on the rock. She baked devil's food cake just for the occasion."

Gabriel stopped talking. Felicity opened her eyes and noticed that their hands were close together.

"That was a wonderful story." She nodded and moved slightly. "I feel much better."

Gabriel glanced down as if he had just noticed his hand was next to Felicity's. "I'm glad. I'll ask for the check. It's getting late; I still have to call in some medications."

Felicity looked up from her sketchpad and gazed out the window of her suite. The sun was edging behind the mountain, and the clusters of fir trees were thick with snow. A snowmobile whizzed by, and Felicity heard people laughing.

After afternoon tea at the Kulm Hotel, Gabriel had offered to walk her back to the hotel. She'd thanked him and said she could manage by herself. She made a cup of coffee and tried to work on a sketch for Camilla, but the oversized satin bow wasn't working, and she had used the sweetheart neckline a dozen times before. She set it aside and wondered what Adam was doing in New York.

It was five days until the fashion show, and there was so much to keep her busy. She had to make sure the models had the right lipsticks and eye shadows. Sometimes a model wore her favorite pink lipstick when Felicity instructed her to wear red, and the whole color scheme of her outfit was thrown off. And she needed to make sure there were shawls in the dressing room in case the models got cold while they waited for their turn on the runway.

She wished she could tell Raj about the sketches for Camilla. But she had promised herself she wouldn't say a word until after the fashion show. It would only make him more anxious, and there was nothing he could do to help. Either Camilla would love her designs and put them in the show, or all her work would be for nothing.

And how should she reply to Adam's texts? She had planned on texting him as soon as she arrived back at the suite, but she still wasn't sure what to say. She closed her sketchpad and pulled off her sweater. First she would take a hot bath; then she would reply to his texts. She didn't want to get it wrong; their whole future together depended on her response.

Five

Nell

NELL SAT AT A WINDOW table at La Stalla and gazed onto the Plazza dal Mulin. It was evening, and couples were strolling along the pavement deciding where to have dinner. There were so many choices: pizzerias with wood-burning ovens, and traditional Swiss restaurants with specialty cocktails and photos of celebrities on the walls.

Today had been exhausting. Raj had insisted all the models meet at the gondola for the first run of the day. Nell wouldn't have minded; she was excited about skiing the magic carpet. But what if her mother woke early and decided to stroll through the village? Or her father wanted to surprise Nell by joining her at Badrutt's Palace for breakfast?

She'd called the concierge and hastily arranged a spa morning for her mother. How could her mother say no to a Swiss full-body massage followed by an alpine herbal wrap? That would keep her occupied until the afternoon, and then Nell would be back from skiing. They could browse in the boutiques or go ice-skating on the lake.

Her father wanted to spend as much time with her as possible; she couldn't leave him alone all day. She sent him a text asking him to meet her at the Alpine Hut for lunch. Once he strapped on his skis and hit the slopes, he'd stay on the mountain all afternoon. Then she'd suggest he relax in the sauna and she'd meet him for a late dinner.

"You're here alone. I thought you'd be at the lodge resting after today's skiing." Felicity entered the restaurant. "Don't tell me your parents already found out about each other. Your mother is at the train station, and your father called his pilot and is sitting on the plane."

"I must have been crazy," Nell groaned. "I'm either going to get fat from eating two dinners every night, or I'll be so exhausted I won't be able to walk down the runway at the show."

"If I were you, I'd tell them the truth." Felicity sat opposite Nell. "They're adults; they have to learn to face each other."

"I can't say anything yet," Nell replied adamantly. "They've both made it perfectly clear they can't breathe the same air. I'm no closer to convincing them to attend the wedding than when they arrived."

"What are you going to do?" Felicity dipped a breadstick in butter.

"Last night my father and I had drinks at the Carlton Hotel." Nell sipped her wine. "He told me about the night he met my mother. He pretended to be rich to impress her, but she saw right through him." She paused. "When he started talking about her, I could tell they had really been in love."

"It's easy to be in love in the beginning," Felicity answered glumly. "It's only when you can't agree on anything that you have problems."

"Adam will come round." Nell squeezed Felicity's hand. "You should have heard my father talking about my mother when she was twenty. He sounded like a starry-eyed teenager meeting his movie-star crush."

"That was twenty-eight years ago." Felicity accepted a wine glass from the waiter. "What does that have to do with getting them to attend your wedding?"

"If I can make them relive the first days of their courtship, perhaps that will rekindle some old feelings," Nell said eagerly. "I don't expect them to fall in love, but at least they'll be able to tolerate each other long enough to hear Eliot and me say 'I do.'"

"How do you know your mother felt the same?" Felicity asked.

"I don't, exactly," Nell confessed. "That's why I'm meeting her for dinner. I'll ask her about their first date in St. Moritz."

"I've always believed in Christmas miracles, but what if it doesn't work?" Felicity asked.

"It has to work. I haven't wanted anything so badly since I moved to New York to become a model," Nell said. "My parents wanted me to go to college, so I used my graduation money and paid for my plane ticket. Then I camped out in a friend's loft and knocked on the door of every modeling agency until someone took me on."

"I remember seeing your head shots," Felicity said. "Raj took one look at them and picked up the phone. He told the agency he'd pay double your rate, but he had to have you for my show. He was right, of course." She smiled. "You were so stunning in that empire-style gown with the ruffled skirt, we made Page Six of the *New York Post*."

"There is one thing. I haven't told Raj my parents are here," Nell admitted. "Could you cover for me, so I can spend a little time with them? I won't miss anything important. This collection is the biggest moment of your career, and I wouldn't do anything to jeopardize it."

"You're my best friend. I'll do anything to help you," Felicity assured her. "And Raj tends to go overboard. He's already got RSVPs from the biggest names in the industry. He thought the photos of me and Gabriel online were good publicity." She pulled out her phone and scrolled through the photos. "Adam sent me a dozen texts, he was so furious."

"I've been too busy fretting about my parents to be on my phone." Nell studied the photos. "So this is the doctor. God, he's gorgeous!"

"Gabriel and I are just friends," Felicity clarified. "You have enough on your hands without trying to solve my problems. And Raj has been so busy following the models around, I needed someone to talk to. There's something soothing about Gabriel's presence."

"He *is* a doctor." Nell handed back the phone. "Don't they learn to have a good bedside manner in medical school?"

"It's not just that. He made me question my feelings for Adam," Felicity said slowly.

"And?" Nell asked.

"I don't want to wait forever for Adam to propose. But Adam and I have been building a life together; I can't imagine life without him," she said pensively. "Gabriel was quite helpful. Sometimes it's good to have an outsider give you advice."

"I'd be careful," Nell advised her.

"What do you mean?" Felicity asked.

"He's a hunky single doctor, and you're a successful wedding dress designer." She picked up her wine glass. "His advice might not be objective."

Felicity was about to reply when Nell looked up and noticed her mother standing at the door. She wore a burgundy dress and suede boots.

"Nell, darling—and Felicity!" She approached the table. "How wonderful that you're joining us. I thought you'd be busy preparing for the fashion show."

Felicity greeted her. "Nell invited me, but if you'd rather have a mother-and-daughter dinner, I completely understand."

"You must stay. I want to hear about your career," Patty urged. "Nell raved about the collection. The next time you're in Los Angeles, I'll arrange a trunk show and invite everyone I know."

"My mother's right. You must stay for dinner," Nell agreed. "La Stalla is famous for its fondue. It's much more fun to eat fondue when you have three people."

The waiter set the table with a silver fondue pot and three bowls. He opened a bottle of wine and gave them a quick lesson in eating fondue. First, you always stirred the cheese from right to left so it didn't stick to the pot. There were only three permissible drinks when eating fondue: white wine, kirsch, or herbal tea. If you drank anything else, the cheese congealed in your stomach. Finally, you never followed up fondue with a rich dessert; you had to cleanse your palate with a piece of acidic fruit, like a wedge of pineapple or an orange.

"I didn't realize fondue etiquette was so serious," Nell laughed after he left. They took turns dunking bread crusts into the mixture of cheese, champagne, and truffles.

"I think that performance was to impress you beautiful young women." Her mother smiled. "I remember being a chalet girl in St. Moritz. We were barely twenty-one, and men wouldn't leave us alone."

"Dad said you met at the Carlton Bar," Nell said. "He was trying to impress you, but you saw right through him."

"When did he tell you that?" her mother asked in surprise.

Nell swallowed her wine and gulped. She shouldn't have mentioned her father. What if her mother asked when she had last seen him? Telling an outright lie was different than withholding information.

"He came to New York last month, and we drank White Russians at the Nat King Cole bar," she said vaguely.

"Your father was drinking White Russians?" Her mother raised her eyebrow. "I thought he was watching his weight. He became vain as we got older; I'd catch him sucking his stomach in in front of the mirror."

"He told me about your first date," Nell continued. "He was the hotel waiter, and you were sitting at a table with your friends. You ended up paying for the drinks, and he was quite embarrassed."

"I can't believe he remembered," she said, but she looked quite pleased. "That was the night we met, but our first date was a few days later. Your father loved to play the knight in shining armor. He thought he was saving my honor."

"How did he do that?" Nell looked at her mother.

"It's quite a funny story." She sipped her wine and leaned back in her chair. "He was so proud of himself, you would have imagined he'd discovered a cure for cancer."

Patty

Patty stood in the chalet's kitchen and flicked her blond hair behind her ears. She shouldn't have taken the job; she hated serving cocktails at parties. But it was nice to have some extra money, and to not have to rely on her parents' credit card.

She did everything she could to reassure her parents that she wasn't going to St. Moritz to drink champagne or stay out all night. She genuinely loved skiing. And it was good for her to be on her own. Sometimes she felt like one of her parents' cats, who spent their whole lives lying in the sun. Her parents expected her to get engaged to the son of one of their friends, and her life would go on exactly the same: driving out to Malibu and attending movie premieres and eventually having children.

Her father wouldn't even listen when she said she wanted to join him at the studio. The best thing was to show him she was independent, and perhaps then he would change his mind. Even if she was only a chalet girl in St. Moritz, at least she was paying for lodging and ski tickets.

Music blared from the stereo in the living room, and she longed to plug her ears with cotton balls. But then she couldn't hear guests shouting for another plate of sausage kabobs. If only her roommate hadn't suddenly come down with food poisoning, she'd be curled up in bed with a book. Instead she was trying to avoid being pawed at by men in tight ski pants.

A young man with dark hair entered the kitchen. He was wearing a leather jacket, and she recognized the waiter from the Carlton Bar.

"What are you doing here?" Todd asked in surprise. He was carrying a martini glass in one hand and a plate of bratwurst in the other. "I thought you hated chalet parties."

"I'm part of the waitstaff," Patty answered. "Why are you here? I didn't think this was your scene."

"The guy we're staying with is friends with the host." Todd shrugged. "To be honest, I came in the kitchen to escape. They're discussing Kierkegaard and debating the best French wines. I'm more of a beer man, and I've never read a German author."

"You're missing out on great literature." Patty busied herself arranging stuffed chard. "I want to apologize for the other night. I had too many White Russians, and it was the night before my birthday. I didn't mean to kiss you."

"I'm happy you did." Todd grinned. "Maybe I can be of service again."

"That won't be necessary," Patty said hurriedly. "I'm in St. Moritz to ski, not to meet men. If you'll excuse me, I have to deliver these canapés."

She opened the swinging doors and froze. Her cheeks paled and she retreated into the kitchen.

"Are you all right?" he asked curiously. "You look like you saw a ghost."

"One of the guests was hitting on me." She leaned against the fridge. "I was hoping he'd left, but he just finished his fourth vodka. I don't want to run into him again."

"I'll talk to him." Todd set his glass on the counter. "What is he wearing?"

"You can't do that!" Patty exclaimed. "You'll make a scene."

"I once worked as a bouncer at parties," Todd assured her. "The trick is to be polite while you escort the guy to the door."

"I suppose you could try," she agreed. "He's got brown hair and is wearing a red ski sweater."

Todd disappeared into the living room and Patty refilled trays of dumplings. There was a crash and she ran through the swinging doors. Todd was sprawled on the floor, and a small group was forming around him.

"What happened?" She crouched beside him.

"I told that guy to stop hitting on you, and he said you were lying." Todd waved at a man with wide shoulders. "Then he punched me."

"You accused the wrong man! Hans is the captain of the Swiss ski team, and he's married." Patty pointed to the other side of the room. "The man who made a pass at me is over there."

"That explains it." Todd rubbed his jaw. "If he's as good a skier as he is a boxer, the Swiss team will win."

A man approached Patty and talked sternly to her in German. She took off her apron and motioned to Todd.

"The host wants us to leave. He's terribly humiliated."

"I'm very sorry," Todd said as they walked down the hill to the village. The sky was black velvet and there was a half moon. Snow covered the sidewalk, and the shop windows were lit with twinkling lights.

"I don't mind, I was only filling in for a friend," Patty said, wrapping her scarf around her neck. "Were you really willing to take a blow for a girl you just met?"

"I didn't know he was going to punch me until his fist landed on my face," Todd admitted. "But you did kiss me, and I quite enjoyed it. I had to return the favor."

"Then we're even," Patty said, nodding. "Do you mind if we keep walking? My roommate has food poisoning, and I don't want to go back to her retching in the bathroom. I left my purse at the chalet, so I can't go to a café."

"I'd offer to pay, but I'm broke until tomorrow's paycheck," Todd said.

"It's a beautiful night. Let's climb up to the leaning tower," Patty suggested.

They turned onto the Via Maistra, and Patty pointed to a stone tower rising above the village square. The tower was illuminated by yellow lights, and the whole sky seemed like it was lit on fire.

"The tower was built in 1570 and was attached to the church." She rubbed her hands to keep warm. "But it started leaning, so they had to remove its bells. It has a 5.5-degree tilt—that's more than the Leaning Tower of Pisa."

Patty paused and noticed Todd was staring at her.

"Why are you looking at me like that?" she asked. "Do you think I'm only capable of making porridge and serving martinis? I took an art history class in college."

"I was thinking that I don't know anything about you," Todd countered.

"There's not much to tell. I live with my parents and I'm a theater major at UCLA," she said lightly. "My parents expect me to marry a boy from a good family and have a couple of blond children. We'll buy a house with a swimming pool, and in the summers we'll all drink too much and flirt with each other's spouses." She looked at Todd and her eyes danced. "It will be harmless, of course, because I'll be very happy. I'm only going to marry for love, even if it takes me years to find him."

"How will you know?" he asked.

"How will I know what?" she responded. Todd stood so close, she could smell his aftershave.

"How will you know you're in love?" he wondered. "If you've known the same men all your life, how will you choose the right one?"

"I'll know it here." She took his hand and placed it on her sweater. His fingers were warm and they curled around her breast.

He leaned forward and kissed her. She kissed him back, and felt warm and alive.

"And what about Todd with the borrowed tuxedo?" she asked when they parted. "I don't know your last name or where you live."

"It's Todd Mason, and I'm from Cleveland," he answered. "My father is the branch manager of a bank, and my mother works in human resources. I have one more semester until I graduate from college."

"What will you do?" she asked, curious.

"I'm not sure. I was never one of those kids who wanted to be a baseball player when he picked up a bat, or an astronaut when he got a telescope. My friend's dad has a sporting goods store—I'll work there, or I'll work at the bank." He paused. "This is my first trip. I've never even been out of Ohio, except to visit relatives in Chicago."

"Does that mean you've never been to California?" she asked.

"Don't make it sound like a calamity," he said, chuckling. "It's not like I'm a virgin."

"It's worse than that." She crossed her arms. "You have to see the Pacific Ocean."

Todd looked at her as if he were about to say something. Then he wrapped his arms around her and kissed her.

"We'll have to fix that," he said when he released her. His dark hair glowed under the lamplight, and his eyes had thick lashes. "You can invite me."

"What was I thinking, inviting someone I'd just met to California?" She shook her head. "The funny thing is, Todd and my father hit it off immediately. They played tennis and backgammon. Your father could charm anyone; he should have been an actor. Once, we attended a premiere and the reporter asked who he was. He was sure Todd was someone famous."

"It sounds like a storybook romance," Felicity offered, eating the last bite of fondue.

"It was, in the beginning." She shrugged. "Then Todd started working at the studio and I got pregnant at the same time. I sat in our apartment without anything to keep me cool but a ceiling fan while he and my father jetted off to Cannes. Even when he was home, all he talked about was movies."

"You loved movies too," Nell reminded her mother. "You were a theater major at UCLA."

"I didn't want to be *in* movies, I wanted to produce them," she said. "That's one of the reasons I went to St. Moritz. I thought if I could show my father that I was independent, he would give me a chance in the company. Instead I brought him a son-in-law with a decent tennis serve."

"You never said anything about this before," Nell piped up. "I always assumed you were happy at home."

"My father was old-fashioned. It wouldn't have changed anything." She turned to Nell. "And I *was* happy—having you and your brother was the best thing I ever did." She paused. "Your father and I just couldn't get back what we had, and it got worse. He was gone for weeks at a time, and one year he completely missed Christmas. You and Pete were so upset, you didn't even want to open your presents.

"We've talked about your father enough for one night." She

finished her wine. "I want to hear about you and Felicity. Twenty-something girls on the verge of getting married are more interesting than an ancient love story with an unhappy ending."

Nell followed her mother and Felicity into the lobby of Badrutt's Palace and dusted snow from her jacket. The fondue had been excellent. Next, they strolled along the Via Serlas. The windows of Escada Sports were filled with ski goggles in fluorescent colors, Faoro had classic ski sweaters, and in Valentino there were little black dresses perfect for New Year's Eve. For a moment Nell forgot about her parents not attending her wedding, and enjoyed the festive atmosphere.

"It's still early. Why don't we stop in the bar for White Russians?" Her mother turned to Nell. "I haven't had one in years—it will be my treat."

"We would love to." Nell nodded and walked toward the bar. Suddenly she saw a dark-haired man talking with the bartender. It couldn't be her father; they'd planned to meet at the Dracula Club after his sauna. She had put her phone on vibrate; what if he'd texted and asked her to meet him earlier?

"On second thought, White Russians have so many calories. I won't fit into Felicity's wedding dresses." Nell took her mother's arm and steered her across the lobby.

"You promised you wouldn't become one of those models who pinches her thighs to see if there's any extra fat," her mother said reproachfully. "Besides, we just ate fondue."

"It's all about moderation," Nell answered hastily. "That's how French women stay slim. They have croissants and café au lait for breakfast, but then they skip lunch and eat salade Niçoise for dinner. I learned that when I did the runway shows in Paris." She walked toward the elevator. "Why don't we go to your suite? There were some dried apricots and nuts in the minibar that looked delicious."

"My suite?" her mother repeated, confused.

"Raj doesn't want us to buy anything from the minibar." Nell pushed the elevator button. She couldn't take any chances and go to her own room; her father might come up to find her. First she had to get her mother safely to her suite. Nell looked at Felicity pointedly. "You and Felicity can talk about holding the trunk show in Beverly Hills. It would be a huge success."

"That's an excellent idea." Felicity followed Nell's lead. "Raj is always saying we need to break into the Hollywood market. If Jennifer Lawrence or Charlize Theron wore one of my gowns, Raj would swoon."

"I suppose I could fix amaretto and cream from the minibar." Her mother shrugged. "I haven't craved cream liqueur in years, but it sounds like the perfect way to end the evening."

They sat on the yellow damask love seats in her mother's suite and talked about Felicity opening an atelier on Rodeo Drive. Finally her mother announced that she was going to take a bath, and Nell and Felicity took the elevator to Nell's floor.

"I thought she'd never go to bed," Nell sighed when they entered her room. She pulled off her sweater and grabbed a miniskirt from her closet.

"Where are you going?" Felicity asked, perching on the bed.

"I was supposed to meet my father at the Dracula Club, but he texted that he was waiting at the Polo Bar." Nell looked for a pair of stockings. "I turned off my phone and didn't notice until we entered the lobby. I had to keep my mother away from the bar; there would have been a showdown, like in a Western movie."

"You can't go out now, it's past curfew." Felicity glanced at her watch.

"I won't be long." Nell pulled on suede boots. "If you see Raj, tell him I went to the village pharmacy for some aspirin. I do have a headache—the fondue was so rich, and I didn't want any nuts, but I had to make up an excuse to get my mother upstairs."

"At least you know why she's angry at your father." Felicity curled her feet under her.

"What do you mean?" Nell turned around.

"She was left at home with the children while he ran around the world making movies," Felicity continued. "It would be like someone saying I couldn't design bridal gowns, or you had to stop modeling."

"I don't believe that. There must be something else." Nell picked up a hairbrush.

"What do you mean, you don't believe it?" Felicity asked.

"My mother never mentioned wanting to run the studio before. And she loved being a mother." She spritzed her wrists with perfume. "I doubt my father was unfaithful; he's the most loyal person I know. And I can't imagine my mother having an affair. Something happened, and I have to find out what."

"Finding out what ended a marriage is different from trying to make your parents remember why they fell in love," Felicity warned her. "What if you uncover something terrible?"

"It can't get any worse," Nell said. "You heard my mother; she refuses to attend the wedding if my father's there."

"Maybe two weddings isn't a bad idea," Felicity offered. "I can make you a fabulous dress for a vineyard wedding, something rustic and elegant. A hand-draped tulle sheath with a twelve-foot lace veil."

"I don't want two dresses, and we're only having one wedding." Nell dropped her lipstick into her purse. "I have to go before my father gets impatient and comes upstairs." She sighed. "Maybe I should get a GPS tracker for his phone so I know where he is."

Nell stepped out of the elevator and walked through the lobby. The pianist was playing "Fly Me to the Moon" and she flinched. Was wanting to perform the father–daughter dance while Eliot danced with her mother too much to ask? She was going to find out what happened in her parents' marriage, and then she was going to fix it. Her father waved, and she waved back and entered the bar.

Six

Four Days Before the Fashion Show
11:00 a.m.

Felicity

FELICITY PULLED A BLUE SWEATER over her turtleneck and brushed her hair in the mirror. It was four days before the collection, and she had planned to spend the morning matching accessories with dresses, but she had overslept. One of her favorite parts of the fashion show was finding just the right piece to go with each gown: an ivory cameo to adorn a princess-style ball gown, or a colored glass necklace draped around an off-the-shoulder crepe sheath. At the moment, all the brooches and necklaces were wedged together in a trunk, and she was going to sort them out.

Last night after the fondue dinner with Nell and her mother, she had planned on going straight to bed after her bath. Soaking in the bubbles had been just what she needed. Her worries about Adam receded, and she even thought of a new design for Bergdorf's. She was tempted to wait until she finished the bath before she started sketching. The more she saw the image in her head—a mermaid-style gown with a swirling skirt—the more she knew she had to work on it.

There was paper and a pen on the bathroom counter, and she grabbed them and started drawing. It would have a strapless satin bodice with silver beading. The skirt would flare at the knees, and be made of faux fur. When the model walked down the runway at the fashion show, it would look as if she were floating on a fluffy white cloud.

Then the notepad fell in the bath, and she had to lay it on the towel rack to dry. By the time she climbed back in, the water was cool, and she had to fill the bath all over again. But it was worth it; there was nothing better than creating a new dress. And she was hopeful that Camilla would like it!

She stayed up past midnight sketching more ideas for Camilla: a pleated V-neck dress the color of Swiss butter, and a tea-length gown with white gloves and a pillbox hat. When she finally fell asleep, she'd missed her alarm, and now she had wasted half the morning. She had to submit the designs to Camilla in five days, and she still had so much to do to get them right.

There hadn't been any more texts or phone calls from Adam. She had decided not to text him after all; whatever she wrote might come out wrong. Now she was tempted to call him, but first she had to think. Gabriel had said it was silly for Adam to be angry about the photos, since he'd been the one who suggested they see other people. But what if Adam thought something had been going on for a while? Anyway, she wasn't involved with anyone; it was a misunderstanding.

There was a knock on the door. Raj was standing in the hallway. He balanced two coffee cups in one hand and a shopping bag in the other.

"Can I come in? I brought a late breakfast." Raj placed the bag on the coffee table. "Yogurt with hazelnuts, apple bread with snow Camembert, and banana-and-goat's-milk yogurt. Greta's cousin works at Pur Alps bakery on Via Maistra."

"You and Greta were together last night and had breakfast this morning?" Felicity peeled off the lid of the yogurt and took a small scoop.

"We didn't sleep together," Raj said, cutting a piece of apple bread. "We met for an early breakfast before she went skiing in Diavolezza. She asked me to join her, but I couldn't leave the models alone. Katie has recovered from her altitude sickness, and is now being pursued by an Italian race-car driver she met at the Cava Bar. He wants to take her over the Julier Pass in a vintage Bugatti. I told her if she sets one foot in that car, I'll send her to her room and take away the key. All I need is one of the models to hurtle down the mountain in a fiery car crash."

"You'll make a wonderful father some day," Felicity chuckled. "You are like that duck in the children's book who spends all his time keeping the ducklings safe."

"Why are you all dressed?" Raj asked. "I've left the day free until our dinner reservations at Chesa Veglia. Their white pizza with buffalo mozzarella and truffle shavings is world famous, and at midnight it turns into the hottest nightclub in St. Moritz."

"Midnight?" Felicity raised her eyebrows. "Isn't that past curfew?"

"I'm making an exception. The place will be teeming with celebrities, and we'll get lots of coverage." Raj ate a bite of Camembert. "Speaking of coverage, you're all over the blogs this morning."

"What do you mean?" Felicity put down her spoon, a sudden chill running down her spine.

Raj clicked through his phone and read out loud: "St. Moritz seems to be heating up for New York wedding designer Felicity Grant. While her models braved the cold temperatures for a hearty lunch of bratwurst and raclette at the Alpine Hut, Felicity was spotted enjoying afternoon tea in the historic Kulm Hotel. Granted, she may just be recovering from yesterday's near miss of getting run over by a sled. The dark-haired hunk eating scones with her seems to be the same doctor who carried her into Badrutt's Palace after her accident. Her cheeks looked rosy, and judging by the intent look in her face, she wasn't suffering from a concussion. A word to Felicity: maybe it's time to check in with your boyfriend, sports manager Adam Burton, and update him on your recovery."

"How could they! I was at the Alpine Hut with the models." Felicity studied the photos of her and Gabriel sitting by the fireplace. Gabriel must have been telling her the folktale, because she was leaning forward and her eyes were sparkling.

"If I recall, you took off before we sat down to eat our raclette." Raj took back his phone.

"Adam sent me a bunch of angry texts, and I discovered them when we reached the Alpine Hut," Felicity said worriedly. "I tried to call him back, but he wouldn't answer." She looked at the photos again. "Gabriel was just showing me around St. Moritz to make me feel better."

"Who is this doctor?" Raj asked. "Maybe Adam has reason to be jealous."

"Gabriel is a friend; he was giving me advice." Felicity's cheeks grew warm. "I didn't think any more photos would show up online! If Adam sees them, he'll be livid."

"This is why I have a strict no-serious-girlfriend policy," Raj chuckled. "If you and Adam can't stay together, what chance is there for the rest of us?" He touched her hand. "I'm kidding— Adam will come round. I'll text him myself. I'll tell him about skiing the magic carpet and having lunch at the Alpine Hut and make him wish he was here."

"I doubt that will help." Felicity was trying very hard not to cry. "He'll think I'm living it up and not working at all."

"Speaking of working, I have to go. I decided the whole runway should be rimmed with colored lights so the models' shoes glitter like precious jewels. Even Badrutt's Palace can run out of something. Every strand of lights in the hotel is draped around an indoor Christmas tree or a fireplace mantle. I have to go down to the village."

"That's a wonderful idea." Felicity pictured pink and green and blue lights like confetti.

"One more thing before I go," Raj said as he opened the door. "Is something going on with Nell?"

"What do you mean?" Felicity asked.

"I caught her sneaking into her room from the fire-exit stairs at two a.m.," he said.

"What did she say?" Felicity gulped.

"She made up some story that she woke up with a headache and went to get aspirin. The elevator was too slow, so she took the stairs up to her room." He paused. "She was wearing a miniskirt and heels, and there was a stamp on her hand from a nightclub."

"She must have gone to a club and got a headache after she went to bed," Felicity suggested. "That's happened to me. You think going to sleep will cure it, but then you wake up an hour later and it's worse."

"I suppose it's possible." Raj shrugged. "I hope she's not seeing someone. Eliot is a nice guy, and it wouldn't look good if our star model was cheating on her fiancé."

"Nell would never do that! She and Eliot are madly in love," Felicity said, and put on her sweetest smile. "Thank you for the Camembert. I'll put it in the minifridge. It must have cost you a fortune, and it will make an excellent snack."

Raj left, and Felicity opened the trunk of accessories. Ordinarily they cheered her up immediately. She adored the aquamarine pendant that Raj had found in a thrift store, and the triple-strand glass necklace that looked exactly like real diamonds. But all she could think about was Adam discovering the new photos online. She really needed to warn Gabriel about the photos; after all, he was a respected doctor in the village. And at the same time, maybe he could help her decide what to do next. It was only noon; she could run down to Gabriel's office and still have all afternoon to work. She closed the trunk and hurried out the door.

Last night's snowfall had made the village look like the window in a pastry shop. The snow-covered lampposts resembled candy canes, and the chalets looked like gingerbread houses coated with white icing. She rounded a corner and saw Gabriel walking down the street. His doctor bag was slung over his wrist, and he wore an overcoat.

"Felicity!" he exclaimed. "What are you doing here? Were we supposed to meet?"

"I was going to text you, but I didn't want to bother you if you were with patients," she said. "I need to talk to you."

"You're walking properly, so you can't have fallen down again. And it's too early to be drinking, even for you," he joked. "What happened?"

"I'd rather talk somewhere quieter." She waved at the sidewalk bustling with tourists. "Could we go back to your office?"

"Why don't you walk with me? I have to see a patient at one of the ski lodges," he answered. "I had a young boy this morning with possible appendicitis. Each time I asked where it hurt, the pain changed sides. It turned out he was afraid of riding the chairlift, and didn't want to tell his parents. He begged me to keep his secret, so I said I'd bring some medicine to the lodge. Then I went down to the Confiserie Hanselmann and bought a box of caramelized marroni cooked in sugar." He showed her the package. "His parents will think it's some kind of edible pill, but it's actually candy."

They strolled along Via Somplaz and stopped in front of an orange chalet with carved wood windows. Gabriel gave the package to the concierge and Felicity waited outside.

"That should allow him to miss two more days of skiing," Gabriel said cheerfully when he returned. "Why don't we keep walking, and you can tell me what's wrong?"

"I thought you should know—photos of us having afternoon tea together ended up online." Felicity handed him her phone. "I'm sorry. I hope it's not a problem for you. And there was a snarky item on a wedding blog; I'm afraid Adam will see it."

"It doesn't matter to me, but you must be famous!" Gabriel scanned the article. "I have afternoon tea at Kulm Hotel occasionally, and no one ever takes my photo."

"Perhaps some journalists who are covering the collection arrived in St. Moritz early," Felicity guessed. "Adam hasn't called or texted, and I don't know what to do."

"Why do you have to do anything?" Gabriel wondered. "You weren't doing anything wrong, unless there's a law about eating chestnut puree in the afternoon." He glanced at the photo again. "I could complain that my nose looks too long, but you look lovely."

"Your nose is fine," Felicity laughed. "I'm worried that Adam will believe the blogger and think I'm involved with someone else. Maybe he thinks it's been going on for a while and I've been hiding it from him."

"That's unlikely." Gabriel shook his head. "How would we have met?"

Gabriel made it sound so simple. But when she explained it to Adam in her head, it became as complicated as a spool of thread she couldn't unravel. She wished she were sitting in her atelier, sipping coffee and nibbling a Christmas cookie. The bell above the door would tinkle, and Adam would rush in with news about a new client. They'd go out for drinks to celebrate, and it would all be so exciting.

"I wish we'd never argued," Felicity sighed. "Adam is a wonderful boyfriend. He doesn't mind when I only have frozen lasagna for dinner, and he never complains when I sleep at his apartment and forget to turn off the coffee pot when I leave."

"That's fine, but those are the actions of a polite roommate." Gabriel turned toward a long wooden building. "Come with me. I want to show you something."

They entered a foyer with a massive wood staircase and high ceilings. In front of them was a skating rink with a retractable roof, and to the right was an outdoor terrace with round tables and colored umbrellas.

"This is the Olympic Pavilion. It reopened last year in the same location where the first Winter Olympics were held in 1928. Back then spectators from all over the world arrived in Bugattis and Mercedes. Charlie Chaplin was there, and Calvin Coolidge."

He led her into a room that served as the museum. Olympic medals sat in glass cases and wooden skis rested against the walls. There was a bobsled with a Swiss flag and a pair of snowshoes.

"St. Moritz hosted the games again in 1948, but the war had just ended and many countries couldn't afford to compete. The Norwegian cross-country team had to borrow skis from the Americans because they couldn't buy their own."

"How do you know all this history?" Felicity studied the photos of young men standing on pedestals and holding bouquets of flowers. There was a photo of luges careening down the track, and of a figure skater lifting his partner in the air.

"See this picture?" Gabriel pointed to a photo of a young man clutching a silver medal. "Lawrence Buchwald was on the Swiss team that won the silver medal for the bobsled. He was eighteen and grew up in St. Moritz. He was my grandfather."

"Your grandfather!" Felicity's eyes widened.

"Lawrence was my mother's father," Gabriel said, nodding. "He traveled to England and America. The press adored him, and all the mothers wanted him to marry their daughters." He chuckled. "But he returned to St. Moritz and married his childhood sweetheart."

"What a wonderful story." Felicity beamed. "And what about your parents? Did they grow up here?"

"My father is Irish; he came to St. Moritz on holiday after he finished medical school," Gabriel said. "My mother was working as a hostess at a restaurant on the mountain. It was love at first sight, and he never went back to Dublin."

"Are they still married?" she asked.

"My mother died in a car accident when I was fifteen," he answered quietly. "She was visiting relatives in Munich."

"I'm sorry." Felicity looked at Gabriel.

"When I was growing up, my father worked all the time. I fixed everything around the house, the toaster and the dishwasher." He paused. "After my mother died, my father took me with him to see his patients. That's when I realized I wanted to fix people.

"I had to come home when my father had a heart attack," Gabriel finished. "Besides me, his patients are the only family he has. Without them, he is all alone."

They left the museum and walked around the building. Upstairs there was a conference room and a viewing area that looked out at the mountains. They could see skiers waiting for the gondola, and children throwing snowballs.

"And what about Felicity Grant?" He turned to Felicity. "When did you decide to become a bridal designer?"

"I can't remember a time when I didn't sketch dresses for my dolls. But I really knew the summer during high school, when my parents took me to New York." She leaned against the railing. "Do you know the moment in *Breakfast at Tiffany's* when Audrey Hepburn stands in front of Tiffany's? Fifth Avenue is deserted, and she's holding a coffee cup and a pastry. She takes off her sunglasses and smiles, and the viewer knows she's exactly where she belongs.

"That's how I felt when I discovered Vera Wang's atelier on Madison Avenue." She hugged her arms around her chest. "There was a beige organza gown in the window that looked like tufts of cotton candy. Another dress had a veil shaped like an enormous bow. I knew I had to design bridal gowns, and it had to be in New York. I went home and applied to Parsons. The day I was accepted was one of the happiest of my life."

"And now?" Gabriel asked.

"What do you mean?" Felicity turned to him.

"If your work gives you so much pleasure, why are you trying to convince your boyfriend to marry you?" Gabriel asked.

"Everything is better when you share it with the person you love," Felicity said slowly, images of wedding gowns with skirts like whipped cream dissolving before her eyes. "It makes getting up with your alarm easier, and gives you something to look forward to when you work late."

Tears filled her eyes. She longed to be strolling down Lexington Avenue with Adam. How many Sundays had they spent visiting the bridal salon in Sak's so she could soak up the atmosphere? And all those nights when she wouldn't go to bed until she finished a sketch, and Adam had massaged her shoulders.

"My parents had the happiest marriage." Gabriel interrupted her thoughts. "My mother waited to eat dinner with my father even when he visited patients until midnight, and he saw foreign movies with her even though it strained his eyes." He looked at Felicity. "My father told me that he was offered a position at a hospital in Dublin, but my mother loved St. Moritz, so he never mentioned it. And my mother won a baking contest, and the prize was a three-month course in New York with a celebrated chef. She didn't tell my father because she didn't want him to have to take care of me alone. They were in love, and wanted the best for each other."

"That's a lovely story," she ruminated. "I do love Adam, and I know he loves me. I'll call Adam, and we'll come to a compromise. Perhaps Adam can propose next summer and we can have a long engagement. Or we'll buy a house and get married later when we're more settled."

Felicity took a deep breath, and for the first time since Raj had showed her the blog, she felt relaxed.

"It's my turn to buy lunch"—she waved toward the outdoor

café—"and we'll order something to go for your father. He sounds like a nice man, and I owe him something for helping me figure it out."

They sat at a table facing the lake and ordered farmer's bread with ricotta and eggs. There were sweet pancakes with apricot cream and mugs of hot chocolate. Felicity leaned back and let the air leave her lungs.

"St. Moritz really is heavenly." She ate a bite of pancake. "If I was in New York, I'd be sitting in my workroom wondering if I should brave the slush on the sidewalk. I always forget the time, and by the time I stop working it's ten p.m. and I wonder if it's worth going home." She stopped and laughed. "The next day, I do it all over again."

"All vacations are wonderful," Gabriel agreed, eating a bacon burger with Emmental cheese. "But eventually one has to go back to work."

"If you lived in St. Moritz, it would never seem like work at all." She waved her arms around the deck. "Everyone looks happy, and the scenery is breathtaking." She looked at Gabriel. "If I were you, I'd take over your father's practice and find a girl to marry. You do want to fall in love, don't you? No one wants to be alone forever."

"Of course I do," Gabriel agreed. "But the local girls either get married when they're twenty or move to Zurich or Geneva. And the jet-setters who arrive on their private planes are too wealthy to marry doctors. Anyway, I'm only staying until my father gets better. The minute he gets the all-clear, I hope to get my job back at the clinic in Geneva."

"I'm sure you'll find someone special, and it will be a fairy-tale romance like your mother and father's," Felicity said, nodding. The fresh air and the prospect of working it out with Adam were making her almost giddy. "Would you tell me one of your stories?" she asked, leaning forward.

"My stories?" Gabriel looked up from his crepe.

"It's Christmas, and they put me in such a good mood." She sipped her hot chocolate. "You don't hear folktales in New York. Everyone is scrolling through their phones and reading gloomy articles about politics and the economy."

"There's an Austrian folktale I used to love," Gabriel said. "It's about a little boy who lives alone with his mother high in the Alps. They're very poor and can never afford enough to eat. One day the boy goes into the forest and meets an old woman. The woman knows of their dire circumstances and offers him a small magic pot. Whenever he says 'cook, little pot, cook,' it makes a bowl of sweet porridge. And when he says 'stop, little pot,' it stops cooking.

"The boy takes the pot home and he and his mother are no longer hungry. Whenever they want to eat the boy says 'cook, little pot, cook,' and it makes a bowl of delicious porridge. Soon they're making porridge for all the poor people in the village. One day the boy goes into the forest and is gone for a long time. His mother instructs the pot to cook, but she doesn't know the word to make it stop. The pot keeps cooking and the whole house is submerged in porridge. Porridge overflows into the street and seeps through the windows of other houses.

"By the time the boy returns home, the mother is in a panic. The boy turns to the pot and says, 'stop, little pot,' and it stops cooking. The porridge dries up and the inhabitants of the village can return safely to their houses. From then on, only the boy instructs the pot to cook, and they have sweet porridge for years to come."

Gabriel finished the story and Felicity burst out laughing.

"That's one of the funniest things I've ever heard," she said, spreading apricot crème on her pancake. "I picture a whole village covered in porridge."

"My mother used to tell it to me at bedtime. In her version the little boy was named Gabriel, and he could fix anything."

Felicity put down her fork and looked at Gabriel. His brow was furrowed as he wrestled with a jar of mustard.

"I'm sorry, I didn't mean to bring up difficult memories. You say you know nothing about love, but you're wrong," she said slowly. "You loved your mother so much you remember bedtime stories she told you twenty years ago. And you love your father enough to put your life on hold to take care of him. Maybe you were right to give me advice; maybe you have it all figured out."

"Nobody has it figured out." The lid popped open and he spread mustard on his burger. He looked up and there was something new in his eyes. "But when something is important, you never give up."

They ordered steak with tomatoes for Gabriel's father and strolled through the village. The mountain was filled with skiers, and Badrutt's Palace was nestled against the forest.

"You should come back in the summer," Gabriel said. "It's completely different, but just as beautiful. There are jazz concerts and boating on the lake."

"It would be wonderful to return to St. Moritz with Adam," Felicity said dreamily. "We'd pack a picnic of rye bread and Edam cheese and go hiking. There would be hidden lakes and fields filled with orange and gold poppies. Adam would kiss me and whisper that he's never been anywhere so magical."

There was an odd silence and Gabriel walked faster along the path. He seemed like he was about to say something, but suddenly there was the sound of horses galloping and people shouting.

"Look! It's a snow polo match." Felicity pointed to the frozen lake. Men in leather jackets were riding horses and waving polo mallets in the air. "Can we stop and watch? I read about these matches, and it sounds exciting."

"I guess so. I'm in no hurry to get back to the practice." He joined her at the fence. "My first patient this afternoon has a recurring backache. I tell him to take a break from skiing and he ignores me. He shows up a few days later asking for a prescription for Vicodin." He rubbed his hands to keep warm. "I don't know why people see a doctor if they refuse to follow the advice."

The polo match grew more intense, and the players sent the balls spinning across the lake. A horse reared on its hind legs, and Felicity worried that the rider would be thrown. But the man rubbed the horse's neck until it calmed down, and the crowd cheered with relief.

Even the spectators were thrilling. The women wore mink coats and huge sunglasses to protect their eyes from the sun. The men yelled at the riders in half a dozen languages, and the air reeked of cigars and sweat.

Suddenly one of the horses skidded and the rider slipped and fell. The horse scrambled on the ice and galloped across the lake. A man tried to stop it, but it shied away and headed straight toward Felicity.

There was the sound of hooves crunching on hard snow, and then everything happened very quickly. The horse broke through the barrier and Gabriel threw his arms around Felicity and pulled her away. They fell together on the snow and the horse shot past them.

"Are you all right?" Gabriel gasped, when they were both sitting up. "Good God, that horse was coming right for us."

Felicity's shoulder hurt. Her jacket was soaked, and there was snow in her hair.

"I'm fine, just a little shaken up." She rubbed her shoulder. "I said you were my guardian angel, and now I'm sure of it. First you helped me after the sled almost ran me over, and now you save my life. If you hadn't grabbed me, I would have been killed."

"I've never understood why men are so fascinated with waving a stick at a ball." He shuddered. "Why don't I walk you back to your hotel? I can make sure you get inside safely, and then you can take a bath."

"That's a good idea." Felicity's heart was still pounding. "And I think I'll ignore Raj's request and open a bottle of brandy from the minibar."

Felicity opened the door of her suite and pulled off her gloves. Gabriel offered to cancel his patients and stay, but she assured him she was all right. She promised to call if she got any headaches, and he said he would rush right over.

Her phone buzzed and she recognized Adam's number.

"Felicity, where have you been?" he asked when she pressed Accept. "I sent you all those texts."

"I tried calling, but you didn't reply," she answered. "There's something I want to talk to you about."

"I want to talk to you about something too." His voice was sharp. "Namely, why is the internet lighting up with photos of you in the arms of some Swiss doctor?"

"It's hardly the whole internet. Just a few wedding sites and posts on Instagram," she replied. "A sled almost ran me over, and I fell and hurt my head. Gabriel is a doctor, and he carried me into the hotel. It was nothing. I don't know why it ended up on-line."

"The blogs thought it was something, and they tagged me in their posts!" Adam corrected. "How do you think it looks when I'm having dinner with Doug, and my Facebook feed is littered with photos of you with a strange man?"

"I didn't expect you'd be looking at Facebook over dinner." Felicity was suddenly angry. "You would be too busy introducing him to New York's finest restaurants."

"This isn't a joke, Felicity," he said. "And I don't believe you. Doctors don't carry patients to their hotel suites, and they don't meet for cocktails at a bar."

"I blacked out for a minute, and could have had a concussion!" she corrected angrily. "And it wasn't cocktails, it was afternoon tea. What would it matter if it were champagne and oysters? You were the one who said we should take a break."

"So we could think about the future," Adam snapped. "Not so you could cavort around St. Moritz like a debutante on a ski holiday."

"I *am* thinking about the future." Felicity bit her lip. "That's what I want to talk to you about."

"I don't see how you've had time to think when you're running around with a Swiss doctor," he said briskly. "And you look aw-fully chummy for two people who just met. The blogs said you might be getting married."

"That's ridiculous! And I never saw Gabriel before," she said, waving her hand. "But what does it matter? You were the one who said we should see other people. You only care because you don't want to be embarrassed in front of your clients."

She heard footsteps on a hardwood floor and knew Adam was

pacing around the room the way he did when he was anxious. She pictured him ruffling his hair and straightening his tie.

"That's not why I'm upset." His voice softened. "I love you, Felicity. That hasn't changed."

Her suite was perfectly quiet, and the afternoon light caught the star on top of the Christmas tree. She studied the striped drapes and the logs stacked in the fireplace.

"What has changed?" she asked.

"I told you I wasn't ready to get married," Adam said. "Well, it seems you aren't either."

"What do you mean?" she said wonderingly.

"Look at the photos on Instagram and figure it out," he answered. "I have to go. I'm taking Doug to the Union Square Holiday Market, and tonight we're seeing the Rockettes. I'll talk to you later."

Felicity pressed End and remembered how much she and Adam loved the holiday market in Union Square. Last year they'd hosted a New Year's Eve party and bought a box of Brookie's Cookies and a pumpkin pie.

What had she done? She had been going to tell Adam that she wasn't in a hurry to get married, that what mattered was that they were happy. Then he'd accused her of carrying on with Gabriel, and she'd had to defend herself.

The box of accessories sat on the coffee table and she peeled back the cover. There wasn't time to think about Adam; she had to concentrate on the runway show. She spread snowflake-shaped earrings and opal necklaces on the rug.

There was a black velvet box, and inside was a ring with a round piece of glass that looked like a diamond. She slipped it on her finger and admired it under the lights of the Christmas tree.

A lump formed in her throat and she stifled a sob. If only Adam had proposed at Christmas, she would be the happiest woman in St. Moritz.

She put the ring in the box and placed it on the side table. Then she crouched down on the carpet and sifted through brooches and earrings. In four days she was going to put on the most fabulous fashion show St. Moritz had ever seen. And she still had to work on the sketches for Camilla! Raj would be thrilled if Felicity Grant was featured in Bergdorf's bridal salon. Those were the only things that mattered, and she wasn't going to let herself think about anything else.

Seven

Four Days Before the Fashion Show
11:00 a.m.

Nell

NELL STOOD ON THE STONE steps of Badrutt's Palace and waited anxiously for her father. It was late morning, four days before the fashion show, and a white Rolls Royce pulled into the circular driveway. A valet wearing white gloves opened the passenger door, and a woman stepped out in a full-length black mink coat and suede boots. Her hair was tucked beneath a fur hat and she wore ruby earrings.

Nell watched the valet hand her a dozen roses and a box wrapped in silver paper. He escorted her through the revolving glass doors and they disappeared into the lobby.

The welcome was called the Royal Arrival, and it was part of Badrutt's Palace Hotel's services. The hotel prided itself on making guests feel like royalty from the moment they stepped off the train or landed at Samedan Airport. A whole fleet of Rolls Royces had picked up the models, Raj, and Felicity at the train station.

They'd reclined against the calfskin upholstery and marveled at the crystal champagne flutes and selection of chocolate truffles. By the time they pulled up at the hotel, the girls couldn't wait to swim in the indoor pool and slip on robes designed by Karl Lagerfeld.

Doing a fashion show in St. Moritz was a dream, and Nell should be relaxing in the Jacuzzi or sitting by the fireplace and writing postcards to Eliot. But her father had called and asked her to go for a drive. It's not that she didn't want to join him. He was an excellent driver, and she was excited about exploring the Engadin valley. But he'd insisted on picking her up at the hotel, and she was terrified he would run into her mother.

She had asked her mother to join her for breakfast. Then she'd booked a deep-tissue massage and escorted her to the spa. She didn't feel safe until her mother disappeared into the treatment room and the heavy oak door closed behind her.

Keeping her parents apart was harder than she'd imagined. Last night her mother had texted while she was with her father and asked if she could borrow her cold cream. Nell had hastily texted back that she was all out and the hotel was bound to have some. Then she had been afraid her mother would knock on her door, so she sent another text saying she was going to bed.

Her father insisted they follow their late dinner with a night-cap at Hotel Europa, and they ran into an Italian director he'd met at the Venice Film Festival. Someone started snapping photos of them, and Nell was terrified they would show up on social media. She didn't want her mother seeing pictures of her sipping vodka with her father at the Hotel Europa's Allegra Bar.

She didn't get back to the hotel until two a.m., and by then she was certain Raj would be patrolling the hall. She ran up the fire-exit stairs and tried to slip into her room like a cat burglar. But Raj stopped her before she opened the door and she had to think up an excuse why she was out after curfew.

But she couldn't quit now. She hadn't wanted anything so badly since she'd moved to New York to become a model. Back then, everyone said she was crazy. Of course, she was beautiful; her friends longed for her jet-black hair and eyelashes that went on forever. But Manhattan was filled with gorgeous girls. They worked out at twenty-four-hour fitness centers and sent their headshots with all sorts of swag: a box of salted-caramel cupcakes, or a lipstick from a sample sale. Nell couldn't afford to send anything except a note saying she would be the hardest-working model they ever signed.

A vintage orange car pulled into the driveway and Nell shielded her eyes from the sun. A man jumped out and she recognized her father's dark hair and green eyes.

"What are you doing in that car?" She laughed. "It's like something out of a Hitchcock film."

"It's a 1971 Lancia. My friend brought it to Switzerland to compete in the Winter Raid. It's a car rally held in St. Moritz in January." He stroked the orange paint. "He said I could borrow it, and it's the perfect car to explore the valley. We're going to drive over the Albula Pass and have lunch in La Punt."

"Are you sure it can handle the roads?" Nell asked nervously. The front seats were separated by a stick shift, and it had old-fashioned windshield wipers.

"Cars have been driving over the mountain passes for decades." He opened the passenger door. "If you drive one of those new cars with temperature-controlled seats and assisted braking, you miss the whole experience."

"If you say so." Nell climbed inside. "It doesn't look very sturdy. I hope it has seat belts."

At first the ride was so bumpy, Nell wished they were in a Mercedes with soft bucket seats, or a BMW with surround sound and power steering. Then they drove through a forest like something in a fairy tale. It was completely quiet except for the crunch of the tires on the snow. Her father had one hand on the wheel, while the other rested on the window.

"I didn't know you could drive a stick shift," she said as they approached a clearing. The mountains were dotted with fir trees and there were barns with snow-covered roofs.

"It's the only way to drive; you're in complete control of the car," Todd said, and handed her a paper sack. "The hotel provided a healthy snack. I've never felt so fit. I swam fifty laps and did forty minutes on the stair machine. Your mother always accused me of being vain when I worked out. I wasn't doing it for myself; I want to live to see my grandchildren."

Nell ate a cracker and thought that this was the perfect time to insist her father attend the wedding. Before she could open her mouth, he kept talking.

"I was always afraid you and Pete would never find love with such lousy role models as parents," he began. "I tried to tell myself you both had everything you needed: tennis lessons and summer camps. Remember the summer you and Pete went to secret agent camp? It cost a thousand dollars, and you came home with a codebook and a magnifying glass." He chuckled. "But you didn't have parents who could order a pizza without arguing whether it should be sausage or pepperoni." He paused. "I love you and Pete so much; I wish we could have done better."

"Pete has a wonderful girlfriend, and I couldn't have found a better guy than Eliot." She ate a slice of apple thoughtfully. "I never knew before that Mom wanted to run the studio. I thought it was her choice to stay home with us."

"It's not something she liked to talk about," he explained. "Your mother loved to suffer in silence. She saw herself as a modern-day Joan of Arc. And she's always been good at hiding her feelings. I had to trick her into going on a second date."

Nell swallowed a chunk of Gruyère and gulped. She wished she could sit them down at the Polo Bar and tell them to get along. But if that were possible, her father wouldn't be living in a bachelor pad in Malibu, and her mother wouldn't be rattling around the house in Beverly Hills.

"You said she was the one who kissed you," Nell remarked.

"She was. But then she wouldn't return my calls." He reached for a grape. "I only had two weeks left in St. Moritz. I would have stopped an avalanche with my hands if it meant she would go out with me again."

St. Moritz
Twenty-Eight Years Ago

Todd

Todd stood in the chalet's dining room and surveyed the oak table. On it were Älplermagronen in a covered pot, and fried cheese balls arranged on a serving dish. There was a loaf of pumpernickel bread and a selection of Swiss cheeses.

Patty was waiting in the living room, and everything had to be perfect: the flickering candles and bottle of red wine and chocolate meringue he'd picked up at the bakery.

Ever since the night Todd ran into her at the party, Patty had been avoiding him. At first he thought she was busy with her duties as a chalet girl. But each time he called, her roommate said she was in the shower. One night he bumped into her at the Zoo Bar and she hurried out before he could say hello.

He couldn't stop thinking about her. She was beautiful and impulsive and said whatever she liked. Now, by some miracle, she was going to have dinner with him. He collected the wine glasses and pushed open the swinging doors.

"Your friend has wonderful taste in books." Patty stood next to the bookshelf in tan ski pants and a green sweater. "Have you read James Michener? I could curl up for hours with The Drifters."

"I don't read." Todd opened the wine bottle and poured two glasses.

"What do you mean, you don't read?" Patty walked to the coffee table. "Everyone reads; it's how you learn about the world."

"Perhaps people who can afford to own a ski chalet they use once a year." He shrugged. "I never had time to read. I always worked."

"Always?" she repeated.

"Since I was fourteen," he said, nodding. "I had a car-detailing business, and I cleaned swimming pools. Once I dog-sat a Doberman for a week. It didn't go well; he loved to terrorize my mother's dachshund."

"No one works all the time." Patty accepted the glass of wine. "You must have hobbies."

"I'm a fan of the Cleveland Indians, and I like to cook," he offered.

"You cook?" she asked.

"Yes, it's the thing you do in the kitchen." Maybe this had been a bad idea; he and Patty were from different worlds. Then she looked at him with her large blue eyes, and his throat constricted.

"I know what you do in the kitchen." She laughed. "I love baking cheesecake, and I make a decent lasagna. I don't know many men who cook. My father practically needs directions to find the kitchen at our house."

"What about boyfriends?" Todd asked, thinking that this was the perfect opportunity to find out if she was seeing someone.

"I haven't had a serious boyfriend. My father scares them away. On my senior prom, he waited outside with a flashlight." She smiled. "I didn't mind. My date was drunk, and I wasn't looking forward to pushing him away."

"When I turned fourteen, I discovered there were two things I loved: making money and eating," Todd mused. "My parents worked, so I learned to cook: pork chops and an excellent meatloaf."

"Those were the only two things you loved?" she asked mischievously. "What about girls?"

"I couldn't afford girls." His cheeks colored. "Let's eat. The soup will get cold and the bread is fresh out of the oven."

"Shouldn't we wait for Amy and Christopher?" she asked. "They went to buy sour cream."

Todd sipped his wine and wondered if now was the time to tell Patty the truth. She might walk out, and all his efforts would be wasted. But if he waited until after dinner, she might be furious and never talk to him again.

"They aren't coming back." He put his glass on the coffee table.

"What do you mean, they aren't coming back? You and Christopher invited us to dinner."

"I knew Amy wouldn't turn down a free meal, so I asked Christopher's friend if we could borrow the chalet for the evening." He paused.

Then I gave Christopher money to take Amy to Pizzeria Caruso so we could eat by ourselves."

"Why would you do that? If you can afford to pay Christopher, you could have taken me to a restaurant."

"I have some pride. I didn't want you to walk out on me in front of a room full of people." He looked up. "Are you going to walk out on me?"

"I should," she responded. "I don't like someone who lies, and I've never gone to a man's place on a second date."

"I didn't lie, exactly—Christopher and Amy are having dinner," he corrected. "And it's our third date, if you count the kiss outside the Carlton Hotel."

"I suppose I could make an exception, and I am hungry." She wavered. "Christopher told Amy you were a wonderful chef."

"More like line cook at the International House of Pancakes," Todd grinned. "I've become quite good at preparing Swiss dishes. My Älplermagronen is delicious."

"I have no idea what that is." She wrinkled her nose.

"The proper translation is 'alpine herder's macaroni.'" He ushered her into the dining room. "The herdsmen used all the ingredients in their huts: macaroni, potatoes, onions, and bacon with melted cheese. It's the best thing I've tasted."

They ate fried cheese balls and talked about all the wonderful things to do in St. Moritz: snowshoeing on Lake Silvaplana and tobogganing in the Bever forest and seeing modern art at the Segantini Museum. Patty's blue eyes were luminous in the candlelight, and Todd felt a surge of happiness.

"This is the best meal I've had in weeks," she said when Todd replaced the bread and cheese with meringues and strawberry cream.

"Don't they feed you at the chalet?" Todd poured two cups of coffee. "One of the perks of the job must be the leftover sausage and bacon."

"If you hang out in the kitchen, the male guests think you're waiting to be asked on a date," she explained. "There are never any snacks in our room. The other chalet girls save their calories for when they go out to dinner."

"Why don't you go on a date if you're not seeing anyone?" Todd asked.

"I didn't come to St. Moritz to meet someone." She ate a bite of meringue. "I just wanted to ski and be on my own."

"You're on a date with me," he reminded her.

"I suppose I am," she laughed. "And I'm enjoying it. So maybe I was wrong."

"Wrong?"

"To not answer your calls," she admitted.

"You were avoiding me!" Todd exclaimed. "I don't understand. You kissed me the first night, and then we kissed again when I punched that guy out at the party."

"The first time I was a bit tipsy, and it was daring to kiss a boy I just met," she explained. "And the second time, there was a full moon and it was so romantic."

"And after that?" he prompted.

"After that I discovered I quite liked it." She sipped her coffee.

"That's a good thing." He was puzzled. "Why would you want to stop?"

"We're never going to see each other again. There's nothing worse than couples exchanging addresses that will be left at the bottom of the

suitcase along with an old boarding pass and a bag of airplane pea-
nuts." She put down her cup. "My roommate at UCLA met a boy in
Croatia last summer and spent the fall semester waiting for him to call.
She gained five pounds sitting by the phone eating Snickers and missed
the auditions for Newsies."

"What if it isn't a holiday romance?" He moved to her side of the
table. "What if it's fate bringing two people together? What if the guy
knows by the way she talks and the color of her eyes that he's going to
be crazy about her?"

Todd leaned forward and kissed her.

"That might be different," she said, and kissed him back.

"God, the young are the most ignorant and arrogant people on the
planet," Todd groaned, maneuvering the car around a sharp turn.
"We didn't even ask each other the right questions. I didn't know
her goals or who she wanted to be president. We were too busy
admiring the scenery to discuss anything important."

"It sounds wonderful," Nell said. "Eliot loves to cook. He
made Christmas dinner this year. Turkey with gravy and sweet potatoes."

"I make an excellent gravy," her father said proudly. "On
Thanksgiving your mother called and said she was missing a platter, but it was really an excuse to get my gravy recipe. I always
made the gravy for Thanksgiving. I pretended I didn't understand
what she wanted. It's ridiculous, the amount of pleasure it gave me.
I felt guilty afterward."

"But you hardly ever cooked at home," Nell protested.

"When we were first married, we cooked together: lasagna, and
your mother's cheesecake. Then I started working late and didn't

make it home for dinner." He rubbed his forehead. "One year she signed us up for cooking classes. I missed the first three classes and she was so angry, she wouldn't let me back in the kitchen. In Malibu, I cook all the time."

He smiled brightly. "I have an idea. After the wedding in Napa, you and Eliot should stay with me. I'll make blueberry waffles and eggs benedict. After breakfast, we'll work it off by running on the beach."

"There's only going to be one wedding," Nell cut in. "It's going to be in Nantucket, and I want you to be there."

"We've gone over this," Todd said. "It's not possible."

Nell was suddenly angry. "Anything is possible. You're choosing not to come."

Her father patted her hand and gunned the engine. "Let's not discuss this at the top of the Albula Pass. I promised I'd show you La Punt. We'll talk about it at lunch."

The car drove over the Albula Pass and into La Punt. The whole village was just four interconnecting streets with a stone church and a train station.

They entered a hotel with painted shutters and carved windows. It was perched on the bank of a river. Inside was a fir tree decorated with Christmas ornaments.

"It's lovely," Nell said after they were seated at a table in the restaurant. The floor was made of pine, and picture windows looked out on the river. The sun gleamed on the bridge, and the buildings were quaint and pristine.

"I forgot to give this to you." Her father reached into his pocket and took out a box. "I picked it up this morning."

"I don't want any more presents." Nell put the box on the table. "I want to talk about the wedding."

"Open it first." He pressed it into her hand. "I think you'll like it."

Nell unwrapped the tissue paper and discovered a diamond pendant. There was a smaller box with matching diamond cufflinks.

"The bride and groom always exchange presents on the wedding day, but I thought I'd start a new tradition." He beamed. "The pendant is for you, and the cufflinks are for Eliot."

"They're gorgeous, but I don't want them." Nell closed the box firmly.

"What do you mean, you don't want them? The diamonds are from Chopard, and the clarity is exquisite."

"I don't want a necklace or a coffee maker or a cashmere blanket," she announced. "All I want is for you to come to our wedding."

"Sometimes we can't have everything we want. It's part of becoming an adult," he said.

"You're the one being childish," Nell fumed. "How can you deprive me of having the two most important people there when I walk down the aisle?"

"Don't you see?" he pleaded. "Even if I could ignore the fact that sharing the head table with your mother might put me in the hospital, I couldn't do that to you."

"Do what to me?" Nell asked.

"If your mother found out I said yes, she might not come," he said, and his mouth sagged. "It would be my fault, and I'd never forgive myself."

Nell chewed her food while her father chatted about filming in Athens. Nothing tasted good: not the Alps lamb racks recommended by the chef, or the dumplings in a cream-cheese sauce. She remembered when she was a child and her parents had had an argument at dinner. All she'd wanted was to leave the table and run to her room.

They drove back to St. Moritz and Nell clutched the dashboard. The road was bumpy and her stomach dropped every time her father took a curve. Even the weather had turned: the blue sky was replaced by clouds, and there were snowflakes on the windshield.

He dropped her off and she hurried into Badrutt's Palace. It was mid-afternoon, and the lobby buzzed with skiers returning from the slopes. They all wore parkas and talked about the fresh powder and spectacular vistas.

"Nell, there you are." Her mother sat by the fireplace. There was a silver tea service and an open book on the coffee table. "You weren't in your room. I was about to walk to the village, and wanted to know if you would join me."

"I need to take a hot bath first," Nell said. "I went for a drive and I'm freezing."

"You went for a drive?" Patty was puzzled. "The last time I was in New York, you said you didn't have your license."

Nell gulped and remembered saying one of the benefits of New York was not having to drive. There were so many choices: you could take a car service or call an Uber or ride the subway.

"I didn't drive myself," she corrected hurriedly. "It's one of the hotel services. The scenery was breathtaking, but the car didn't have proper heating. I'll change and meet you here."

What if her father saw them browsing in the shops? If she let her mother go alone, her parents might run into each other in the village. It was better if she went; she could always drag her mother into a store if she saw her father coming.

"What's in your purse?" Her mother pointed to her bag.

Nell noticed the jewelry box sticking out of her purse. "It's just something I picked up this morning."

"You bought something at Chopard for no reason?" Her mother said in surprise. "Modeling must pay even better than I thought. Maybe I should sell the bookstore and become one of those older models for face cream."

"You should; you've never looked more beautiful," Nell said warmly.

"You've been spoiling me with massages." Her mother smiled. "I'm dying to see what you bought."

Before Nell could stop her, her mother reached for the box.

"A diamond pendant!" She looked at Nell. "Are you sure you bought it for yourself?"

"What do you mean?" Nell colored.

"I bumped into Raj and he asked if you were feeling well," she commented. "Apparently you went to find aspirin at two o'clock in the morning. Now you're returning from a mysterious outing with expensive jewelry."

"What are you implying?" Nell asked.

"If you're having second thoughts about the wedding or seeing someone else, you should admit it now. Infidelity will ruin any marriage," her mother offered. "It's better to sort things out before it's too late."

"Of course I'm not seeing someone!" Nell exclaimed. "Look, there are diamond cufflinks for Eliot." She rummaged in her purse for the smaller box. "I thought it would make a nice wedding-day gift between the bride and groom."

"Those are stunning." Patty examined the cufflinks. "The only thing your father gave me on our wedding day was his shirt to take to the cleaners. He forgot to get it ironed, and he didn't have any pressed shirts. But shouldn't Eliot buy your present?"

Nell was suddenly tired of bending the truth. She wanted to crawl into bed with a hot-water bottle and a magazine.

"I'm a successful career woman." She closed the box. "Why shouldn't I buy myself diamonds?"

Nell sat on the rim of the bathtub and turned on the hot water. The marble counter had a selection of lotions and a stack of fluffy bath towels.

She wished she could tell Eliot that her parents were in St. Moritz. But he was filming a week-long segment on Christmas trees in Maine, and there was terrible cell phone service.

There had been something odd in her mother's voice when she'd asked if Nell was seeing someone. What if her mother or father had had an affair? She'd never imagined it was possible, but maybe she was wrong. Perhaps her mother was lonely and had taken up with Pete's tennis coach, or her father had been flattered by a young starlet who'd complimented his flat stomach.

She slipped off her robe and stepped into the bath. There were four days until New Year's Eve, and she had to find out what had ended her parents' marriage. Then she was going to do everything in her power to persuade them to put aside their feelings and come to her wedding.

Eight

Four Days Before the Fashion Show
6:00 p.m.

Felicity

IT WAS EARLY EVENING, FOUR days before the fashion show. Outside Felicity's window, a light snow was falling on the hotel awnings. Festive ornaments twinkled on the Christmas tree, and the whole Engadin valley was bathed in a yellow glow.

Her sketchpad lay open on the coffee table, and she stared at the page. Camilla had loved the purple brocade gown the bride wore at the Knickerbocker Club, but could she submit something so daring for Bergdorf's fashion show—a crepe dress with a bodice painted with flowers from a spring garden? Or should she create something more classical, like an empire-style gown with crocheted undergarments and white crocheted gloves?

Gabriel had called while she was working on her sketches to ask if her shoulder was all right, and she'd told him about her phone call with Adam. He couldn't understand why Adam had made such a fuss about the photos online, when it was Adam's decision to take a break. He'd offered to meet her for a drink, but she'd said she had to get ready for dinner at Chesa Veglia.

She had spent part of the afternoon matching accessories with the dresses and making a list of the undergarments. There was nothing worse than models milling around backstage and realizing they didn't have the correct bustier, or noticing that a satin fascinator was missing. And the stockings! She'd packed six pairs for each model—one pulled thread and the whole stocking could unravel. But four pairs were missing, and she wondered if they'd ended up in Raj's carry-on.

She stuck a pen behind her ear and admired the wedding dress hanging over the marble fireplace. It was an A-line organza gown with a crystal-beaded bodice. The beads had cost a fortune and it had taken her weeks to attach them, but when the model stood in front of the three-way mirror, she knew it was worth it.

The dress had been designed last spring after a brainstorming session with Adam about his new company. When Adam had fallen asleep, Felicity pulled on his shirt and crept out of bed. She couldn't sketch the dress fast enough: a wide skirt like layers of marshmallow and a headpiece adorned with pearls.

It had all seemed so easy: they were two young professionals about to reap the rewards of their hard work. But now she was sitting in a hotel suite and Adam was barely talking to her. She glanced at the phone and wondered if she could call him. But she didn't know what to say without making it worse.

There was a knock on the door, and she opened it.

"Can I come in?" Nell stood in the hallway. She wore a fuchsia dress, and her dark hair was curled in ringlets.

"You look gorgeous." Felicity ushered her inside. "God, I lost track of time. I haven't started getting ready. Raj will be furious if I'm late for our reservation."

"I got reprimanded by Raj last night," Nell admitted. "He saw me entering my room at two a.m. I said I had a headache and went out for aspirin."

"He told me." Felicity nodded. "Don't worry, I confirmed your story. I said I get headaches late at night all the time."

"The headache is real," Nell groaned. "My father took me on a drive over the Albula Pass this morning, and then my mother insisted I go shopping in the village. All I wanted was to curl up with a hot chocolate, and I had to try on sweaters and ski pants."

"You're a model, you love trying on clothes," Felicity reminded her.

"Not when I'm peering over my shoulder to see if my father is walking by," Nell sighed. "I feel like I'm in a spy novel and I'm not making any progress. Neither of them will come to the wedding."

"I hate to say it, but maybe you should give up," Felicity suggested gently.

"I can't do that. My mother said something odd this afternoon," Nell answered. "My father gave me a diamond pendant, and she thought it was from another man. She asked if I was seeing someone, and said infidelity would end any marriage."

"That's not strange," Felicity countered. "I could never be with someone who cheated."

"It was the way she said it. As if it happened to her," Nell explained. "Perhaps after I left for New York, my mother was bored and took up with a member of her book club. Or my father felt like he was getting old, and succumbed to the advances of a young actress."

"I don't know any co-ed book clubs, and your father never gets older." Felicity grinned. "He could pass for a man in his thirties."

"You know what I mean," Nell responded. "I never thought either of my parents were capable of cheating, but maybe I'm wrong."

"You were twenty-two when they separated. Why wouldn't they tell you if something happened?" Felicity asked.

"There's something gnawing at me, but I don't know what it is." Nell picked up her phone. "I can't see either of them tonight. I just hope they don't run into each other while we're at Chesa Veglia. I ordered room service for my mother, and suggested she watch a movie. And my father is going to Hemingway's Club with an Italian director."

"I'm sure it will be fine. Adam finally called," Felicity said. "He is furious about the wedding blogs. He even implied that I had known Gabriel for a while."

"This probably isn't going to help." Nell handed her the phone. "It was just posted on *Silver Weddings*."

Felicity took the phone and saw a photo of her and Gabriel having lunch at the Olympic Pavilion. There was another photo of them watching the snow polo match. Gabriel was pointing at the players, while Felicity watched with rapt attention.

"Things are heating up in St. Moritz for bridal designer Felicity Grant. And it's not caused by the steam rising from the indoor swimming pools. Felicity and her Swiss doctor were spotted having lunch at one of St. Moritz's favorite watering holes. They say laughter is the best medicine, and from the expression on Felicity's face, she seems to be on the road to recovery. Now if she'd only follow our advice and tell sports manager boyfriend Adam Burton about her misadventures in St. Moritz.

"Maybe Felicity has more on her mind than hoping the bump on her head will recede. The dark-haired doctor and Felicity were later caught at the snow polo matches. Everyone knows you practically need a Patek Philippe watch and partial ownership of a private jet just to blend in as a spectator. What if the doctor cures concussions as a hobby and he's rolling in dough?

"Remember, this all started when we spotted Felicity wearing her own wedding gown. Could our first assumptions be correct, and she and the doctor are enjoying a week of pre-wedding festivities? We're going to be watching this one closely. Word to Felicity: what happens in St. Moritz does not stay in St. Moritz."

She looked more closely at the photo of her and Gabriel at lunch. He must have been telling her the story about the magic porridge pot, because she was laughing.

"Oh God, how did this happen? I offered to buy Gabriel lunch, because he has been so kind." She looked frantically at Nell. "When Adam sees this, he's going to think I was lying and there's something going on between us."

"Is there something going on?" Nell wondered. "Gabriel is handsome, and doctors have great hands."

"I've hardly noticed Gabriel's hands, and nothing is going on." Felicity looked at Nell with huge eyes. "Adam and I were a team. He knows every dress in my collection; I'm the one who furnished his office. Now we're on opposite sides of some kind of war."

"It's the middle of the night in New York; there's nothing you can do now," Nell said. "Get dressed and we'll go to Chesa Veglia together. Everyone is probably waiting for us."

"I hope they serve very strong cocktails," Felicity said, walking to her closet. "I'm going to need a steady stream of alcohol to get me through the night."

Felicity sat at the bar sipping a Swiss Alps with crème de cacao and schnapps and thought she really should be enjoying herself. Chesa Veglia was so charming. It was housed in a hundred-year-old farmhouse in the middle of St. Moritz. There was a beamed ceiling and plank floors, and booths made of carved wood.

Dinner in the pizzeria had been delicious. They shared deer bresaola with porcini mushrooms as an antipasto, and Alpenrose Pizza with mozzarella and goat cheese and ham. Raj wasn't happy at first, complaining that the servers were rude and the table was cramped. But then Gwyneth Paltrow arrived with her children, who were all squeezed into a table near the back, and his mood brightened. By the end of the meal, Raj was sitting with Gwyneth and chatting about *Goop* and the merits of online newsletters.

Then they all went upstairs to the nightclub. The walls were purple velvet, the floor was black granite, and colored lights bounced off the tables. The dance floor was crowded with men and women with deep tans and gold jewelry, and even the bartenders were ridiculously good-looking.

Felicity watched Raj chat with a Russian industrialist whose daughter was getting married, and had to smile. At least she didn't have to worry about the future of Felicity Grant Bridal. As long as she designed gorgeous gowns, Raj would never let them fail.

At dinner Raj had announced he'd received an RSVP from the editor-in-chief of *Vogue Italia,* and the society editor of *Tatler* was flying in on New Year's Eve. It was possible the society editor was only in St. Moritz to attend a New Year's Eve party, and had never heard of Felicity Grant. But Raj was certain that a dozen roses delivered with a handwritten card would convince her to attend the fashion show.

Her phone was sitting on the counter. She missed Adam so much it was like a physical ache. He should be sitting beside her and sipping a gin and tonic. He'd lean into her and whisper that she was the sexiest woman in the bar.

She remembered how once, when they were first dating, Adam had been stuck at a nightclub with his boss's client. Felicity had rescued him, and it had turned into one of the best nights of her life.

Felicity's eyes adjusted to the dimly lit bar and she searched for Adam. They had only been dating for two months, and she still felt a jolt of excitement whenever she saw him. It wasn't just that he was handsome and a gentleman: sending her flowers, carrying her groceries up five flights to her apartment. It was that they never ran out of things to talk about.

She told him all about the lace sheath she was designing for a wedding in Bermuda. The veil had a seashell appliqué, and the hem was stitched with iridescent aquamarine thread. And they spent hours discussing Adam's new position. He had been promoted to assistant, and had already accompanied his boss to baseball spring training in North Carolina.

"Felicity, over here." Adam waved. He was wearing jeans with a narrow tie, and there was a line of perspiration on his forehead.

"This place is amazing," she said, joining him. "I've lived in Manhattan for four years and I've never been anywhere like it. The sign outside says it sells hot dogs, and I had to enter through a vintage phone booth."

"It's called Please Don't Tell, and it used to be the best-kept secret in the East Village." Adam kissed her. "Then word got out, and it's practically impossible to get a reservation. The whiskey sours are terrific, and the hot dogs and truffle fries are the finest in New York."

"They really serve hot dogs?" Felicity laughed, glancing at the table set with retro bottles of ketchup and mustard. "What are you doing here alone? I thought you had to take that South African rugby player out on the town."

"I'm not alone." Adam pointed across the room. "Roger is drinking straight vodka like 7-Up, and hitting on every woman in the bar. He propositioned the wife of the deputy mayor. If I don't get him out of here, he'll get deported and I'll be fired."

Felicity followed his gaze and saw Roger chatting to a woman wearing a red dress. Felicity turned to Adam. "I'll be right back."

A few minutes later, she brought Roger to where Adam was standing.

"Roger wants to leave," she said. "Would you pay the bill and meet us out front?"

"Roger wants to leave?" Adam repeated incredulously.

"He has a craving for rice pudding," she answered mischievously. "I told him we'd take him to Rice to Riches on Spring Street. The 'Sex, Drugs and Rocky Road' flavor is delicious, and the 'Fluent in French Toast' is out of this world."

"How did you know Roger liked rice pudding?" Adam asked after they'd put Roger in a taxi and returned to Felicity's apartment.

"I read an interview of him online. The thing he misses most about South Africa is malva pudding—it's a type of sweet rice pudding. I mentioned to him I knew a store with the best rice pudding," she chuckled. "I was lucky. The woman he was flirting with raved about Rice to Riches' 'Take Me To Tiramisu.'"

Adam leaned forward and kissed her. He tasted of rocky road and vanilla, and he curled his arm around her.

"Where's Raj?" he asked, when they separated.

"You mean, when is he coming back?" Felicity repeated nervously. Even though they had been dating for almost two months, they hadn't made love. Adam's roommate was usually home, and they never knew when Raj would appear at Felicity's apartment.

"Something like that," Adam whispered, kissing her again.

"He's breaking up with a girl." She waved at the chocolate cheesecake on the counter. "She started dropping off desserts every day. He was worried that she was getting too serious and he was getting fat," she laughed. "She lives in outer Williamsburg; he won't be back for hours."

Adam drew her close and wrapped his arms around her. He tipped her face up to his and their lips met. Suddenly all she wanted was to feel his chest against her breasts.

She led him into the bedroom and gulped. The bed was littered with sketches, and there were swatches of fabric on the side table. A teddy bear was propped against the headboard, and there was a framed photo of her family on the dresser.

"It's not very sexy," she said shyly. "My parents gave me the teddy bear when I left for college. They were afraid I'd get lonely in New York."

"You're sexy," he said, lifting her hair from her ears, "and I wouldn't change a thing."

Adam unzipped her dress and it fell to the floor. His hand cupped her breast and a shiver ran down her spine. She fumbled with his buttons and ran her fingers over his chest. Her mouth found his and she never wanted to stop kissing.

"Come here," he said, moving the sketchpad off the bed, and pulled her onto the bedspread. His fingers brushed her thighs and she tried to draw him on top of her. He pulled away and rolled onto his elbow.

"I want to look at you first." He touched her cheek. "Ever since I walked into Raj's apartment and you were standing in the kitchen, I've been crazy about you."

"I'm crazy about you too," she admitted.

Adam rubbed the sweet spot between her legs and she gasped. His body was taut and when he entered her, the pleasure was so exquisite she could barely breathe. Their arms and legs became tangled, and their skin was slick with sweat. She came first, the waves catching her before she was ready. Adam waited and then groaned and collapsed against her.

"I have a confession to make," he said when she was curled against his chest.

"That sounds serious," she murmured. Every nerve tingled and she felt bright and alive.

"Sort of serious." He kissed her neck. "I've never waited so long to have sex with a girl."

"Because you were afraid the sex wouldn't be good, and you wouldn't want to see me again?" she said, half-joking.

"No, the opposite." He turned her on her back and perched above her.

"The opposite?" She studied his face and had never seen eyes so blue.

"That I'd want you so much, I'd never be able to let you go."

"What do you think now?" she whispered.

"I think I was right," he said hoarsely. "But it's too late. I'm hooked."

Her heart beat faster, and she reached up and kissed him. "Me too."

Felicity glanced nervously around Chesa Veglia as if people could see what she was thinking. Suddenly the music was too loud, the bar was too smoky, and she had to get some air. She ran down the staircase and into the street.

She had to call Adam and tell him she loved him. Nothing was going on with Gabriel; all she wanted was to be together. She turned the corner and saw a young woman standing under the awning. Her hair was tucked into a wool cap, and she was scrolling through her phone.

"Katie?" Felicity approached her. "What are you doing out here? Are you feeling all right?"

"Felicity!" Katie looked up. "Don't worry, I'm not having another bout of altitude sickness. That Italian race-car driver was pressing me to go for a drive, and I couldn't shake him off. I ducked outside when he went to buy cigarettes."

"Raj said you were falling for him." Felicity stood beside her.

"Of course not; I just didn't want to offend him. I have a serious boyfriend in Kentucky." Katie took a small box out of her purse. "Don't tell anyone, but we're engaged."

"Why aren't you wearing the ring?" Felicity studied the tiny diamond on a gold band.

"Jake proposed at Christmas, and we haven't told my parents," Katie giggled. "The ring is so pretty, I can't go anywhere without it."

"It's lovely, and I'm so excited for you," Felicity said warmly. "When's the big day?"

"In the late summer," Katie said. "Jake is taking over his uncle's farm, and I'm going to help him. He's remodeling the barn, and we'll move in in the fall."

"You can't move back to Kentucky," Felicity protested. "You're one of the hottest models in New York."

"Jake could never live in the city." Katie shook her head. "We tried long-distance, but we hated being apart."

"You're helping to support your siblings." Felicity remembered the photo of the twelve-year-old twins. "And you're giving up an amazing career. Raj wants to book you for my summer collection."

"My brother and sister can live without new jeans." Katie grinned. "Modeling has been fun and the money is great, but it doesn't mean anything without love. I wish I was as lucky as you."

"As me?" Felicity asked.

"You're successful, and you have an amazing boyfriend." Katie looked at Felicity. "Sometimes one has to choose. I have to marry Jake. We're in love and all we need is each other. I've never been so happy."

Felicity walked quickly through the village. Her head throbbed and her throat was dry and she couldn't face going back inside.

Why hadn't she seen things more clearly? Adam couldn't be in love with her; he wasn't willing to change anything to be together. Katie was one of the rising stars in the modeling world, and could have closets full of shoes and paid trips to Milan. She was giving it all up to get married and live on a farm in Kentucky.

She had to put Adam out of her mind and concentrate on the fashion show and finishing the sketches for Camilla. From now on she'd put all her energies into creating the perfect tulle gown with capped sleeves like Cinderella's dress at the ball, or an off-the-shoulder chiffon dress with long white gloves.

Christmas lights were strung across the sidewalk. She remembered how excited she had been to debut the collection in St. Moritz. A whole week in a glamorous ski resort, with her designs modeled on the famous catwalk of Badrutt's Palace. Now she had to choke back the tears.

She would give herself one night to cry. Tomorrow she'd get up early and make sure the glass tiara that accompanied Nell's ball gown sparkled, and the court-length veil that matched Katie's mermaid dress was pressed. And she had a new idea for a dress for Camilla: a charmeuse gown with a faux-mink cape, accessorized by diamond earrings bigger than the women wore at the Polo Bar.

The entry to the hotel was teeming with guests. Felicity edged her way into the lobby. She didn't feel like smiling at the valets or commenting about tomorrow's ski conditions. All she wanted was to go up to her room and take off the silver lamé dress she'd bought in the village and get out of her new stilettos.

"Felicity," a female voice called. "What are you doing here? Nell said everyone was having dinner at Chesa Veglia."

Felicity turned around and saw Nell's mother crossing the lobby. She was carrying a book, and was wearing a twill sweater and matching skirt.

"The music was pounding and everyone was on the dance floor, and I suddenly felt old," Felicity explained. "I left early, and I'm going to bed."

"You're much too young to be thinking about your age," Patty said warmly. "Come join me in the bar. I was going to order a brandy and finish this book, but I'd much rather have your company."

"A brandy does sound nice," Felicity agreed. "It's snowing outside, and I'm freezing."

They sat at the bar and the bartender set two shot glasses in front of them.

"It's called Träsch, and it's made from cider pears." She handed one to Felicity. "There used to be a bottle at the chalet where I worked as a chalet girl. I'm remembering so many things about St. Moritz; I feel like I'm twenty all over again."

"St. Moritz at Christmas is gorgeous." Felicity glanced at the tables set with red chrysanthemums and flickering candles. "Everywhere you go, it's like an advertisement in some glossy magazine."

"It's the perfect setting for the fashion show. I've already overheard guests talking about it," Patty acknowledged. "I envy you. You're young and beautiful and you've accomplished so much."

Felicity thought about Katie's small engagement ring and Adam's accusations over the phone, and a sob caught in her throat.

"Are you all right?" Patty leaned forward. "You're crying! Tell me what's wrong."

"You don't want to hear it." Felicity shook her head.

"I'm a mother; of course I do," Patty offered. "Maybe I can help."

Felicity told her about the fight with Adam at Christmas, and the photos of her and Gabriel online, and Katie giving up modeling to move to Kentucky.

"I thought Adam just wanted to wait to get married until his firm was doing well, but now I don't know if he ever loved me at all," Felicity finished. "Eliot couldn't wait to get engaged to Nell, and look at you and Felicity's father. Nell said it was love at first sight."

"I suppose it was," Patty conceded. "But falling in love and be-ing happily married can be two different things. I'm afraid I'm not a good role model."

"Todd loved you enough to want to marry you," Felicity said fiercely. "Adam doesn't care what I do. He suggested we see other people."

"I wouldn't take that too seriously. Todd and I said things we didn't mean when we argued," Patty replied. "The only thing I'm sure of is that it helps to marry your best friend."

"I thought that's what Adam and I were." Felicity gulped her brandy. "But now I wonder whether I wanted it all so badly—being in love, getting married, having a family—that I didn't see Adam clearly at all."

"Those aren't bad things to want," Patty remarked. "Don't say anything to Nell, because I never want her to worry about me, but I miss being part of a couple. There's nothing better than having someone to share things with, and it's wonderful to have someone to sleep beside."

"I'll have to get a giant teddy bear," Felicity groaned. "I don't know when I'll have a man in my bed again."

"You're not even thirty; there's time to figure things out. Make sure Adam is the man you really want," Patty said thoughtfully. "Marriage can be wonderful, or it can be as cold and lonely as be-ing stranded in a snowstorm." She sipped her drink. "The impor-tant thing is marrying the right man."

Felicity entered her suite and tossed her purse on the love seat. A silver tray sat on the coffee table with an assortment of chocolate truffles. Through the bedroom door she noticed a hot-water bottle propped on the bedspread, and a vase with fresh flowers.

The lights were dimmed in the living room, and the wedding dresses glowed like fireflies. There was the ivory brocade gown with a strapless bodice and open back. It had occupied an aisle seat on the airplane, and Felicity had been terrified a flight attendant would brush past and the Swarovski crystals would fall off.

Hanging next to it was one of her favorites: a princess gown with an inner corset and pearl button closure. She had seen the pewter color in a magazine, and Raj scoured every garment store in Manhattan for the right fabric. It had been worth it! The color was so flattering, it made the model look like she'd just returned from a spa vacation.

And she adored the A-line dress with a regal lace motif and crystal buttons. When the light caught the buttons, the dress reminded her of fireworks on the Fourth of July.

She couldn't count how many times Raj had shown up with some incredible fabric—batiste light as air, or champagne-colored Mikado—and she'd decided that was going to be the fabric for her own wedding dress. And there was the time she'd spotted a pair of gold heels in the window of Reem Acra and imagined wearing them for her first dance.

Being a wedding dress designer was everything she'd dreamed of, but it didn't take the place of love. Even Patty believed in love and marriage; there was nothing better in the world. She switched off the lights and walked into the bedroom. The bed was turned down. She pressed the hot water bottle against her cheeks.

Nine

Nell

NELL ZIPPED UP HER SKI pants and buttoned her parka. The sky was pale blue outside her window, but she knew the puffy clouds and bright sun were deceiving. It was early morning and the temperatures on the slopes would be freezing.

There were three days until the fashion show, and the other girls were getting free massages provided by the hotel spa. It sounded so relaxing: reclining in one of those thermal beds, being slathered with lotions made from goat's milk and locally grown honey and thyme.

But her father had suggested they have breakfast and take some early morning runs, and she'd asked Raj for the morning off. He hadn't understood why she wanted to miss a seaweed wrap and deep-tissue massage, but he reluctantly agreed.

At least she didn't have to worry about running into her mother on the slopes. Her mother had given up skiing when Pete and Nell were children. She'd said it was impossible to enjoy herself when she had to run back to their room because Pete forgot his mittens, or the ski rental shop gave Nell the wrong poles and it took all day to exchange them. It was better to curl up in the lodge with a cup of hot cocoa and a book and wait for them to come down the mountain.

Nell rummaged in her purse for Chapstick and sighed. They did have some good times as a family, like the Christmas holiday when they'd rented a cabin in Lake Tahoe and made snowmen. Her mother and father had even got into a snowball fight. Afterward they all drank mulled cider and sang Christmas carols in front of the fireplace.

Should she have paid more attention to her parents' marriage, and would it have made a difference? They hadn't separated until Nell left for New York, and even then they'd still shared the house in Beverly Hills. Her father had moved into the pool house, and seemed content taking his early morning swims and eating dinner whenever he liked.

Even when they'd signed the divorce papers and her father moved to Malibu, Nell hadn't been concerned. Lots of her friends' parents got divorced, and the families still spent holidays together. It never occurred to her that her parents would refuse to occupy the same air space.

There was a knock at the door, and she wondered if it was Felicity. Felicity had left the nightclub early last night, and she hadn't seen her afterward. Nell tried calling, but her phone was off and the Do Not Disturb sign was on her door.

"Mom!" Nell opened the door. "What are you doing up? You said you were going to sleep until noon."

"There's something so luxurious about having nothing to do; it makes me want to get out of bed." Her mother entered the room and laughed. "At home, I'm so busy running the bookstore and taking care of the house that all I want to do is take a nap. Here, I can't wait to explore the shops and maybe take a horse and carriage ride."

"A horse and carriage ride?" Nell asked, wondering if her mother had met someone. "Aren't those for couples?"

"Why shouldn't I go by myself?" she asked. "One of the greatest myths about divorce is that a single woman can't go out on her own. I'm treated well wherever I go, and I've had many interesting conversations. It was only your father who grunted one-word answers when I asked him a question. Just because we made two children together didn't mean I knew his opinion on everything."

"I'm sure he didn't mean to ignore you," Nell answered.

"I shouldn't have said anything. I'd rather not talk about your father before breakfast," her mother commented. "I thought we could go to Hotel Hauser in the village. I haven't been there in years; they served the most delicious cheese and ham toasties."

"The Hotel Hauser!" Nell gulped. That's where she was going to meet her father. Then they were going to take the Chantarella funicular and ski Corviglia.

"When I was a chalet girl, it was very popular with the locals." Her mother nodded. "I still remember their porridge. They serve it with cinnamon and honey, and it's delicious."

Nell tried to think. If she suggested another restaurant in the village, they could still run into her father.

"It's such a beautiful morning," Nell said quickly. "Let's eat at a café on the mountain. Restaurant Chasellas is supposed to be excellent."

"The Chasellas; that's a name I haven't heard in years," her mother repeated. "I knew the chef; he used to serve all the chalet girls extra bacon. It's quite out of the way. You have to take the gondola to the chairlift to get there."

Nell calculated the logistics in her head. She'd text her father and say she was running late and had to skip breakfast. After she and her mother ate, she'd leave her mother at the Chasellas and take the chairlift to Corviglia. She'd have to carry her skis to breakfast, but she didn't have a choice.

"I'd love for you to show it to me," Nell said sweetly. "I read that the same chef has been there for years. Maybe he'll remember you."

"His name was Stefan, and his English was terrible." Her mother touched her hair. "Why not? I'll call and make a reservation for three people."

"Three people?" Nell asked.

"I hope you don't mind. I ran into Felicity last night and we had a brandy," she said. "I suggested she join us for breakfast."

"Felicity," Nell repeated. "I wondered where she went. She left the nightclub, and then her phone was off."

"I gather she and Adam are having problems, but I told her not to worry," Patty said. "You girls are too bright and successful to let men make you unhappy."

"Of course I don't mind, I adore Felicity," Nell answered. "I can't wait to get on the mountain. I'm starving."

Restaurant Chasellas was a large hut wedged into the side of the mountain. The restaurant had wooden beams and arched windows and a terrace with tables under striped umbrellas. Waiters carried trays of white sausages to skiers wearing mirrored sunglasses and fur-trimmed parkas.

"Are you all right?" Nell said to Felicity when her mother went inside to see the chef. "You disappeared last night and never answered your phone. My mother said she ran into you in the lobby and you shared a brandy."

"I'd rather not talk about it right now." Felicity was wearing a pink ski sweater, and there were dark circles under her eyes. "Let's enjoy breakfast with your mother."

"I'm your best friend—you can tell me anything," Nell prodded. "No offense, but you look like warmed-up oatmeal."

"If you must know, Adam isn't in love with me," Felicity blurted out. "Everything I've been doing to make up has been a waste of time."

"Did Adam tell you that?" Nell inquired.

"I haven't talked to him today," Felicity admitted. "It was something Katie said. It's sort of private; I should let her tell you."

"Katie the model?" Nell asked. "What does she have to do with anything?"

"Let's talk about it later," Felicity said as Nell's mother appeared. "I'm glad your mother asked me to join you. The mountain air is wonderful, and I already feel better."

"The chef retired years ago. The new chef is Stefan's son." Her mother sat down and laughed. "He recommended the homemade blueberry cake. He promised to add extra blueberries."

The waiter brought blueberry cake with fresh cream. There were plates of eggs and bacon and mugs of black coffee.

"This was a good idea," her mother said approvingly, stirring sugar into her coffee. "I forgot what it's like to eat on the mountain. Everything tastes better, and the air is so invigorating. When we were chalet girls, we all wanted to be Audrey Hepburn in the opening scene of *Charade*."

"I've never seen it." Felicity ate a strip of bacon.

"We used to watch it on the TV in our room," she mused. "Audrey Hepburn is sitting at a mountain hut in a Swiss ski resort. She looks impossibly elegant: huge sunglasses and a beehive hairdo and skiwear by some European designer. A gorgeous man skis up and it turns out to be Cary Grant. They fall madly in love, of course," she sighed. "The girls would sit for hours at a café on the mountain hoping the same thing would happen to them."

"It seems like a waste of a good day's skiing," Nell said, laughing.

"I quite agree." Her mother nodded. "Most of the chalet girls were in St. Moritz to find a fiancé. They even ranked the men by their nationalities. Italian men were sexy, but they often had wives at home. The French had titles, but hardly any money. It all went to keeping up their chateaus." She chuckled. "I wasn't thinking about marriage. I came to St. Moritz to ski."

"I've never seen you on skis," Nell said, and turned to Felicity. "When we were kids, my mother used to stand at the bottom of the bunny slope with chocolate bars."

"You and Pete were always hungry," she recalled fondly. "I was a good skier when I was young. And completely fearless. I broke my ankle skiing the Corvatsch."

"You broke your ankle in St. Moritz?" Nell asked, startled.

"It was a week before I was supposed to go home." Her mother sipped her coffee thoughtfully. "If I hadn't, I might never have seen your father again."

Patty

Patty sat at an outdoor table at Café Trutz and dug into a plate of veal cutlets with polenta and Gorgonzola cheese.

It was the kind of morning when Patty was glad she'd come to St. Moritz. All the bad parts of being a chalet girl—the male guests who pinched her when she served their crepes, the endless loads of laundry—seemed inconsequential when she could spend hours skimming the fresh snow and schussing to the bottom of the run.

Todd was standing at the self-service food bar. Her stomach did a little flip. Even though they'd spent the entire week together, she still couldn't believe they were falling for each other. He was funny and sweet, and as handsome as a movie star.

It was lovely to share a chairlift in the morning, and to rub each other's feet at the end of a day. And it was heavenly to sit at an outdoor table and share the house specialties: barley soup and apple strudel with dollops of whipped cream.

Patty's roommate was having an affair with a Swedish ski instructor, so they usually went to Patty's room after Todd finished work. They watched American movies with German subtitles on television and nibbled leftover lamb chops.

The second night, when Todd tried to unsnap her bra, she'd removed his hand and told him she wasn't about to lose her virginity to a boy she'd never see again. But every night she invited his hand to venture a little further, and it gave her so much pleasure.

Sometimes when his mouth was on hers and his hand roamed over her thighs, she didn't want to stop. But it wasn't a good idea. What if she felt differently after they made love? What if it was harder to say goodbye?

"These self-service restaurants can be infuriating." Todd appeared at the table. "I was stuck behind a Canadian woman who wouldn't choose a dish she couldn't pronounce. Who cares how you say gerstensuppe or streuselkuchen? They're all delicious."

"How can you complain on such a gorgeous day?" Patty waved at the mountain. "The conditions are perfect. You should have joined me on the Grand Alva, the moguls were amazing."

"I prefer to keep my skis on the ground." Todd buttered a slice of pumpernickel. "I have to work tonight, and it's difficult to serve cocktails with your leg in a cast."

"The moguls are the best part of skiing," Patty said. "The wind is in your hair and the sun is on your cheeks and you feel like you're flying."

"It sounds sexy when you describe it," Todd concurred. "You can tell me about it this evening in bed."

"How do you know we're going to spend tonight in bed?" Patty asked impishly. "I might have other plans."

"I'd be jealous if I thought that was possible." He kissed her. "We've spent every minute together, and you haven't had time to meet anyone else."

"It's not about meeting someone else," she said thoughtfully. "We should do something at night besides watch a Clint Eastwood movie where everyone speaks German. We could go to a museum or tobogganing."

"The movies are awful; I can't understand a word the actors say," Todd agreed. "But you've been happy watching television. What's changed?"

Patty stabbed her sausage with her fork and blushed. She had never talked about sex with a man.

"We're in St. Moritz. We should go snowshoeing or take a horse and carriage ride," she suggested. "Instead all we do is lie on a lumpy bed with itchy sheets."

"They are terrible sheets," Todd laughed. "I always wonder if they're preventing us from doing what we both want."

"What do you mean?" she asked.

"We kiss until my lips are numb, and then you disappear to the kitchen for a glass of water. I want you to feel safe, but I can't tell if you want to stop or if you're just thirsty." He looked at Patty plaintively. "You have to tell me what you want."

"I don't know what I want." She blushed furiously. "I've never talked about sex with a boy before."

"I know I want to make love to you," he said hoarsely. "You're beautiful and intelligent, and when we're together I'm so happy."

"I want it too, but what if I get pregnant?" She shook her head. "I can't risk my future for a few minutes of passion."

"If you like, I can go down to the pharmacist to get some condoms," Todd said. "I'll even keep them in my pocket so you won't be embarrassed by your roommate finding them in your dresser."

"It's not just that." She looked up at Todd. "What's the point? We're leaving in a week, and then we'll both be unhappy. It's better to leave as friends."

"I don't want to be friends." He tucked a piece of hair behind her ear. "I'm falling in love with you, and I hoped you'd feel the same. I can live without having sex, but I can't imagine not seeing you again. We'll figure something out."

"That's easy to say when we're sipping hot chocolate at a mountain café," Patty said, trying to be logical. "But how will that work when we live in different states? Statistics show holiday romances never last. It would be less painful to part as friends."

"There's that word again," Todd said vehemently. "We're not a statistic, we're two people from different places who found each other in the Swiss Alps. Do you know how lucky we are? I'm not letting what we have disappear." He stared at the skiers barreling down the slopes.

"Let's make a bet. I'll race you to the bottom of the mountain," he announced. "If I win, we vow to see each other again after the week is over."

"You want to race for our relationship?" Her eyes danced. "That's the craziest thing I ever heard."

"It's not crazy at all. I want to race for the opportunity to get to know you better," he said. "There's nothing more important in the world."

"I'm bound to win. I've been skiing since I was six years old," she responded. "I'd be at the bottom while you're adjusting your bindings."

"Are we on?" Todd leaned forward.

Todd's face was close to hers, and his eyes were emerald green. Her heart beat a little faster and she took a deep breath.

"We're on." She stood up and grabbed her goggles. "I'll meet you at the chairlift."

Patty clutched her poles and pushed off down the mountain. The Hahnensee was the most difficult black diamond run in St. Moritz, but it was almost the most exhilarating. At the top it was wide and open, and Patty felt like a ballet dancer making patterns in the snow. Then it passed through a forest and became so narrow, two skiers couldn't pass at the same time.

Todd was crazy to race her. She had taken lessons since she was a child, and he'd never tried on a pair of skis until high school. He wavered at the top of the chairlift and she almost pulled to the side and waited for him to catch up. Then the sun glinted on her skis and she didn't want to stop.

The thick swath of fir trees ended, and she could make out the bottom of the run. She turned to see if Todd was behind her and noticed him skiing around the moguls. She was about to lift her poles in victory when a tree branch jutted out in front of her. The last thing she remembered was her skis flying out from under her and the sound of something crunching like a car tire on an icy road.

Patty opened her suitcase and flinched. It had been five days since her accident, and she was finally able to move without swallowing pain pills. Todd told her everything that had happened after she blacked out: the stretcher that carried her to the hut, and the doctor who debated whether her ankle required surgery. Thankfully it was a hairline fracture, and all she needed was a boot and plenty of rest.

Todd had called her parents, and her father had insisted on coming to St. Moritz. The last thing she wanted was to sit at the chalet while her parents hovered over her. It was better if she went home.

"You're up." Todd entered the room carrying a paper sack. "I brought chocolate croissants. The cashier at Hanselmann's felt sorry for you and included a free nut torte."

"Thank you, but I'm not hungry," Patty said.

"Then I'll eat them." Todd bit into a croissant. "Why is your suitcase out?"

"I'm going home." Patty opened the drawer. "I have a seven p.m. flight from Zurich."

"What do you mean, you're going home?" he asked in shock. "You haven't said anything about leaving. The doctor said you should lie with your ankle up."

"I've been lying here for days. I'm going stir-crazy." She folded a pile of sweaters. "And I'll keep my ankle up on the plane. It will be eighteen hours of enforced rest."

"It's going to be impossible to travel by yourself with that ankle," Todd said imploringly. "How will you manage luggage and customs?"

"The taxi driver will carry my suitcase into the station, and my father hired someone to meet me at the Zurich airport." She took underwear out of the drawer. "Don't worry, I'll be handed over to my parents at LAX like an impossibly delicate soufflé."

"We haven't worked out how we'll see each other again." He was almost frantic. "You can't just disappear."

Patty noticed the look of hurt in Todd's eyes. There was a catch in her throat.

"There is such a thing as a telephone," she offered.

"We'll be too busy when we get home. We need to make a plan now." He gulped. "I'll tell you what. What if I take you to the airport? I'd like that very much."

"You're going to take the train all the way to Zurich?" She raised her eyebrow.

"I can't let you just leave." His voice softened. "I'm not ready to say goodbye."

"All right, you can take me to the airport." She hobbled over and kissed him.

He kissed her back and his breath tasted like chocolate.

"I did win the race, remember," he whispered. "I take bets very seriously."

"How can I forget?" She tried to laugh "I'm wearing the boot to prove it."

"I mean it." He kissed her again. "I'm not giving up on us."

"I believe you." She nodded, and a frisson of excitement ran up her spine.

Patty was glad Todd had offered to accompany her to Zurich. They took the Rhaetian Railway and had to change trains at Chur. Her ankle started to throb and the suitcase was heavier than she thought, and by the time they reached the airport she was grimacing with pain.

"Someone is supposed to meet me." She glanced around the terminal. If he didn't show up, she'd have to change planes at Heathrow by herself. There was only an hour's layover, and she might miss her connecting flight. "My father paid him to escort me to Los Angeles."

"Turn around," Todd instructed her. He was wearing a wool coat and carrying a knapsack.

"I don't see him, and they are about to board," Patty said worriedly. "It's going to take me ages to get to the gate."

"You turned too far." He took her arm and positioned her in front of him. "That's better."

"What are you talking about?" Her cheeks flushed and she gasped. "You can't take me to Los Angeles!"

"Why should your father pay a stranger to sit on a plane, when I'm going to the same country?" Todd asked. "I called and offered to accompany you."

"You called my father without telling me?" Patty was suddenly angry. "I'm not a package you get paid to deliver."

"He's not paying me. I just changed my flight." Todd shook his head. "Anyway, I didn't want to stay in St. Moritz without you. You don't even have to sit next to me on the plane. I'll get you settled and not bother you at all."

"Where's your suitcase?" she wondered. "All you have is a back-pack."

"There wasn't time to pack." He shrugged. "I asked Christopher to ship it. I'm sorry, I should have said something." He hung his head. "I was afraid you might say no."

"I might have," she agreed. "California is a long way from Ohio."

"I have a six-hour layover," he said brightly. "Maybe you can show me the beach."

She reached up and kissed him. He kissed her back and she felt something new, like a flower opening after the winter.

"I did say you should come to California," she acknowledged.

"You did," he agreed.

"Then let's go." She pointed to her bag. "Would you mind carry-ing my suitcase?"

"How did we start talking about this?" her mother asked, eating a slice of blueberry cake. "Your father could charm anyone. Within a week he had moved all his stuff to Los Angeles and got a job at a restaurant so we could get to know each other. He even convinced his new boss to let him sleep in the room above the restaurant where they kept the extra furniture."

"He was in love with you," Nell said to her mother. If she could only get her mother to see how much her father had loved her, perhaps she would change her mind about coming to the wedding.

"Who knows what he was?" she answered briskly. "It doesn't matter; that was years ago. When you are young, you don't realize people change as often as chameleons shed their skin. Your father and I are completely different people."

Her mother went inside to use the powder room and Nell finished her coffee.

"Your mother really is beautiful," Felicity commented. "She must have been stunning when she was young."

Nell gazed at the skiers and suddenly had an idea.

"My father was her first proper boyfriend," she said thoughtfully. "Maybe she regretted never seeing other men."

"You think she had an affair?" Felicity asked. "Your father was so in love with her, she didn't have to look anywhere else."

"Not an affair—what if other men admired her? A director at a cocktail party, or a teacher at school? She didn't rebuff their advances, and my father got jealous."

"I suppose it's possible," Felicity agreed. "But why would she be so angry?"

Nell stood up and grabbed her goggles. "I don't know yet. I'm supposed to meet my father at the gondola in twenty minutes. Will you stay and finish breakfast with my mother?"

"What will I say if she asks why you left?" Felicity wondered.

"Say Raj scheduled a last-minute photo shoot." Nell waved her hand. "I can't keep my father waiting."

"You really should tell them the truth," Felicity said. "You can't keep running around St. Moritz."

"I have to find out what happened so they come to the wedding," Nell faltered. "Every time I think of walking down the aisle without my father, or not seeing my mother sitting in the front row, I can hardly breathe."

Nell sat on the chairlift and tried to imagine her mother at twenty-one: young and beautiful and skiing effortlessly down the mountain. People might change, but true love lasted forever. That's what made it wonderful.

Her father stood at the base of the gondola and she waved. If only she could make her parents see that, perhaps they would forgive each other and attend the wedding. Then she'd be the happiest bride in the world.

Ten

Felicity

FELICITY WALKED THROUGH THE VILLAGE in the early afternoon and admired the shop windows. She left Patty at the hotel after their breakfast at Restaurant Chasellas and decided to buy some souvenirs. There was a light dusting of snow, and it all looked so inviting: interior-design stores with modern Swedish furniture, a Chanel with bottles of perfume perfect for New Year's Eve, a diamond-and-sapphire pendant at Harry Winston.

If only things were different, she'd be tempted to splurge on something fabulous to take home: the bright orange dress at Gucci, or a quilted jacket from Escada. But Adam would never see it, so what was the point? She'd spend the next year in the slacks and blouses she wore to work and the bathrobe she put on when she got home.

Perhaps she should buy Gabriel a thank-you present for being such a good friend: a Christmas cake, or a box of pralines. She would miss their lunches and his stories. But she didn't need his advice. Perhaps it was time to admit the break with Adam might be serious and she had to learn to live without him. Like a favorite sweater you can't put away until you notice the holes in the elbows.

She entered a pastry shop and admired the glass cases of chocolates. There were milk-chocolate truffles with colored sprinkles like confetti, pink peppermint sticks, and chocolate pyramids drizzled in caramel.

The clusters of Brazil nuts dipped in dark chocolate looked delicious, and she handed them to the cashier. He wrapped them in a clear bag and tied them with a ribbon. She walked back onto the street and heard someone calling her name. Raj strode toward her, waving his cell phone.

"What are you doing here?" she asked in surprise.

"Finding you," Raj said. "I tried calling, but it went straight to voicemail."

"I'm sorry, the phone reception is so spotty," she apologized. "Don't tell me one of the models got hurt. We shouldn't let them ski; someone is bound to be injured."

"Everyone is fine," Raj assured her. "I gave them the afternoon off until this evening's bobsled race. I need to talk to you. This has got to stop."

"What are you talking about?" Felicity asked.

"This thing you're carrying on with the Swiss doctor, it's all over the blogs." He pointed to his phone. "At first I thought it was harmless, and any mention was good publicity. But it's gone too far. You are a wedding dress designer—you can't cavort around St. Moritz with a handsome stranger while your boyfriend is in New York."

Felicity's cheeks colored and her stomach dropped.

"I'd rather not talk in the middle of the sidewalk," she said, and pointed to a café. "Let's sit down and discuss it."

"Listen to this," Raj said when they were seated at a table. He clicked his phone on and read out loud. "Someone doesn't have much Christmas spirit this year. Sports manager Adam Burton looked positively Grinch-like at the Union Square Holiday Market. We can't blame him; the blogs have been swirling with photos of his wedding-dress-designer girlfriend, Felicity Grant, getting cozy with a mystery man in St. Moritz. We thought we had good news for Adam: Felicity was seen at St. Moritz's hottest nightspot, Chesa Veglia, with her whole crew. She was eating their famous white pizza and hanging out with the models, and there wasn't a dark-haired man in sight.

"The other girls headed for the dance floor after dinner, but Felicity begged off. She was later spotted at the Polo Bar sipping brandy with a female friend and looking very upset. It seems unlikely that she was missing Adam, since she's been having such a good time in St. Moritz. Perhaps the mystery doctor didn't approve of her friends at Chesa Veglia and they had a lover's quarrel. It doesn't look good for her boyfriend, Adam, in New York. No one wants to be someone else's sloppy seconds. Thankfully, the New Year is around the corner. Seems like it's a perfect time to put in motion the old adage: out with the old and in with the new."

Felicity grabbed the phone and studied the photo of her and Patty sitting at the Polo Bar. The photo was dark but her mascara was smudged, and she looked like she had been crying.

"I don't know why they keep making things up!" Felicity handed him the phone. "I got upset about Adam and decided to go back to the hotel. Then I was freezing and stopped at the bar for a brandy."

"Who were you with?" Raj asked. "You don't know anyone in St. Moritz."

God! Nell hadn't told Raj that her mother and father were in St. Moritz. She didn't want anyone to know.

"The blogs made that part up too," Felicity said, waving her hand. "I was just sitting at the bar."

"I wondered why you left Chesa Veglia. It looks like something is going on with that doctor, and it has to end." Raj put away his phone. "Every journalist and blogger is covering the collection. We're not going to get favorable reviews if you're behaving like a lovesick teenager."

"Gabriel and I are just friends." Felicity looked up and her eyes were bright. "If you must know, it was something one of the models said. I promised to keep it a secret. It doesn't matter anyway. Adam and I are over."

"What do you mean, it's a secret? I need to know everything about the models!" Raj blustered. "This fight with Adam will blow over once you're together. In the meantime, if the blogs keep making snide comments about you and Gabriel, the show will be a disaster. Everyone is coming to experience magic and romance, not to get in the middle of some sordid love triangle."

"There's no love triangle," she said hotly. Then she remembered how hard she and Raj had worked on the collection. "If you really think it will hurt the collection, I won't see Gabriel again. I promise there won't be any more pictures online."

Raj relaxed and leaned against the chair.

"You've never let me down in six years, so I'm going to trust you," he said, nodding. "I know we're both on edge. Every time a model leaves the hotel, I'm afraid she's going to slip on the ice or run off with an Austrian count. But we're creating a terrific buzz. The fashion show is going to be a huge success."

"You're doing a great job, and I'm grateful." Felicity suddenly felt emotional. Felicity Grant Bridal was all she had left, and she had to put everything into it.

"I have to go, I'm meeting Greta." Raj looked quizzically at her package. "Don't tell me you bought something at Läderach? Their chocolates are terribly overpriced."

"It's a present for Gabriel," she said sheepishly.

Raj picked up the bag and inspected the chocolate-covered nuts. "Why are you buying a present for someone you just met?"

Felicity's cheeks colored and she snatched the bag away. "It's Christmas, and he's been very kind. Why shouldn't I buy him something?"

Felicity climbed the steps to Gabriel's office and knocked on the door.

"Felicity! It's nice to see you." Gabriel appeared in a long white coat, carrying a stack of magazines. "Come in, I was tidying up the waiting room. What's wrong? You look upset."

Felicity sat on the vinyl sofa and handed him the bag of nuts. So much had happened, and she didn't know where to start.

"These are for you," she said. "To say thank you."

"They look delicious, but why are you giving them to me now?" He turned the bag over. "You're in St. Moritz for three more days. Did something happen? Do you want to talk about it?"

Felicity told him Katie's story, and how she was sure Adam had never loved her.

"I appreciate everything you've done for me," she said, folding her hands, "but I don't need more advice. Adam and I are finished. I was making Adam into something he never was from the beginning."

"I doubt that," Gabriel said slowly. "Adam wouldn't stay with you for six years if he didn't love you."

"How do you know?" she wondered. "Maybe we stayed together because I was convenient."

"Convenient?" he asked.

"I live across Central Park, so he doesn't have to take the subway to get to my apartment." She fiddled with a cushion. "I don't do any of those clingy girl things, like keeping my vitamins at his place or asking him to do my taxes. And we like the same toppings on pizza, so he doesn't have to order half sausage and half pineapple."

"I doubt he's with you because you're convenient. From what you said, Adam can afford taxis, and he wouldn't notice if you left your toothbrush in his vanity," Gabriel responded. "My bathroom cabinet is full of things I never use: earplugs and extra-large Band-Aids."

"How would you know how Adam feels?" she asked despondently. "You've never met him."

"I know you." He opened the packet of nuts. "You wouldn't be in love with him if he wasn't worth it."

"If you were really in love with someone, would you tell her you wanted to take a break?" She accepted the nut he offered.

"If I was in love, I would wrap my arms around her and tell

her that no matter how hard it was, we'd work it out. I'd tell her I couldn't live without her, and she's the most important thing in the world." His eyes were suddenly serious.

There was an odd silence. Felicity stood up and smoothed her slacks.

"I have to go," she said. "I've so enjoyed our walks and your stories, but Raj doesn't want me to see you again."

"What do you mean?" Gabriel frowned.

"The blogs are having a field day, and he's worried the negative press will hurt the collection."

"That's ridiculous," he objected. "We're just friends."

"We know that, but the bloggers can be quite ruthless," she answered. "I can't jeopardize the fashion show. Raj and I have worked so hard."

"Of course. I understand." He nodded. "It's a shame. I had tickets to the new exhibit at the Segantini Museum tonight. I was going to invite you. Afterward we could listen to caroling in the village and eat Sacher torte and almond nougat at Hotel Hauser."

She remembered her promise to Raj that there wouldn't be any more photos of her and Gabriel online.

"I'm sorry, I can't." She shook her head. "Raj wants us to watch the bobsled races."

"I'll just have to go by myself," Gabriel said and smiled. "The bobsled races are quite exhilarating. Just don't get too close to the track. You don't want to get run over."

Felicity looked at Gabriel's brown eyes and something small inside her shifted. She brushed the feeling aside and nodded.

"I certainly don't," she agreed. "I won't have my guardian angel there to protect me."

"And don't go outside without a jacket," he admonished.

"St. Moritz is eighteen hundred meters above sea level. You can't walk around in a sweater and slacks."

"I have it right here." She pointed to the jacket folded over her arm.

"I'm sure we'll run into each other; it's a small village," Gabriel offered. "Is it all right if I wave from across the street, or will the bloggers read something into that?"

"It's perfectly all right." Her eyes were bright. "I promise I'll wave back."

"Good luck then, and thank you for the chocolates," Gabriel said. "How did you know Brazil nuts were my favorite?"

"I was just lucky." A smile crossed her face and she turned to the door.

Felicity climbed the steps of Badrutt's Palace and entered the lobby. It never failed to thrill her: the giant Christmas tree festooned with ornaments, the women in fur coats and tight ski pants, the men with dark tans and gold watches. In three days it would be New Year's Eve, and all these people would line the catwalk to view her collection. Katie would appear first in an A-line gown with a marching ermine cape. Crystal would wear iridescent Mikado silk with a skirt stacked like seashells. She could hardy contain herself when she pictured Nell's dress for the finale. The sweetheart neckline was embroidered with gold stitching and the organza bow was as wide as the runway.

She had so much to be grateful for: Raj's devotion to the business, Nell's friendship, and the success of Felicity Grant Bridal. And now the chance to be part of Bergdorf Goodman's bridal collection! All she needed was a bath and a cup of hot chocolate and she would feel better. Maybe she'd even buy herself a treat: a coffee-table book from the hotel gift shop, or a cashmere scarf she saw in the boutique. It was Christmas, after all; she could afford to buy herself a present.

There was a man standing at the concierge desk wearing a gray overcoat. He had light brown hair, and his black carry-on looked familiar. The man waved at the concierge and Felicity's heart beat faster.

It couldn't be Adam! He wouldn't fly to St. Moritz without telling her. She remembered the latest blog, and her stomach turned over. Perhaps Adam was so angry he'd come to break up with her in person.

"Felicity!" He turned around. "Thank God. Your cell phone didn't pick up, and there's no answer on the phone in your suite. This gentleman wouldn't let me up to your room without your permission."

"What are you doing here?" she asked. His cologne was familiar and his eyes were the same shade of blue, and for a moment she remembered how much she'd missed him.

"I came to talk to you. And I'd rather not do it in the lobby." He grimaced. "St. Moritz isn't the easiest place to get to. I've been on two planes and a train and a taxi. Can we go up to your suite and talk in private?"

"Thank you, Gunther," Felicity said, turning to the concierge. "Everything is fine. Adam is a friend from America."

They entered the suite. Adam surveyed the striped drapes and velvet love seats and the balcony with its view of the lake.

"This is quite a place," Adam said, and whistled. "Don't tell me Raj paid for all this. You're living in the lap of luxury."

"Raj got a discount on the suite, and we're both working hard," she answered. "Katie almost had to be sent home because of altitude sickness, and Crystal got in trouble for wanting to do the Cresta Run. Not to mention making sure every photo opportunity is documented," she said. "We've been busy from morning to night."

"You have been busy." Adam settled on the sofa. "And extremely well documented. Everyone in New York knows what Felicity Grant is up to in St. Moritz."

"If you came all this way during the most important week of my life to harp about a few silly blogs, you could have saved yourself the trip," she said sharply.

"It's not a few silly blogs. It was in Page Six in the *New York Post*," he said. "Anyway, Doug signed with the firm yesterday, so I decided to get on a plane. It's the only way to find out what's going on."

"I told you, nothing is going on," Felicity replied. "The blogs made it all up."

"I find that hard to believe. The pictures are everywhere," Adam responded. "On Christmas Day, all you wanted was to get married; now you're practically planning a wedding to a complete stranger."

"Gabriel is just a friend," she answered. "But you said we should take a break. You even suggested we see other people."

"I didn't mean the thing about seeing other people. It popped out of my mouth, and I was too wound up to take it back." He looked at Felicity. "I came because I didn't want to lose you. I've missed you, Felicity."

"You can't miss me. I've only been gone for four days." Felicity sat on the sofa beside him.

"I missed *us*—we're an amazing team." He touched her hand. "I can't see the future clearly, but I know you're part of it. I'm jet-lagged and haven't had a decent meal in twenty-four hours. Why don't we continue this conversation at dinner? I'll ask the concierge to recommend a restaurant, and we'll order a bottle of wine and a couple of steaks."

Felicity removed her hand and walked to the window. A group of children hurried by carrying a red sled. Gabriel might help her figure out what to do, but she'd promised Raj she wouldn't see him.

"I'm sorry, I can't have dinner." She turned around. "I have plans."

"What do you mean, you have plans?" Adam demanded. "Tell Raj that I'm here. He can survive an evening without you."

"I've been invited to a private showing at the Segantini Museum," she said, crossing her fingers behind her back and telling a little white lie. "It's very important. They might sponsor the collection."

"Then I'll come with you," he offered.

"I already RSVP'd for one. I'm not allowed to bring a guest because the space is tiny," she said quickly. "Why don't you relax, and we can meet for drinks later at the King's Club? It's one of the hottest nightclubs in Europe."

"I guess that will work. It will give me time to take a shower," Adam said, relenting. "There were no rooms at Badrutt's Palace. I had to book a room at the Suvretta House above the village."

Felicity crossed the room and kissed him on the cheek. "You must be tired, and you don't want to walk in the cold. I'll tell the valet to call you a taxi."

After Adam left, Felicity sank onto the sofa in her suite. In all the scenarios she'd pictured—Adam waiting for her at JFK with a dozen roses, Adam filling her apartment with flickering candles—she'd never expected him to be standing in the lobby of Badrutt's Palace.

The crystal ornaments on the mantelpiece glowed under the chandelier and the lights on the indoor Christmas tree twinkled red and green and gold. She had dreamed of Adam coming to St. Moritz, but now that he was here she felt all mixed up, like a snow globe that had been shaken too much.

Her phone sat beside her and she dialed Gabriel's number.

"Felicity," Gabriel answered. "Why are you calling? Are you feeling all right? You have to be careful with a head injury, sometimes you don't realize it's a concussion until days later."

"I'm fine. I hope I'm not disturbing you," she faltered. "I wondered if that invitation to the museum opening was still good."

"My last patient left and I was planning on going," he concurred. "I never pass up free hors d'oeuvres and vintage wines."

"Can I join you?" she asked. "Something happened and I'd like to talk to you."

"What if someone sees us?" he wondered.

"I'll wear a disguise," Felicity chuckled. For the first time since Adam had appeared, her spirits lifted. "Look for the woman in the hooded parka and dark sunglasses."

"Now I'm intrigued. It sounds like a spy movie," Gabriel answered cheerfully. "I'll see you at seven p.m."

Felicity put down the phone and poured a cup of tea. The sound of caroling drifted through the window, and she took a small sip.

It was Christmas week in St. Moritz, and she should be happy and excited about the winter collection and her sketches for Camilla Barnes. Instead, she was desperately trying to make everything all right with Adam. All she wanted was to be happy with the man she loved. She put down her teacup and wished for a Christmas miracle.

Eleven

Three Days before the Fashion Show
5:00 p.m.

Nell

NELL SAT ON A LEATHER stool at the Quattro Bar and sipped hot buttered rum with nutmeg. It had been the most amazing afternoon of skiing. She and her father had started at the Chantarella station and skied the width of the Corviglia. The snow was like vanilla cream filling in some fabulous wedding cake, and the runs were so wide that the whole valley was spread out below them.

Chatting with her father on the chairlift and crisscrossing the mountain together, she almost forgave him for being stubborn. She was so lucky! He would rather spend time with her than do almost anything else, and he was fit enough to keep up with her on the most challenging runs in the Alps.

It was late afternoon, three days before the collection, and they'd decided to take a break before returning to the village. The Quattro Bar was perched halfway up the mountain, and from the outside it reminded Nell of an airline hangar. But inside there were sleek wood floors and a granite bar and panoramic views.

"This place was built for the 2017 World Cup," her father said, eating smoked salmon with horseradish cream. "People said no one would eat at a one-star Michelin restaurant while they were wearing parkas and ski boots. The menu is pretty pricey, but the tables are full all day."

"We didn't have to choose anywhere fancy. We could have shared a cheese and fruit plate at the Alpine Hut," Nell laughed. "You always discovered the most expensive places to eat on vacation. Remember that little village in Portugal? Mom was happy to eat anywhere; all she wanted was for Pete and me to stop whining."

"Well, your mother was the one that made us drive two hours out of our way to visit an antiquarian book shop," he retorted. "I had to keep you and Pete occupied while she and the owner rattled on about Balzac. All he wanted was to get into her pants; he didn't want to sell her a book at all."

This was the perfect time to find out if her mother had ever had a serious flirtation. But how could she bring up her suspicions? It wasn't the kind of thing you'd casually mention over a plate of smoked salmon.

"Mom must have been beautiful when she was young." Nell traced the rim of her glass. "Men would have flirted with her all the time."

"She was stunning. That blond hair and blue eyes and model's figure," her father agreed. "The most attractive thing about her was that she paid no attention to her looks. That's the kind of thing that drives men crazy."

"So men did flirt with her?" Nell leaned forward.

"Of course, but she never gave them the time of day." He shrugged. "We were wild about each other in the beginning. You could have lined up the biggest movie stars and neither of us would have noticed."

"Still, you both got married so young," Nell persisted. "You were Mom's first proper boyfriend."

"Who told you that?" her father asked, startled.

Nell bit her lip. Had her father mentioned it, or was it her mother? She really should keep notes on her phone.

"You said you met when she was twenty-one," she reminded him. "She couldn't have had any serious boyfriends before that."

"I did say that, didn't I?" He stirred his drink. "Her father wouldn't let anyone near her. I couldn't blame him. With those legs and that smile, she was impossible to resist. Somehow her father took a liking to me." He grimaced. "The more her father appreciated me, the more your mother found reasons to fault me. It was like being a human ping-pong ball," he said. "Still, we got two incredible children out of the marriage. That's worth years of feeling like my skin was on fire."

"You must have had good times," Nell urged, not wanting to change the subject. "I remember watching her getting dressed for cocktail parties. Her hair was set in huge curlers and she wore French perfume."

"It was Dior." He nodded. "I bought it for her when I was on location in Paris. She wore it every day until the next year when I forgot Valentine's Day. Then she poured the rest of the bottle down the drain."

"It must have been hard to trust each other," Nell said idly. "You were surrounded by actresses, and Mom was home alone with all the single dads. That would wear on any marriage."

Her father looked at her in surprise. "I trusted your mother completely. I hope you're not talking about you and Eliot. Just because you get paid to strut down a runway, that doesn't mean he shouldn't trust you. If you'd like me to talk to him . . ."

"Don't be silly; Eliot is completely supportive of my career." She grabbed her phone and found a photo of a bouquet of white tulips. "He sends me flowers every day because he can't be in St. Moritz. I told him he shouldn't spend his money; the maids bring flowers every morning. He said it's not the same, that he wants me to wake up to a bouquet he chose himself."

"I'm glad. All I want is for you to be happy." Her father studied the photo closely. "What's that hanging up?"

Nell glanced at the tea-length wedding dress hanging next to the bed in her hotel room. Next to it were a pillbox hat and elbow-length silk gloves.

"It's one of the gowns I'm wearing in the fashion show," she answered. "Don't tell anyone you saw it; the whole collection is top secret. I wanted to make sure it still fit. The waist was a bit tight, and I've gained a couple of pounds since we arrived."

"I doubt that. You're like your mother, neither of you ever gain an ounce," he said, waving his hand. "She loved to flaunt it in my face. She'd eat a bowl of ice cream while I was trying to enjoy a black coffee and my whole night would be ruined."

"You're drinking buttered rum now," Nell reminded him.

"I've grown a little easier on myself," her father conceded. "But you don't have to worry, you're slender as a swan. I can't wait to see you in that dress. It reminds me of your mother's wedding dress."

Nell glanced up and frowned. "She didn't have a proper wedding dress. Mom told me when I was a little girl that you were married by a justice of the peace. Mom had to take your shirt to the dry cleaner's because you didn't have a pressed shirt, and she wore something out of her closet."

Her father stirred his cocktail and his eyes were suddenly misty.

"I only owned two dress shirts, and the maid, Inez, usually ironed them. How was I to know Inez had the week off?" he said. "That was the dress for the second wedding. God, the way it showed off her legs!"

"You had a second wedding?" Nell's eyes were wide.

"We tried to have a second wedding," he sighed. "It was my idea, and it was a complete disaster. I was only trying to do the right thing, and your mother was furious." He swallowed his cocktail. "Under the circumstances, one could hardly blame her."

Beverly Hills
Twenty-Eight Years Ago

Todd

Todd stood in the florist's on the corner of Wilshire Boulevard and thought that a bunch of peonies there must cost as much as an entire flower shop in Cleveland. After four months in Beverly Hills, none of it seemed real: the foreign sports cars driven by teenagers barely old enough to have a license, the small dogs wearing jeweled collars. Even the sales girl at the florist was probably only there because her parents had threatened to stop her allowance unless she had a job.

Tomorrow was the opening night of Grease *at UCLA, and he wanted to present Patty with a fabulous bouquet. She had been so irritable lately. Even though she claimed the play wasn't important and she was only fulfilling her course requirements, he was sure she had pre-opening jitters. Of course she wanted to become an actress; who wouldn't want their face on the big screen?*

The May sun shone through the florist's window, and he wondered how he'd ended up in Beverly Hills. After working at the restaurant in Hollywood for a few weeks, the assistant to Patty's father, Alistair, had quit, and Alistair had asked Todd if he would like the job. It took Todd about an hour to say yes. The offer included free board in the pool house and a ride to the studio every morning in Alistair's convertible.

The best thing about the arrangement was the proximity of the pool house to Patty's bedroom. Two weeks later, Patty had surprised him with a bottle of wine and new lingerie, and pulled him into bed with her. Since then, they couldn't get enough of each other.

Sometimes when Patty draped herself naked across his chest, Todd laughed that she was only using him for his body. Then he would turn her on her back and she would look up at him with her luminous blue eyes, and he knew they were meant to be together.

The salesgirl suggested a bouquet of sunflowers, and he handed her the money. He had to do something to get Patty out of her dark mood. The past week, he wasn't sure whether she would throw her script at him or shut her door and refuse to come downstairs.

He walked the six blocks to the hacienda on Beverly Drive and entered the pool house. Todd had expected a lecture from Patty's father to keep his hands off Patty or be fired. But Alistair approved of the relationship. It was better that Patty date Todd than some unemployed actor Alistair didn't know.

"There you are." Todd entered the den. The wood-paneled walls were covered with family photos, and there was a miniature putting green.

"It's the only room with decent air-conditioning," Patty said from the couch. A magazine was draped over her stomach, and she was wearing shorts and a halter top. "Inez keeps the rest of the house too hot. I'm going to wilt like last week's flowers."

"This isn't hot." Todd perched on the armchair. "You should visit Cleveland in the summer. The humidity is so high, you can't eat a Popsicle without it melting."

"I'm never moving from this couch," she groaned. "I told Inez she doesn't have to make dinner. I'm going to have a salad and an iced tea."

"You have to eat; your performance is tomorrow night." He wished he could tell her about the flowers, but he wanted them to be a surprise. "How will you accept the thunderous applause and bouquets of flowers if you collapse onstage?"

"I'm not going to perform." She looked up. "My understudy, Suzy, is taking my part."

"What do you mean?" Todd demanded. "You've been rehearsing for weeks."

"I don't want to do it," Patty said stubbornly. "I told my professor and it won't affect my grade."

"Your father booked a table at Wolfgang Puck's to celebrate," Todd persisted. "You can't back out."

"This has nothing to do with my father." Patty sat up. "It's my education, and I can do whatever I like."

"If it's stage fright, you have nothing to worry about." His voice softened. "The audience will adore you."

"I've been trying to tell you something, but I can't find the right time." She looked at Todd and her eyes were huge. "I have some very big news. I'm pregnant."

The room spun, and Todd desperately needed a drink. "What did you say?"

"There's nothing wrong with your hearing, and apparently you have healthy sperm." Her voice rose anxiously. "They managed to avoid my diaphragm, and I'm going to have a baby in seven months."

"Are you sure?" Todd gulped. "Those home tests can be wrong."

"I went to my ob-gyn for my annual exam," she continued. "I should have guessed. My breasts ache and I hate the smell of coffee. I can't have an abortion. I'm Catholic, and I'm not going to burn in hell for eternity because you have exceptional swimmers."

Todd stood up and walked to the bar. Alistair wouldn't complain about Todd drinking his whiskey when he found out that Patty was pregnant. He'd be too busy tossing Todd's suitcase into the driveway and demanding he never set foot in the house again.

"I don't expect you to have an abortion." Todd gulped the whiskey.

"Then what will we do?" Patty asked. For a moment she looked like a little girl, instead of a headstrong woman who always had the last word.

The whiskey burned his throat and he poured another shot. He was twenty-two years old; he wasn't ready to be a father. But he looked at Patty with her blond hair and blue eyes and couldn't desert her.

"We'll get married," he said before he could change his mind.

"We can't get married," she almost laughed.

"What do you mean, we can't get married?" he retorted. "We're both of age, and I have a good job. I even opened a savings account."

"You're living in my parents' pool house, and you work for my father," she sniffed.

"We'll get an apartment," he answered. "And I'm good at what I do."

"What if you and my father have a falling-out?" she persisted. "You don't even have your degree."

"I'll get my degree at night. If we have a falling-out, I'll work for someone else." He sat beside her. "It's not what I planned, but we don't have a choice. If you're having a baby, we need to get married."

"Is that why you want to get married?" She inched away. "Because I'm an obligation?"

"I want to get married because from the moment I saw you at that bar in St. Moritz, there was no other girl for me. You are beautiful and opinionated and our life together is never dull." He took her hand. "Besides, I'm madly in love with you."

"Then we'll elope," she decided. "I'm not going to be held hostage for months by some Beverly Hills wedding planner. And how would I look in a Vera Wang gown with a round stomach? We'll have a civil ceremony at the courthouse."

"We can't elope!" he exclaimed. "Your parents would be furious."

Patty stood up and the magazine fell to the floor. Her breasts pushed against her halter top, and there was a new fullness to her figure.

"We either elope or we don't get married." She walked to the bar and poured a glass of iced tea.

"You can be impossible," he said, following her. "But I love you, and I hope our child is just like you."

He bent down and kissed her shoulder. She smelled of lotion, and suddenly he wanted her more than anything.

"I'll call the courthouse and see when they have an opening," she said, and kissed him.

"Why don't we go upstairs, and I'll rub your back?" he murmured. "Pregnant women need a lot of pampering."

Two weeks later, Todd surveyed the items spread out around the hotel cottage and thought everything looked perfect: the tea-length crepe *wedding dress, satin pumps, and bridal bouquet of lilies of the valley. There was a pillbox hat, lace gloves, and a prayer book like the one Grace Kelly carried at her wedding to Prince Rainier in Monaco.*

The wedding planner at the San Ysidro Ranch had insisted that the prayer book was the perfect touch. Grace Kelly was one of Patty's favorite actresses, and every bride wanted to believe she was marrying a prince and her life would be a fairy tale.

In a few minutes, Patty would return from the hotel spa and receive a huge surprise; their closest friends and family were gathered on the lawn for the wedding ceremony. Afterward, they would move to the barrel room for lobster and pomegranate wedding cake.

Todd was pleased with himself for orchestrating the whole thing: telling Patty they were going to the San Ysidro Ranch for a romantic weekend; choosing her dress; even finding her favorite song for the first dance. After dinner, there would be a bottle of sparkling cider waiting in the cottage, and rose petals leading to the canopied bed.

After Todd had proposed, he realized he couldn't marry Patty without secretly asking for her father's blessing. Alistair approved, but was furious that Patty wanted to elope. Todd knew how stubborn Patty could be, and was afraid she would cancel the whole thing.

Finally, Alistair suggested having a second surprise wedding, and included their closest family and friends. Todd couldn't refuse: all he had to do was convince Patty to spend the weekend at one of the most romantic hotels on the California coastline.

The cottage door opened and Todd hastily entered the living room. The decor really was charming: a beamed ceiling, pot-bellied stove, and wood floors covered by Persian rugs. There was a private patio with views of the Santa Inez Mountains and an outdoor shower.

"How was the massage?" Todd asked, pouring a glass of water.

"I don't want to talk about it," Patty groaned. A pink robe was knotted around her waist, and she wore felt slippers.

"What do you mean?" he asked. "The spa is world class—all the Hollywood celebrities come here."

"The masseuse used eucalyptus oil, and I must be allergic," she said. "My skin is on fire, and I'm covered in blotches."

"There must be something you can do." He pictured the wedding dress, with its sweetheart neckline and knee-length skirt. "Benadryl will stop the itching."

"I can't take Benadryl, I'm pregnant," she said irritably. "I'm going to take a bath and go to bed. I'm sorry, we can't go out for dinner."

"You can't go to bed!" Todd panicked. At this moment, twenty guests were twirling parasols and taking their seats in the garden. A string quartet would play Brahms and everyone would turn and wait expectantly for the bride.

"I can't put on clothes, and I don't think the other guests want to see me naked." She shrugged. "The room-service menu must have a club sandwich. We'll watch a movie and I'll feel better in the morning."

Patty opened the bedroom door. Her eyes widened and she gasped. "What's this?" She waved at the wedding dress fanned out on the bed and the satin pumps perched on a shoebox.

"We're getting married," he gulped.

"We got married last week," she said, turning around.

"Your father and I planned a surprise wedding." Todd beamed. "You don't have to do anything except put on that dress and walk down the aisle."

"You talked to my father without asking me?" she demanded.

"I had to—I didn't want to get married without his blessing," he said cheerfully. "My parents are here, and Christopher and Amy, and your roommate from UCLA. There will be a garden ceremony, followed by a lobster dinner and pomegranate wedding cake."

"I'm pregnant, I can't eat seafood! Fruit gives me stomach acid, and the scent of flowers makes me nauseous. Even if I wasn't covered in a rash, the last thing I want is to stand outside in the heat." She glowered. "Please tell everyone to go home."

"They can't leave! Your father rented out every cottage," he pleaded. "There's a dozen bottles of expensive wine in the barrel room, and a golf cart decorated with tin cans."

"If I wanted a wedding, I would have planned one myself. I'm going to take a bath." She walked angrily to the bathroom. "Go enjoy yourself and give everyone my regards."

The wedding planner had timed the ceremony so the evening light would reflect on the hills. Afterward the guests would mingle under the loquat trees, and there would be appetizers of pan-seared abalone and Spanish octopus. And the wedding menu! Alistair had paid extra for the choice of lobster tails or spiced chicken with roasted cauliflower florets.

Todd stripped off his shirt and unbuckled his belt.

"What are you doing?" Patty asked. "If you think I want to have sex, I'd rather jump out of a plane without a parachute."

"You need someone to wash your back." He helped her into the bath. "And I'll ask the maid for calamine lotion for the itching. It worked wonderfully on mosquito bites when I was a child. There must be a cold soup on the room-service menu. We can order ice cream and watch television."

"What about the guests?" she said, her resolve wavering. "Aren't you going to join them?"

"The only person I need to celebrate our wedding with is my wife." He finished undressing and climbed into the bath. "Anyway, there'll *be more wine for everyone. After a few bottles of pinot noir, they won't miss us."*

"It was very thoughtful, and I should be thankful," Patty sighed. "But you can't imagine what it's like being pregnant. The morning sickness never goes away, and I'm uncomfortable all the time."

"I'm the one who should be grateful. You're doing all the work." He kissed her. "I'm just the lucky guy along for the ride."

"The rash lasted all weekend, and we never had the wedding." Her father sipped his buttered rum. "Your mother wore the dress to a charity function and put it in the attic. It's probably still there; you should ask her if you can borrow it."

Nell gazed out the window at skiers taking the last run of the day, and anger welled up inside her.

"How you can be so unfeeling?" she said, turning to her father.

"I didn't mean to upset her," he said, waving his hand. "What woman wouldn't want a surprise wedding? And the pomegranate cake was delicious. I took it home and ate the whole thing."

"I don't mean your wedding. I'm talking about my wedding," she said. "You understood how important it was for her parents to be there, but you refuse to attend my wedding."

"That was different. We were so young, and we were living in her father's house," he faltered.

"It's not different at all. Most fathers would do anything to see their daughter walk down the aisle," she fumed. "You're too busy harboring some grudge to know what's important."

"I explained it to you," he pleaded. "I'm afraid if I say yes, your mother won't come."

"You haven't even tried." Nell jumped up and grabbed her

gloves. "Parents make sacrifices for their children; that's what parenting is about."

"Nell, wait." He stood up. "Sit down and let's talk about it."

"All we've done is talk." She turned and tears streamed down her cheeks. "I'm going back to the hotel. I'll see you later."

Nell stepped out of the elevator and knocked on Felicity's door.

"Nell! Come in." Felicity opened the door. "Are you all right? It's five-thirty and you're still in your ski clothes."

"I'm fine." Nell opened her bag and took out a bottle of brandy. "Can you pour a shot of this? I bought it at the gift shop."

"You're buying alcohol in the afternoon?" Felicity raised her eyebrow.

"Raj doesn't want us to drink from the minibar, and this is an emergency." Nell sank onto the sofa. "I spent the afternoon on the slopes with my father."

"Don't tell me your parents ran into each other." Felicity poured two glasses and handed one to Nell. "I was afraid that would happen. St. Moritz is a tiny village."

"It's not that." Nell sipped her brandy. "He told me this long story about holding a second surprise wedding so their family and friends could be there. But he still can't see that having my parents at my wedding means everything to me."

"Don't be too hard on him. It seems all men are irrational," Felicity said bleakly. "You'll never guess what happened. Adam is in St. Moritz."

"What did you say?" Nell gasped.

"He showed up in the hotel lobby," Felicity replied. "I couldn't have been more surprised if it was Santa Claus."

"Adam is much better looking than Santa Claus," Nell laughed. "Oh God, am I interrupting? Is he in the bedroom, or taking a shower?"

"Of course not." Felicity shook her head. "He went to his hotel room."

"The boyfriend you've been trying to get back together with flew five thousand miles to see you, and you're not in bed having wonderful make-up sex?" Nell said in surprise.

"Adam wants to discuss our future, and I don't want to say the wrong thing," Felicity said. "I have to do a few things in the village, and I'm going to ask Gabriel's advice first."

"You really think a stranger should keep giving you relationship advice?" Nell asked quizzically.

"At first I told Gabriel what was going on with Adam by accident. When I slipped and hurt my ankle, the whole story spilled out. But he was right about telling Adam how I felt, and I think more clearly when I get an outsider's opinion," Felicity said. "It's like writing to the advice column in the newspaper. He's been quite helpful, and I don't want to make a mistake."

Nell suddenly recalled something her father said. "That's it!" she exclaimed. "That's why my parents got divorced."

"What are you talking about?" Felicity asked. "Did your mother have an affair?"

"I don't think either of them did. I just remembered my father said he felt like a human ping-pong ball between my mother and her father," Nell said excitedly. "What if something terrible happened between them, and he got caught in the middle?"

"It's possible, but how will you find out?" Felicity asked. "Your grandfather died a few years ago."

"I'll find a way to ask my mother." Nell stood up. "It's a long shot, but it's the only one I have."

"Good luck, I'm sure you'll figure it out," Felicity said as she walked to the door. "Don't forget your bottle of brandy."

Nell turned and smiled. "You're going to need it more than me. Why don't you keep it?"

"I think I will. Christmas is supposed to be a time of miracles," Felicity said darkly. "Why do I feel like everything is falling apart?"

"There's still three days until New Year's Eve," Nell reminded her. "Maybe it will work out and all our Christmas wishes will come true."

Twelve

Three Days Before the Fashion Show
7:00 p.m.

Felicity

A LIGHT SNOW WAS FALLING on the cobblestones, and Felicity wrapped her coat around her. The church spire was dusted with snow, and fat snowflakes blanketed the rooftops. It was early evening, three days before the fashion show, and Felicity was late to meet Gabriel at the Segantini Museum.

It would have been wonderful to spend Adam's first evening in St. Moritz together. They could have gone to the bobsled race with Raj and the models, and then had a cozy dinner at a traditional Swiss restaurant. She pictured them offering each other bites of fondue and sharing apple strudel for dessert.

Instead she'd told Raj she had to go to the village to buy garters, and she was hurrying to the museum to meet Gabriel. Her stomach turned over and she felt uneasy, like the time Raj came down with the flu and she had to meet an important client alone.

Felicity had sat in the lobby of the Plaza and listened to the mother of the bride list the other designers they were considering:

Carolina Herrera for her romantic silhouettes, Oscar de la Renta for his impossibly long trains, and Jenny Packham because she'd designed Kate Middleton's gown.

The woman showed her a photo of the bride, and Felicity had pictured the perfect dress: a strapless bodice to accentuate the bride's slender neck, and a slit in the skirt to show off her legs. The most important piece would be the veil.

She grabbed a napkin and sketched a point d'esprit veil attached to a diamond tiara. The diamonds would look like stars against the bride's black hair, and the whole effect would be sexy and elegant. The mother of the bride took one look at the sketch and said that Felicity understood her daughter completely. Felicity had practically run to the studio to show Raj the deposit check.

A tray of diamond rings sparkled in the window of Harry Winston, and she stopped to admire them. Adam had come all the way to St. Moritz and said that he loved her. Maybe the Christmas miracle she wished for was about to happen, and Adam would propose. He'd open a bottle of champagne and they'd feed each other chocolate-covered strawberries and snow would fall softly outside her suite.

"There you are." A male voice interrupted her thoughts. "I thought you stood me up."

Felicity turned and almost didn't recognize Gabriel. He wore a dark suit under a cashmere overcoat and wingtip shoes. A scarf was wrapped around his neck, and he wore a watch with a leather band.

"I'm sorry I'm late. It took me ages to find a hooded jacket." Felicity took off her dark glasses. "Why are you all dressed up? I thought we were just looking at paintings."

"Later I have to attend a private function for one of my father's patients," he explained. "He's British, and spends an inordinate amount of time in St. Moritz. I think it's because of the proximity to his Swiss bank account."

"Well, you look handsome." Felicity was suddenly in a good mood. The air smelled of pine trees and the store windows looked so pretty. "You should change out of your doctor's coat more often; some gorgeous tourist will fall in love with you."

"No thank you. The scarf is itchy, and wearing a tie reminds me of medical school." He walked toward the museum. "Let's go—I haven't eaten dinner, and I don't want to miss the canapés."

The museum was in a stone building perched above the village. The walls were covered with gold frames, and above them stretched a wide dome with intricate frescoes.

"Giovanni Segantini was one of the most influential artists of the Realism movement in the late nineteenth century," Gabriel said as they admired the paintings. "He died while he was painting his *Alpine Triptych,* and the museum was built in his honor."

A man had followed them inside and Felicity was suddenly afraid he was a journalist. She covered her face with the brochure and tried to see if he was watching them.

"You're not listening." Gabriel stopped. "Either I'm terribly boring, or you have no interest in art."

"You're not boring." Felicity flushed. "I was studying the brochure."

"I doubt that, since it's upside down." He pointed to the brochure.

"I got worried." Felicity closed the brochure. "I think that man might be a journalist, and I don't want him to see us."

"You're the one who wanted to meet like Bonnie and Clyde,"

Gabriel responded. "The spy look suits you, but don't get any ideas. I have no desire to steal a painting and go on the lam."

"I don't want to steal anything. But I do need your help." She pointed to an anteroom. "Why don't we go somewhere quiet?"

"That sounds serious." He followed her. "What's wrong, Felicity?"

"I'm perfectly healthy. But you'll never guess what happened. Adam is in St. Moritz."

"Your boyfriend flew all the way to St. Moritz?" Gabriel asked nervously. "I hope he didn't come to punch me out. I'm a terrible fighter. If I see a fist coming in my direction, I tend to duck."

"I told him nothing is going on between us," Felicity assured him. "He asked me to dinner, and I don't know what to do. I'm worried I'll say the wrong thing."

"Tell him how you feel. Do you want to get back together with him?" Gabriel asked.

"Of course, I do. I'm in love with him," Felicity said. "I'm just afraid . . ."

"Afraid is a word you use to describe glacier hiking, or careening down the bobsled track. It's not supposed to describe your feelings for your boyfriend."

"I'm worried Adam will never ask me to marry him," she said slowly. "More than that, I'm afraid he never loved me in the first place."

"We went over this before," Gabriel reminded her. "He wouldn't have stayed with you if he wasn't in love with you."

"Does he love me enough to spend the rest of his life with me?" Felicity asked urgently. "And how do I find out without ruining everything?"

"You tell him the truth about your feelings. What else can you do?" Gabriel turned and looked intently at a painting. "If you're meant to be together, that will be enough."

They walked out of the museum, into the square. Snow was falling softly on the window boxes. Children were playing under the Christmas tree. A couple rode by in a horse and carriage.

"Will you do something for me?" she asked.

"That depends. I'm not going to wrestle the journalist at the museum and take away his cell phone," he replied. "He had the muscles of a bodybuilder, and I'm on the skinny side."

"I don't think he noticed us." She rubbed her hands to keep warm. "This might sound silly, but could you tell me one of your folktales?"

"You want me to tell you a story now?" Gabriel glanced at the couples strolling along the pavement.

"Please. They make me more relaxed," she said. "It will calm me down before I meet Adam."

"I suppose I can." Gabriel rubbed his brow. "Once there was a beautiful princess who lived in a castle in the forest. She loved to sew, and all the important women in the land came to her for their ball gowns. Her father the king loved her very much, and was afraid she might end up in an unhappy marriage. He asked a good witch to cast a spell on her. She would never sew her own wedding dress until she was kissed by a man who was worthy of her beauty.

"The princess had a large dowry as well as beauty, so every man in the kingdom courted her. After a suitor left, she would take out her needle and thread and begin to sew her wedding gown. But the needle would prick her finger and the thread would get knotted and she'd have to give up.

"One day, a suitor came from a kingdom far away. He rode a

white horse and said all the right things. When he kissed her, she was sure he was the one. She took out her needle and a bolt of white silk and began sewing. But the needle pricked her finger and left a spot of blood on the fabric.

"She took it to the laundry in the village and begged the young man to remove the stain. They talked while he worked and he was warm and charming. The stain came out and he offered to walk her back to the castle. When they arrived, he kissed her before she went inside.

"All night she couldn't sleep, thinking about the kiss. In the morning she remembered the bolt of silk, and picked up the needle and thread. The needle darted over the fabric, and she sewed the most beautiful wedding dress. She showed it to her father, and he asked the identity of the man who kissed her.

"The king summoned the young man at the laundry to the castle. He came and promised the king he would take good care of his daughter. The king gave them his blessing and threw a magnificent wedding. The bride looked beautiful in the silk gown, and the good witch made a bouquet of magical wildflowers to ensure they would live happily ever after."

"Where did you hear that folktale?" Felicity asked. "It's not like anything you told me before."

Gabriel was silent, as if he was trying to figure out what to say.

"It must have been something my mother told me." He shrugged. "I haven't thought of it in years, and it just popped into my mind."

"I'm going to run in and change before I meet Adam," Felicity said as they approached the Christmas tree in front of Badrutt's Palace. "Thank you for meeting me. It really helped."

"I hardly said anything important."

Felicity inhaled the scent of pine needles and smiled. "For some reason, just being around you makes me feel better."

Felicity entered the King's Club and searched for Adam. The nightclub was even more spectacular than in the brochures. The walls were flecked with silver and there were mirrored ceilings and suede booths. Disco balls illuminated the dance floor, and the cocktails were served in colored glasses.

Adam was seated at the bar, and Felicity gulped. He looked incredibly handsome in a leather jacket and corduroy slacks.

"You're already here." She joined him at the bar. "It's so crowded, I was afraid we wouldn't find each other."

"You look beautiful." Adam kissed her on the cheek. "I would have picked you out of the crowd. You're the loveliest woman here."

"Thank you." Felicity beamed, glancing down at her red wool dress and heels.

"I ran into Raj at the bobsled track," Adam said, signaling the bartender.

"He hardly lets the models out of his sight," Felicity laughed. "I can't blame him. One model booked a heli skiing trip without asking him. Raj said if she went near a helicopter, he would make sure all the helicopters in St. Moritz were grounded. I reminded him we could have had the fashion show in New York, but he says it will all be worth it. The catwalk is going to be a who's who of the jet set."

"He had his hands full keeping an eye on all of them," Adam agreed, "but we had time to talk. He assured me that I have nothing to worry about. You really did get a concussion, and the guy was the local doctor." Adam sipped his bourbon. "The blogs made it all up."

"I already told you that," Felicity said, and wished the bartender would hurry and bring her drink.

"Yes, but Raj assured me that you were telling the truth," Adam said.

"You believe Raj, but you don't believe me?" Felicity asked in disbelief.

"That's not it exactly," Adam said uncomfortably. "I just needed confirmation."

Felicity gulped the whiskey the bartender put in front of her. She tried to think of something to say, but Adam kept talking.

"I came all the way to St. Moritz for no reason." He grinned. "But I'm glad I did. I'll be so busy when we get back, we'll hardly see each other. I'm thinking of adding office support staff and getting a bigger conference room. I might open an office in LA—not immediately, but by the end of next year. Doug has connections there."

"Excuse me, I need to use the powder room." Felicity put her glass on the bar.

She hurried across the dance floor and entered the small room. It was only when the door closed and she collapsed on the ottoman that her heart slowed down.

She remembered the first day in St. Moritz, when Katie hadn't shown up for the photo shoot. Raj had sent Felicity to the powder room to put on the wedding dress. She'd stood in front of the full-length mirror and marveled at the way the white satin made her skin look creamy, and how the sweeping train fanned out perfectly behind her.

The photographer had taken photos of her holding a champagne flute and gazing at the snow-covered mountains, and she had been positive she would wear a similar dress to her own wedding. How could she even think of getting married if Adam didn't trust her? And besides, Adam was more interested in opening another office than getting engaged.

Hurt and anger welled up inside her. She couldn't argue with Adam now. The fashion show was in three days, and she should be putting all her energy into making sure the gowns were pressed and the veils fell perfectly when the models walked down the aisle. And then there were the sketches for Bergdorf's! It was one of the greatest opportunities of her career, and she couldn't mess it up.

She reapplied her lipstick and opened the door. A man was standing in the corner, and she recognized Gabriel's dark suit and wingtip shoes.

"What are you doing here?" She approached him. "I thought you were attending a private function."

"I am. It's in the member's room in the back." He waved at the double doors. "I needed some air. The magician was about to saw a drunken British aristocrat in half."

"That sounds dramatic." Felicity grimaced.

"That's why I left. I am a doctor. I didn't want to be the one who had to put him back together." Gabriel looked at Felicity. "That was a joke. You looked so serious when you came out of the ladies' room, I was trying to be funny."

"You were watching me?" she asked.

"Of course not. A beautiful woman came out of the ladies' room, and she looked so unhappy," he explained. "I didn't realize it was you. No one is miserable at the King's Club, they're too busy guzzling champagne and sweating on the dance floor."

The DJ played an old Madonna song, and Felicity blinked back tears. Suddenly all she wanted was for someone to hold her. "Will you ask me to dance?"

"You want to dance?" Gabriel repeated. "What about Adam?"

"He's in the bar, he can't see us. Please, just dance with me," she begged. "It's one of my favorite songs."

Gabriel placed his hand on her shoulder and stepped onto the floor. The music changed to a Maroon 5 song, and Felicity remembered the first time Adam had kissed her. It had been the night of his company's Christmas party. There was a snowstorm, and when he took her home, all she'd wanted was for him to put his mouth on hers.

Felicity opened the door of the taxi and climbed the steps to her building. The Christmas party had been so much fun. A DJ played dance tunes, and there had been Christmas-themed cocktails and a buffet of Kobe beef sliders and miniature pumpkin cheesecakes.

All evening, she wondered why Adam didn't take advantage of the mistletoe hanging above the dance floor and kiss her. Maybe she had misread him, and he wasn't interested in her after all. He'd just needed a date to the party, and she wouldn't see him again.

"We could have taken separate taxis," she said as he joined her on the curb. "You live all the way uptown."

"My mother taught me three rules: to always write thank-you cards, tip the doorman at Christmas, and see a pretty girl to her door." He brushed snow from his overcoat. "The taxi will wait. I'll walk you upstairs."

They climbed the five flights to her apartment and Felicity heard music coming from inside. She reached into her purse for her key and noticed a new text on her phone.

"Raj wants me to stay away for a while." She glanced at the text. "He's breaking up with a girl and it's going badly."

"We'll wait here together," Adam offered. "It's snowing too hard to go to a diner, and you can't stay out here alone."

"You can't wait, the taxi meter is running," Felicity reminded him. "I can knock on Mrs. Peabody's door down the hall."

"It's after midnight. You'll wake her up," Adam said. "Why don't we play a game?"

"A game?" she wondered.

"Tell me something you love about New York."

"That's easy," Felicity laughed. "When I moved to New York, I thought life would be exactly like Sex and the City: my very own apartment, close girlfriends, and brunches at swanky restaurants in the Village. Then I discovered I couldn't afford an apartment without a roommate, and my food budget didn't include brunches unless I gave up hot water and electricity." She smiled. "I love it anyway. It's the most exciting city in the world, and I never want to live anywhere else."

Adam was looking at her intently, and Felicity flushed. "Your turn. Tell me something you love about New York."

"I grew up on the Upper West Side, and life was laid out as neatly as the intersection at Lexington and Fifth Avenue: private school, followed by Dartmouth and a partnership in my father's insurance firm. One day I took the subway downtown and explored by myself: raw chickens hanging from hooks in Chinatown, hip galleries in the Meatpacking District, and Washington Square, crammed with students wearing jeans and backpacks. I didn't want to attend college in New Hampshire; I wanted to stay in New York. But not in my parents'

Manhattan, with doorman buildings and town cars idling on the sidewalk. I wanted to be where there were people from different cultures and exotic foods and graffiti. That's why I chose NYU."

The music changed, and Felicity gulped. She forgot that they were standing in the hallway and Raj was breaking up with a girl inside.

"I'm glad you did, or we would never have met. I'm so happy that Raj wasn't home that night when you came to see him at the apartment," she said, and looked at Adam. He moved closer, and she could smell his aftershave.

"There's another thing my mother taught me," he whispered. "You never kiss a girl without asking her permission."

Felicity closed her eyes and nodded at the same time. The kiss was sweet and soft, and she kissed him back.

"I heard a noise." She pulled away. "I think the girl is leaving."

Adam took her hand and led her down the staircase.

"Where are we going?" she asked when they reached the landing. "It's snowing too hard to go outside."

"We're not going anywhere," Adam answered. "We're going to walk back upstairs as if we just arrived."

"But what if she's still there?" Felicity wondered. "And the taxi meter is still running."

"I'll take care of the taxi later. First I'm going to kiss you again." He touched her cheek. "And that's going to take a long time."

The DJ changed songs, and Gabriel put his arm around Felicity's waist. The lights above the dance floor bubbled like fizzy champagne on New Year's Eve. For a moment Felicity forgot where she was, and all she wanted was for Gabriel to pull her closer. She looked into his eyes and he leaned down and their lips met and held. Then they pulled apart and her legs turned wobbly.

Felicity raced through the doors and into the street. She kept running until she reached the lake. The air was sharp and she didn't have a jacket and she was suddenly freezing cold. She hugged her arms to her chest and wondered what she had done.

How could she have kissed another man? What if Adam had seen her? She didn't do things like that. It was against everything she believed in.

There was a noise behind her, and Felicity turned around. A male figure appeared in the dark, and she recognized Gabriel.

"There you are." Gabriel waved her jacket. "You ran away before I could stop you. And you left your coat in the cloakroom. It's the middle of the night, and it's minus ten degrees."

"Thank you." She took the jacket.

"Felicity, about what happened just then . . ." Gabriel continued. "I . . ."

"You don't have to say anything, it was my fault," Felicity interrupted. "I shouldn't have asked you to dance. I drank whiskey too fast. . . ."

"Felicity, I . . ."

"No, really." Felicity's heart raced. "I'm terribly sorry. I have to go. I'll see you later."

She hurried across the path, and didn't stop until she reached the hotel lobby. There were footsteps behind her, and she wondered if Gabriel had followed her. But it was only the valet carrying some Louis Vuitton luggage.

The Christmas tree was lit up in her suite, and she slipped off her heels. How could she have kissed Gabriel? She had been upset about Adam, and swept up by the music. It didn't mean anything at all.

She pulled out her phone to text Adam that she wasn't feeling well, and stared at the blank screen. Gabriel had come after her, but Adam hadn't texted or tried to follow her. She poured a shot of brandy and took a long gulp. Adam hadn't even noticed she'd left. He didn't care about her at all.

Thirteen

Three Days Before the Fashion Show
7:00 p.m.

Nell

THE BELLS CHIMED ON THE hour. Nell watched wet snow
settle onto the windowpane. The view reminded her of why she
had been so excited to come to St. Moritz: polo players galloping
across the frozen lake; the Christmas tree in Badrutt's driveway,
festooned with ornaments; and the village, a collection of wooden
chalets and quaint stone buildings.

She couldn't enjoy any of it, because she was too busy making
sure her parents didn't run into each other. It was three days until the
collection, and tonight her father was taking a drive with the Italian
race-car driver, and her mother was tired and going to bed early. It
was the perfect opportunity to do the things she liked: get a massage,
or bundle up in a parka and wander around the village at night.

Instead she texted Raj and said she had a slight cough and had
to skip the bobsled race. Raj and Felicity were so good to her, she
hated not doing everything Raj asked. But she had to find out if
anything had happened between her parents and her grandfather.

Nell scooped up a handful of nuts and tried to recall everything she could about her grandfather. He had been tall with dark hair, and wore a different suit every time she saw him. He'd died four years ago. Her father had always said Alistair was one of the smartest men he knew.

What if she was wrong, and there hadn't been some major event that ended the marriage? Maybe her parents got divorced because they were tired of arguing. Then all this time spent trying to figure out what happened would be wasted. The fashion show was in three days, and she was running out of time to make them change their minds.

Her phone buzzed, and she pressed Accept.

"Eliot!" she said when she heard her fiancé's voice. "This is the best surprise. I thought you were still in Maine."

"I got home last night, and couldn't wait to call," he replied. "I didn't realize covering a Christmas tree farm in Maine was so dangerous. I narrowly missed a close encounter with a bear."

"I'm glad I didn't know about it," Nell chuckled. "I miss you terribly. I wish you were here."

"I miss you too. If I didn't have to cover the ball dropping on New Year's Eve, I would be on the first flight," he agreed. "I'll record it, and we'll watch it in bed when you get home."

"I can't wait," Nell said, and suddenly wanted to tell him everything. "My parents are in St. Moritz."

"Your parents are there together!" Eliot exclaimed.

"They came separately, and they don't know the other is here," she began. "I thought I could use this time to convince them to attend our wedding, but they are both being so stubborn. Perhaps I should give up; your father did offer to walk me down the aisle."

Eliot was quiet, and Nell wondered what he was thinking. Finally his voice came over the phone. "Do you remember when we met, at the charity luncheon in Southampton? You were in the fashion show, wearing a white crocheted dress and a straw hat.

"That's not when I fell in love with you, though you looked gorgeous with your long legs and deep tan. It was later, when the valet lost your car keys and you couldn't get home. I offered to help, but you said you'd figure it out on your own. You slept in the pool house, and the next morning you took the Hampton Jitney to Brooklyn. You picked up your spare keys and took the Jitney all the way back to Southampton for your car."

"How do you remember that?" she laughed.

"It's one of the things I love about you," he said. "You see a problem and calmly think of a solution. If there's a way to get your parents to attend our wedding, you'll find it."

"I love you." Nell closed her eyes and pictured Eliot's blond hair and brown eyes.

"I love you too," Eliot said. "And however you get down the aisle, I'll be waiting at the altar. I'm the luckiest guy in the world."

Nell hung up and paced around the room. Eliot was right; she couldn't stop now. Her mother was eating dinner in her suite. She'd go see her and she wouldn't leave until she knew exactly why they got divorced. Then, somehow, she'd convince them both to come to her wedding.

"Nell, sweetheart," her mother said as she opened the door. She was wearing a print dress and smelled of French perfume. "Come in. I thought you were at the bobsled races."

There was a fire in the fireplace, and the air smelled of lamb chops and garlic. The table was set with royal blue china and crystal wine glasses. A bottle of red wine was open, and there was a silver bread basket.

"I was just going to order a bowl of soup," her mother said, waving at the table. "Then I thought, I'm at a Swiss ski resort at Christmas—why shouldn't I have a proper dinner?" She sat down. "Why don't you join me? There's potato soup, and rack of lamb with herbs and gnocchi." She looked at Nell guiltily. "And German chocolate cake for dessert. I shouldn't eat chocolate at night; I'll never get to sleep. But it's served warm, and it's the best thing I ever tasted."

"I'd love to," Nell said, and sat down opposite her.

"The strangest thing happened this afternoon," her mother said. "Your father called me."

"What did you say?" Nell's cheeks flushed, and she tried not to panic.

"It was the oddest thing. It was his number, but he didn't say anything." Her mother tore apart a bread roll.

"He must have dialed it by accident," Nell offered. "When my phone is in my pocket, that happens to me all the time."

"That wasn't the odd part," her mother said. "I could hear voices in the background, and they were speaking in French and German."

"He's been shooting a movie in Europe." Nell gripped her soup-spoon. "He could still be on location."

"It was very strange." Her mother shook her head. "The reception was so clear, it sounded like he was next door."

"Cell phones these days are miraculous," Nell agreed. "I was talking to Eliot in New York, and it was as if we were in the same room." She tried to change the subject. "It wasn't like that when Dad traveled when I was young. Were you ever jealous? He went on movie shoots and press tours, and you were stuck driving car-pools and watching swim practice."

"I suppose I was, in a way. Every mother longs for time to her-self. And who wouldn't want to stay in luxury hotels?" her mother said. "I couldn't imagine what it was like to have your newspaper waiting at your door, and your coffee already brewed."

"We traveled every summer as a family," Nell reminded her. "We went to Portugal and Spain."

"It wasn't the same. I still had to cut up your spaghetti at din-ner, or run to the chemist for medicine when you got a stomach-ache," she said. "Then you became teenagers and we stopped going on vacation."

"Dad must have traveled a lot with your father," Nell said casually. "That must have been particularly frustrating."

"What do you mean?" Her mother stopped eating her gnocchi.

"You wanted to be involved in the company, and they flitted off to glamorous locations." She warmed to her theme. "It must have caused tension in the marriage."

"I suppose it did sometimes," her mother said thoughtfully, put-ting down her fork. "Of course, the worst was the time they stayed at The Little Nell in Aspen."

"The Little Nell," Nell repeated.

"Haven't I ever told you? You were named after it," her mother asked. "We stayed there before you were born, and it was one of the best vacations we ever had. Aspen is gorgeous, and we had so much fun. But then your father and grandfather returned years later for the Aspen Film Festival."

"What happened?" Nell leaned forward.

Her mother sat back in her chair and sipped her wine. "I really shouldn't talk about it, but you're old enough now that there's no reason to keep it a secret. It's what happened afterward. I should have divorced your father then; it would have saved us years of torture. But I thought I was wrong, so I gave him another chance."

Beverly Hills
Fifteen Years Ago

Patty

Patty stood at the marble island in her parents' kitchen and sliced avocados. There was a platter of stuffed artichokes and spinach quiche.

Patty wasn't thrilled about Sunday dinners with her parents at the hacienda on Beverly Drive. Her father and Todd always rattled on about movie grosses, while her mother would prod Patty to attend ladies' luncheons, and Nell and Pete would get bored and start squabbling.

The children's voices sounded from the garden, and Patty knew she had so much to be grateful for. Todd had worked for her father for twelve years, and they had their own home a few blocks away with a swimming pool. The children were healthy, and she didn't have to worry about money.

But sometimes when she waited for Todd to come home, the only way she could account for her day was by checking the receipts in her purse: the supermarket, for eggs and peanut butter; the gas station, because she drove the kids to swimming and soccer; and the pharmacy, for Todd's Dramamine for flying, and her earplugs because he snored in bed.

Of course, she wished she could accompany him on trips: to Rome when they filmed a remake of Three Coins in the Fountain, *and to Tahiti when they shot a romance set in the tropics. Her father was all about the bottom line, however, and the movie budget didn't include Todd's wife tagging along, not to mention hiring someone to take care of Pete and Nell and two guinea pigs.*

The doorbell rang, and Patty waited for someone to answer it. Her father and Todd were drinking bourbon in the den, and her mother was still upstairs. She wiped her hands and walked to the entryway.

"Can I help you?" she said, opening the door.

An attractive woman stood outside. Her blond hair was cut in a bob, and she wore a navy dress and sandals.

"I'm looking for Todd Mason—I believe this is his house," the woman said.

"His house?" Patty repeated.

"This is his phone number and address." The woman showed her a slip of paper. "I didn't realize it was in the flats of Beverly Hills. I thought the only people who lived here are the actors whose homes you see in those guided tours."

"Where did you get this paper?" She glanced at Todd's name, scribbled with a phone number.

"He gave it to me in Aspen," she explained. "I did try calling, but a woman who only spoke Spanish answered."

Patty took in the woman's wide mouth and long eyelashes, and her heart hammered. She was about to say something when her mother appeared beside her.

"Can we help you?" she asked.

"This woman is looking for Todd," Patty said tightly. "She thought he lived here."

Todd and her father emerged from the study and turned toward the entryway. Todd was nursing his martini and laughing at something her father said.

"A woman is here to see you," Patty said to Todd, her blood boiling up inside her. "You gave her your phone number in Aspen and she thought this was your address."

Todd's face was blank and then he hurried toward them.

"Thank God, the hotel sent you," he said. "Is the script in your car? I'll come with you and get it."

"The script?" the woman repeated.

"I left a script at The Little Nell," Todd explained to the group. "It's top secret, and there are some important people attached." He turned to Alistair. "I'm sorry I didn't tell you. I didn't want you to worry until I resolved the issue."

Todd followed the woman outside and Patty bit her lip. She wasn't going to accuse Todd of lying in front of her parents. She would wait until they got home, and talk to him in private.

"Shall we have dinner?" Patty turned to her parents, wondering how she would get through the meal. "I took the quiche out of the oven, and everything looks delicious."

Patty leaned against the headboard and turned the pages of a book. Dinner with her parents had seemed to drag on forever. Todd was in a particularly good mood, telling stories about the Aspen Film Festival and saying that they should take Nell and Pete skiing there next winter.

Finally they said goodbye and drove the few blocks home. Now Todd was brushing his teeth, and Patty wondered how she could believe him. What if he had walked back in her parents' house with the *script? That didn't prove anything. The script might have been in Todd's car all along.*

In the twelve years of their marriage, Patty could fill a notebook with things that irritated her about Todd: he disregarded her rules and took the kids out for ice cream before dinner. He gave them presents, when she insisted they only spend their allowance. And he regularly forgot important dates like Valentine's Day and the children's birthdays. But he never flirted with other women. Whenever they were at a cocktail party, he said that she was the most beautiful woman in the room.

"What was that about?" she said when he entered the bedroom.

"What are you talking about?" he said, climbing in beside her.

"The woman at the door of my parents' house." She placed the book on the bedside table.

"The hotel sent her to deliver my script," he said nonchalantly. "I'm lucky no one found it. I would have been in a lot of trouble if Jerry Bruckheimer or George Clooney got their hands on it."

"You expect me to believe The Little Nell flew a woman to Los Angeles to personally bring your script?" she demanded.

"I expect you to believe it because it's the truth. The Little Nell is one of the most exclusive hotels in the world." He shrugged. "They accept all sorts of crazy requests; the producer staying in the next suite had his coffee flown in daily from Kenya."

"I don't believe you," Patty said flatly.

"It's the movie business," he said. "I once stayed at the Ritz in Paris and a famous actress took up an entire floor. She insisted no one used key cards, because the magnets made her skin age. They had to deprogram all the rooms and get regular keys."

"Well, you're not a famous actor," she retorted. "And the woman at the door couldn't have worked for a hotel. She had expensive highlights and wore a designer dress."

"What does that have to do with anything? How would you know she had expensive highlights?" he asked. "Did you get the name of her hairdresser?"

"I'll tell you what I think." Patty turned to him. "She's an attractive woman who you met at the film festival. You gave her my parents' phone number so I wouldn't find out if she called. You were going to set up a rendezvous at the Beverly Hills Hotel."

"That's a ridiculous story. I don't even know her name," he fumed.

"Well, she knew your name," she said, glowering. "How could you? You embarrassed me in front of everyone."

"You're being absurd. I have never given you a reason to doubt me," he said indignantly. "If you don't believe me, you can call the hotel and ask them."

"Don't be silly," Patty scoffed.

"We have to do something to put an end to this." He grabbed the phone and punched in the number. "Information for Aspen, please give me the number for The Little Nell." He handed Patty the phone.

"What do you want me to do with this?" She held the receiver.

"I want you to ask them if they delivered a script to Todd Mason in Beverly Hills."

Patty waited while she was connected to the concierge. "This is the wife of Todd Mason. I was inquiring about a script my husband left at the hotel."

"Yes, of course, Mrs. Mason," the concierge replied. "I was told it was delivered today to Mr. Mason's home in Beverly Hills. I trust it was in good condition—there were no pages missing?"

"It was fine, thank you," Patty said, and handed the phone back to Todd.

"Are you satisfied?" He replaced the phone on the receiver.

"I suppose so." She turned to her side so Todd couldn't see the tears in her eyes.

Todd's hand brushed her arm and he kissed her neck.

"I've never seen you jealous before," he whispered. "I quite like it."

"I didn't like it," she breathed. "I didn't like it at all."

"Then maybe I can make it up to you." He turned her on her back and kissed her. "I'll serve you breakfast in bed tomorrow, and then I'll take the kids to lunch and a movie. You'll have the house to yourself all afternoon."

She kissed him back and the tightness in her chest dissolved.

"I would like that," she relented. "But don't let Pete make the pancakes. He always uses too much syrup."

"Why are we talking about something that happened fifteen years ago?" her mother said to Nell, putting her wine glass on the table. "I shouldn't have brought it up; it's ancient history."

"You said you should have divorced him then," Nell prodded, excited that they were finally getting somewhere. "But he was telling the truth about the script. What happened next?"

Her mother picked up her wine glass and it tipped and spilled wine on her dress.

"Oh, goodness, I spilled wine on my dress!" Her mother jumped up and ran into the bathroom.

Nell watched the logs flicker in the fireplace. The wine and the brandy were making her head spin, and she suddenly felt deflated. What if she was close to learning the truth, but her mother refused to continue with the story?

"I'm sorry to interrupt our dinner." Her mother returned to the living room. A robe was knotted around her waist, and she was holding the dress. "I have to call housekeeping to get the stain out. The dress is vintage Cavalli, and I could never replace it."

"I'll go with you, I want to hear the end of the story," Nell offered. "You were saying that you gave him another chance."

"I shouldn't have mentioned it, and I really don't want to talk about it," her mother said, and looked at Nell. "No matter our differences, your father and I want what's best for you. That's all that matters."

Nell wanted to say that all she wanted was for her parents to be at her wedding. But she had said it so many times before, and it hadn't made any difference.

"I should go anyway." Nell stood up. "Raj booked the models on a morning sleigh ride."

"I'm glad I'm here, and I can't wait for the fashion show." Her mother kissed her on the cheek. "I'm so proud of you. You are beautiful and successful, and you found a man who makes you happy."

"I am happy." Nell walked to the door.

"Then hold on to him as hard as you can," her mother ruminated. "Happiness is hard to find."

Nell opened the door to her room and kicked off her shoes. It was too late for the bobsled races, and she didn't feel like joining everyone for Viennese coffee at the Sunny Bar.

Had her father called her mother? What would happen if she discovered he was here? That was impossible; her father would have said something. But what if her mother grew suspicious and asked Nell if she was hiding anything from her? She couldn't stop now. She had less than three days in St. Moritz, and she had to convince them to attend her wedding.

Her diamond ring sparkled under the chandelier, and she remembered when Eliot had proposed. It was the first day of spring in New York, and Nell had just gotten over a cold. She wanted to stay home, but Eliot insisted they go rowing in Central Park. It had been raining for weeks, and finally the sky was blue and the grass was soft under their feet.

Eliot had rented a rowboat and Nell leaned back against the cushions. The trees were covered with cherry blossoms and the air smelled fresh and clean. There was a picnic basket of bagels and cream cheese and orange juice. Nell bit into a bagel and Eliot kneeled in front of her.

"What are you doing?" she asked, worried that he was going to tip the rowboat.

"I've been carrying this around for weeks." He drew a blue box out of his pocket. "I didn't think proposing would be romantic when you had a cold and were sniffling and anyway, we couldn't go boating in the rain. Nell Mason, I've loved you since the moment I laid eyes on you, and all I want is to make you happy." He opened the box. "Will you marry me?"

"Yes." She nodded and kissed him. "Yes, I'll marry you."

Eliot slipped the ring on her finger and took out the bottle of champagne hidden under the seat.

"Don't you think this is a little cheesy?" she said, laughing. "The Upper West Side behind us, a Tiffany's ring on my finger, and plastic cups of champagne and orange juice."

"I never want to be afraid of being cheesy," he said, kissing her. "Being madly in love is the cheesiest thing of all, and that's how we're going to feel for the rest of our lives."

Nell's mother was right; she'd found a guy who was warm and handsome and kind. She unzipped her dress and pulled on a robe. If only her parents would be there when she met Eliot at the altar, she'd be the happiest bride in the world.

Fourteen

Two Days Before the Fashion Show
10:30 a.m.

Felicity

IT WAS MID-MORNING TWO DAYS before the fashion show, and Felicity was admiring the room-service tray on the coffee table. There were fluffy pastries and a poached egg on brioche and a glass of grapefruit juice. Raj couldn't even get upset with Felicity for ordering from the menu; breakfast was included with her suite and didn't cost a thing.

Felicity hadn't touched anything except for the coffee and whole cream. Even the cream made her stomach turn. She poured it out and drank her coffee black.

She should be getting ready to go on a sleigh ride with the models. They were going to drive through the Staz forest and stop at Hotel Staz for bratwurst and apple bread. The snow had stopped, and the trees were covered with icicles. It would be so pretty.

She'd barely slept, and the last thing she wanted was to have to smile and make conversation. She told Raj she'd had to make some last-minute alterations and she'd see him this evening. It wasn't a complete lie. She'd had to take in the waist of Chelsea's oyster-colored sheath because Chelsea had had food poisoning and lost a couple of pounds. And Emily's empire-style gown needed a shorter train to show the amethysts sewn into the hem. When Emily glided down the runway, Felicity wanted everyone to notice the gems twinkling against white satin.

All night she'd tossed and turned, remembering her kiss with Gabriel. When she woke up there were two missed calls from Adam on her phone. But he hadn't left a message, and she was too anxious to call him back. What if Adam had seen the kiss and was furious? And why had she kissed Gabriel in the first place?

Finally she got up and grabbed her notepad. She loved the sketch of the mermaid gown with the faux-fur skirt she had created for Camilla, but she still had to create one more design. She worked for an hour, but nothing seemed to work: she couldn't get the strapless bodice right, and the illusion sleeves reminded her of a fisherman's net. She crumpled the paper and tossed it in the garbage.

There was a knock on the door and she answered it. A bellboy held the largest bouquet of flowers she had ever seen. There were two dozen red roses, mixed with tulips and baby's breath.

"Good morning, Miss Grant." He nodded to her, carrying the flowers into the suite. "These are for you."

"Are you sure?" Felicity asked, wondering who'd sent them. Raj never sent flowers before a show. He knew how much florists in Manhattan marked up roses, and thought the company money was best spent elsewhere.

"Your name is on the card." He handed her the envelope. "I'm supposed to wait for the reply."

"You want me to read it now?" she repeated, pulling the robe tightly around her waist.

"If you don't mind." He nodded. "I have strict orders not to leave until you've answered."

Felicity opened the card and scanned the lines:

Dear Felicity,

You disappeared from the nightclub, and I couldn't reach you on your cell phone. I even called your suite, but there was no answer. I apologize if I said something to upset you. I came all the way to St. Moritz to see you. Can we have dinner tonight? I asked the concierge and he recommended Le Restaurant. If the answer is yes, I'll meet you in the lobby at 8 p.m.

Love,
Adam

Felicity looked from the note to the bouquet and her heart hammered. It was a Christmas miracle! Adam had said he was sorry, and he'd sent the most beautiful roses. Maybe their relationship wasn't over after all.

"What should I tell him?" The bellboy's voice broke into her thoughts.

"Sorry?" She looked up, having forgotten he was there.

"What's your answer?" he prompted.

The sun made patterns on the Persian rugs and the silver coffee pot gleamed under the chandelier. She held the card tightly and smiled. "The answer is yes."

Felicity ate the last bite of brioche and put the plate on the tray.

Her appetite had returned, and she finished the poached egg and half a bowl of muesli. Then she searched her closet for something to wear to dinner: her vintage Gucci dress with knee-high boots, or the cashmere sweater Adam had bought her last Christmas with a chenille skirt.

The afternoon stretched in front of her, and she was tempted to play hooky and get a massage or go ice-skating. But Raj would see the charge on the hotel bill, and she couldn't take the chance of getting injured. It was better to stay in her suite and work on the sketches, and finish sewing the hem on Emily's gown.

She gathered the tray and carried it into the hallway. There was a familiar man standing near the elevator wearing a wool coat. Felicity recognized Gabriel's doctor's bag.

"Gabriel!" she exclaimed. "What are you doing here?"

"I saw a patient at the hotel and thought I'd check on you," he said. "I was afraid you caught cold last night without your jacket."

"I'm happy you're here," she said, glad that she had changed into slacks and a sweater. "I want to show you something."

"You're inviting me into your suite?" he asked, pretending to be alarmed. "What if someone sees us?"

She glanced up and down the hallway and grinned. "It's all clear. Please come inside."

Gabriel followed her into the living room, and she poured two cups of coffee. She turned around and saw him staring at the bouquet of roses.

"They're lovely, aren't they?" she reflected. "I couldn't believe it when the bellboy knocked on the door. He made me read the card and waited for my answer."

"What was your answer?" Gabriel accepted the coffee cup.

"I said yes, but that's what I wanted to talk to you about," she began. "Adam said some things at the nightclub last night, and I got angry. But then he sent roses with a card apologizing and asking me to dinner." She hesitated. "I accepted the invitation. Do you think that was the right thing to do?"

"What do you want to do?" Gabriel asked.

"He's never truly apologized before. Maybe I've been wrong." She pondered. "He wouldn't have sent such gorgeous flowers unless he really loved me. I've been wishing for a Christmas miracle, and I think it's actually happening."

"No one would send flowers like that if they weren't in love," Gabriel said, nodding his head. "I'm sure you're making the right decision." He held out his coffee cup. "Do you have brandy to go with this?"

"Brandy in the morning?" Felicity asked in surprise.

"I'm coming down with a cold," he explained. "It started last night when I ran out of the King's Club to deliver your jacket. I forgot my coat, and when I went back, it was gone. I had to walk home in my suit."

"About what happened last night," Felicity said awkwardly. "I don't know what came over me. You've been so good to me, and I don't want to lose you as a friend."

"Don't even think about it," Gabriel said, cutting her off. "I should go. I promised my father a slice of pear bread from Hanselmann's."

"He's lucky to have you." Felicity suddenly felt sentimental. The fashion show was in two days, and then she would fly back to New York. January would be filled with clients' dress fittings, and the week in St. Moritz would become a pleasant memory.

"He's my father." Gabriel shrugged. "I couldn't do anything else."

"He's still lucky. And so are the patients you traipse all over the village to see," she continued. "And so am I. If you ever come to New York, you'll have to look me up. I'll take you to the top of the Empire State Building. The view is almost as spectacular as from the chairlift in Diavolezza."

"It's a deal." Gabriel walked to the door. "I'll look up and down the hall to make sure no one sees me leaving."

Gabriel put his hand on the door handle, and Felicity wondered if she would see him again.

"You're lucky you're not sneezing," she said suddenly.

"Sneezing?" He turned around.

"When I'm coming down with a cold, all I do is sneeze."

Felicity stood at the entrance of Le Restaurant and was glad she'd worn her Gucci dress. The room was impossibly elegant, with crystal chandeliers and silk drapes and a floral carpet. A Christmas tree rose to the ceiling, and gilt mirrors rested against the walls.

"I'm glad I packed a jacket and tie." Adam whistled. "They wouldn't let me in wearing a sweater and slacks."

"We can go somewhere else." Felicity turned to Adam. "A café in the village, where they serve pizza or fondue."

"I asked the concierge for the best restaurant in St. Moritz." He placed his hand on the small of her back. "You look too beautiful to sit at a wooden table and share a pizza. My mother called this afternoon," Adam said, after they had been seated and the waiter had brought them giant prawns in a whiskey and cream sauce. "She sends her love. She's jealous we're both in St. Moritz during Christmas week."

"I'll buy her one of those wonderful lotions they sell in the gift shop," Felicity offered. "And I'll get your father a chocolate torte or a bottle of Swiss cognac."

"I didn't come all the way to St. Moritz to watch the bobsled races or see the Cresta Run," Adam said suddenly, putting down his soupspoon. "We need to talk, Felicity. We had that terrible fight on Christmas, and then I said some stupid things on FaceTime. There were those photos of you and that doctor online, and I didn't know what to think." His face grew serious. "But I've been doing a lot of thinking, and I know we're perfect for each other. I'm not ready to get engaged, but it's not because I don't want to be with you. It's because when we do get married, I want to be able to give you all my attention."

The wine glass sparkled in the candlelight, and Felicity remembered all the times she'd hoped Adam would propose: last August at her parents' cabin on Lake Michigan, and after a friend's wedding in Maine sitting in front of a roaring fire. But did she need a diamond ring to be happy? Hadn't this week taught her that the important thing was that they loved each other?

"I accept your apology." She nodded. "I love you and I want to be together."

"I love you, too." Adam reached forward and kissed her. "There's no one I would rather be with."

The waiter replaced their plates with chateaubriand in a béarnaise sauce. Felicity sipped her wine, and they talked about the fashion show and Adam's prospective clients and New Year's parties in New York.

There was sponge cake with chocolate cream for dessert, and the waiter brought out a bottle of port. Adam held her hand across the table and Felicity felt a surge of longing.

Afterward they lingered in the lobby and listened to the pianist.

Felicity rested her head on Adam's shoulder and let herself relax. She and Adam were together, and her Christmas prayers had been answered.

"Would you like to sleep in my suite?" she asked.

"I thought you'd never ask." Adam grinned boyishly.

A fire crackled in the fireplace of her suite, and Felicity thought it looked so romantic. Crystal ornaments hung from the Christmas tree, and there was a vase of white lilies next to a tray of toffees wrapped in red cellophane.

"I'm glad Raj splurged on a suite after all." Adam caressed her shoulders. "We can make love in the living room and the bedroom and in that massive marble bathtub."

Felicity put down her purse and wondered why she felt a little flustered, like when she skied down a run too fast and couldn't catch her breath. It must be the wine they'd had with dinner mixing with the port they'd drunk at dessert.

"Are you all right?" Adam asked. "You're very quiet."

"I'm perfect." She nodded. "I'm going to change. I'll meet you in the bedroom."

When she came out of the walk-in closet, Adam was reclining against the headboard. His eyes were bright blue, and his chest was smooth. The unsettled feeling disappeared.

"Come here." He held out his hand. "I've missed you."

Felicity climbed on the bed and he kissed her hungrily on the mouth. His hands stroked the fabric of her robe, and a frisson of sexual desire ran through her. A small moan escaped her lips; she had forgotten how wonderful it was to be stroked and desired.

The robe fell open, and Adam caressed her breasts. She pressed his hand against her stomach and guided it between her legs. Their legs tangled in the sheets, and she pulled him on top of her.

"I love you, Felicity," he whispered, tracing her mouth with his thumb. "You're all I want."

"I love you too." She nodded and opened her legs wider. He pushed into her, and she wrapped her arms around him. The waves started deep inside her, and she gripped his shoulders and urged him to go faster.

She came first, and her body trembled so deeply she never wanted it to stop. Adam rocked against the headboard and let out a groan and collapsed against her breasts.

Felicity padded to the living room and poured a glass of water. The last embers glowed in the fireplace, and the star on top of the Christmas tree sparkled like the emerald-cut diamond she'd seen in the window at Harry Winston's.

There was a velvet box on the side table, and she opened it. Inside was the glass engagement ring a model would wear with the princess wedding gown. For a moment she slipped it on her finger and studied it under the light. Then she put it back and closed the box firmly.

They had just made love, and Adam was asleep in the king-sized bed. This was what she had been wishing for and she was so thankful. She took the glass of water into the bedroom and climbed under the sheets beside him.

Fifteen

One Day Before the Fashion Show
9:00 a.m.

Nell

IT WAS THE DAY BEFORE New Year's Eve, and the village was swarming with people enjoying the end of their holiday. Women browsed in the shops, debating between sequined evening gowns and chic black dresses to wear to holiday parties, and families loaded up on Swiss chocolates to take home.

Nell was meeting her father for breakfast at Le Lapin Bleu, and she was already late. Tomorrow was the fashion show; this would be Nell's last chance to figure out why her parents got divorced.

Her father glanced up from his newspaper, and Nell was reminded of how much she enjoyed his company. Even when her parents were being stubborn and childish, she knew they both loved her, and she was lucky to have them.

"Nell, I'm glad you came." He waved to her. "I brought you a present."

"You didn't have to do that," she said, eyeing the red box.

"Don't worry, it's nothing extravagant," he chuckled. "Well, maybe a little extravagant. I was passing Valentino and saw a dress that would look stunning on you. I know you get hoards of free clothes, but I don't have anyone to buy things for, and you can wear it to a New Year's party."

Nell unwrapped the paper and gasped. The dress was gold lamé with a scooped neckline and open back. There was a quilted evening bag and silver bracelet.

"I can't accept this." She slid the box across the table. "It must have cost a fortune."

"Of course you can." He pushed it toward her. "Send me photos. I'll miss being with you when you're back in New York, and it will give me something to look forward to."

"Thank you." She nodded. "It's very thoughtful."

"The strangest thing happened when I walked through the village this morning." He folded his newspaper. "There was a woman inside Bogner who looked just like your mother."

"My mother?" Nell froze.

"I only saw her through the window, but she had your mother's cheekbones and ash-blond hair," he said. "I went inside to find her, but she had disappeared."

"I'm sure it was just a woman with the same coloring." Nell tried to keep the panic out of her voice.

"I suppose you're right," her father agreed. "Your mother would never go inside Bogner; she hates everything to do with skiing. I'll miss hitting the slopes, I feel ten years younger." He added cream to his coffee. "Though I'll be very busy. We just wrapped a film that we're going to show at Sundance and the Aspen Film Festival. I'm very excited about it."

"Mom and I were talking about Aspen." Nell toyed with a packet of sugar. "I didn't know I was named after The Little Nell."

"When did she tell you that?" he asked in surprise.

Nell bit her lip. Why had she mentioned Aspen? It slipped out when she wasn't thinking.

"I called and told her I was in St. Moritz," she said hurriedly. "She said it was very similar to Aspen. The Little Nell was one of her favorite hotels."

"Why on earth was she talking about The Little Nell?" Her father seemed strangely bothered. "We only went there once before you were born."

Nell sipped her coffee and wondered if her father had had an affair with the woman who delivered the script. Maybe her mother hadn't told her the whole story.

"I asked what it was like with you always traveling, and she recalled the time you and her father stayed at The Little Nell," she said casually. "It was an interesting story. A woman came to her parents' house to return your script, and she thought something was going on between you. She couldn't believe that The Little Nell would send someone to Los Angeles to personally deliver the script."

"I never saw that woman before in my life," he said tightly. "Your mother wouldn't believe me. I made her call the hotel so she knew I was telling the truth."

"She told me that," Nell concurred. There was something in her father's tone that made her want to know more.

"She shouldn't have told you any of it. She still blames me, and none of it was my fault. I was only trying to do the right thing, but your mother never forgave me." Her father continued as if he hadn't heard her. "That's what's impossible; she still thinks I was wrong. It all came to a head at her father's funeral. There was a reception at the house afterward. I think you and Pete had just left."

Todd

Todd examined the bottle of Hennessy and poured a shot of whiskey. It was a pity that Alistair wasn't here; he appreciated a good whiskey more than anyone. It was one of the things Todd admired about Alistair. He worked hard for the good things in life—the hacienda in Beverly Hills, membership to the country club—and he wasn't afraid to enjoy them.

Alistair's death had been so sudden. They were drinking scotch in the den, and Alistair had dropped dead of a heart attack. Todd would miss him, and he was nervous about running the studio by himself. But if there was one positive thing about Alistair's death, it was that Todd could work on saving his marriage.

Todd looked up from the bar and saw Patty standing at the buffet. At forty-three, she was still a beautiful woman. Her hair was the same honey blond, and her legs looked stunning in a black dress. They had grown apart over the last few years, and Todd was determined to change that. Alistair was gone and he would do whatever it took to keep her.

Patty was with a woman who looked vaguely familiar. Suddenly there was a pit in his stomach, and he froze. He ducked behind the bar and waited for the woman to leave.

"I'm so very sorry, this must be a terrible time," the woman was saying to Patty. Her blond hair was cut in a bob and she wore a navy dress. "I didn't go to the funeral, of course. I hope you don't mind me stopping by to pay my respects." She paused. "I debated coming, but

in the end I thought it was the right thing to do. After all, it wasn't just a holiday romance. We were together for years."

"You were together for years?" Patty said. Todd noticed the look of shock and surprise on her face.

"He was so generous, and we really cared about each other." The woman held a plate of canapés. "Then he wanted to marry me, and I felt terrible breaking it off. But I couldn't go through with it; after all, he had a family. You never want to be wife number two: what if it happens all over again?"

"Patty, there you are." Todd stepped out from behind the bar. "Mr. and Mrs. Harvey want to see you."

"Do you remember Grace Cannon? You met in Aspen, and she delivered the script to you." Patty's voice was like ice. "She was just telling me about your relationship. Apparently you wanted to marry her. But she was too clever; she didn't want the same thing to happen to her."

"Oh, goodness!" Grace flushed. "I'm sorry if you misunderstood, you have it all wrong." She glanced from Patty to Todd. "I wasn't talking about your husband, I was talking about your father."

"My father?" Patty gasped.

Todd downed his whiskey and wished for some kind of distraction: a flood or an earthquake. Patty would cling to him for safety, and this whole ugly scene would be forgotten.

"This isn't the time or the place to discuss it," he said to Grace, and took Patty's arm. "There are a dozen people waiting to pay their respects. We must go."

"No one is going anywhere until you tell me what is going on," Patty said firmly. Todd was reminded of how stubborn she could be.

"I'm sorry, I thought you knew." Grace was puzzled. "Alistair said he told the family everything."

"I've never heard of you except for the day you brought my husband his script." Patty looked from Todd to Grace, and the realization came over her. "That's not what you were doing here at all."

"I really think you should leave," Todd said pointedly to Grace. "It's an emotional time for everyone."

"Of course." Grace turned to Patty and held out her hand. "It was nice seeing you. Alistair talked about you all the time; he was very proud of you."

Todd sat on the sofa in the living room and nursed a glass of scotch. He could barely remember the rest of the reception. Finally the last cars pulled out of the driveway and he drove the few blocks home. Nell and Pete were seeing old friends, and the house was quiet except for Patty's heels clicking on the parquet floor.

"That woman didn't come to return your script. You made the whole thing up." Patty turned to Todd. "She had a rendezvous with my father. Did you know they were having an affair?"

"I never saw her before in my life," Todd said. "Alistair met her in Aspen and gave her a card with my name and his phone number."

"So that if she called and my mother answered, it wouldn't look suspicious." Her voice was anguished. "And you protected him. How could you lie to everyone!"

"I had no idea the affair continued," Todd admitted, and looked at Patty. "But I was aware of other women."

"That's why he traveled with you! So you could be an accomplice to his infidelity."

"That's not the reason; I was very good at what I did," Todd said hotly. "Your parents had been married for over twenty years when we met. I couldn't change who he was."

"You could have told my mother the truth. Instead, you were play-ing God," Patty spat. "She wasted her life on a man who collected women like bottles of liquor from a hotel minibar."

"You're overreacting. Your parents had a wonderful life, and it had nothing to do with me." He refilled his glass. "I was practically a kid when I started working for your father. I wasn't about to start grilling him on his personal life."

"So you let him romance women all around the world while my mother sat at home and sewed my theater costumes."

"I'm completely against cheating, but you must see the position I was in," he fumed. "Your father gave me a job that supported his daughter and grandchildren. I had to be loyal to him; he gave us every-thing."

"The only person you owed loyalty to was your wife," she said furiously. "You could have told me what was going on, so I didn't discover it at my father's funeral."

Todd walked over to Patty and touched her hand. "Maybe I didn't handle things correctly, but I had the best of intentions. Your father is dead, so it really doesn't matter. Things have been strained between us, but perhaps we can start fresh. You can travel with me to shooting lo-cations, and we can do all the things we dreamed of." He pulled an envelope out of his pocket. "It was going to be a surprise, but we can start with Paris. I have to be on the set next week, and I booked four nights at the Ritz. We'll take a dinner cruise and go to the ballet."

Patty stared at the ballet tickets, and for a moment Todd thought everything would be all right. He would tell the company jet to pre-pare an extra meal, and make sure the Ritz had Patty's favorite lotions waiting in the suite.

"Starting fresh is a good idea." Patty walked briskly to the bar. She poured her scotch down the sink and smoothed her skirt. "I suggest you

move out of our pool house and get your own place. I'm going to do some remodeling, and there won't be anywhere for you to sleep."

"What are you talking about?" Todd asked.

"Nell is in New York, and Pete is in China; there's no reason to stay married," she answered. "We never liked the same things anyway. You never read a book from start to finish, and I have no interest in tennis or fancy cars. We can get a divorce and do exactly as we please."

"I don't want a divorce! I know we haven't been getting along, but I plan on changing that. And lots of couples have different hobbies, and everyone in Beverly Hills drives an imported car," he fumed. "We've loved each other since we were in our twenties; that has to count for something."

"We didn't know what love was then, but I do now," she said. "It's not keeping vital information away from the person you love most." She walked to the door and turned around. "You can pick the divorce attorney. I won't have time. I'll be busy ripping up the floors in the pool house and replacing the furniture."

"I couldn't do anything to change her mind. Her anger was like a wildfire that grew out of control." Todd ate a bite of his Danish and looked at Nell. "Now you see why I can't attend your wedding. I wouldn't put it past your mother to come after me with a dessert fork."

Nell wanted to say something, but it was all too much: her grandfather having affairs and her father knowing about them, and her parents keeping secrets from her all these years.

"I have to go." Nell put her coffee cup on the table. "We're having a dress rehearsal later, and I have to go to a final fitting."

"I shouldn't have told you, but there was no other way to make you understand. Please know that I don't regret a minute of the marriage," her father said, stopping her. "You and Pete are the best things that happened to me, and I'm grateful to your mother for raising you."

"I'll see you later." Nell stood up and walked to the door.

"Nell," her father called.

"Yes?" She turned around, and for the first time, the father who'd always resembled a movie star with his chiseled cheekbones and emerald eyes seemed like an ordinary man.

"Your mother was wrong about one thing. I knew what love was in my twenties, and it never changed. She's still the most spectacular woman I ever met."

Nell strode through the lobby of Badrutt's Palace and punched the elevator button. She wished she could call Eliot, but it was the middle of the night in New York. Felicity was the only other person who might understand. The elevator stopped at her floor and Nell knocked on the door.

"I just got out of the shower and was about to text you," Felicity said, answering the door. "Come in, I have so much to tell you."

"I have so much to tell you too." Nell followed her into the living room. Felicity sat opposite her on the love seat, and Nell noticed the tray with two empty shot glasses.

"It looks like you had a visitor," Nell said, pointing to the tray. "Did you and Adam finally make up?"

"He went back to his hotel an hour ago," Felicity said, nodding. "We ate at Le Restaurant and he apologized and said he loved me.

He doesn't want to get engaged yet, but he wants to be together forever."

"Is that what you want?" Nell asked.

"I'd like a ring eventually," Felicity acknowledged. "But he was sweet and sincere. Afterward we came up to the suite and made love and it was like we'd never been apart."

"As long as you're happy," Nell said. "I had breakfast with my father. He thought he saw my mother inside a ski shop! Yesterday, my mother said he dialed her number and she could hear people talking in French and German in the background. What am I going to do if they find out what I've been up to? Neither of them will speak to me again."

"Of course they'll speak to you," Felicity assured her. "You are their daughter, and you're not doing anything wrong. It's only natural that you want them to attend the wedding. Did you learn anything new from your father?"

"Yes—wait until I tell you," Nell said, and the color went out of her cheeks. "I know why my parents got divorced. My grandfather used my father as an accomplice for his affairs."

"What do you mean?" Felicity raised her eyebrows.

"My grandfather gave women my father's name with his own home phone number. If his wife answered, she wouldn't be suspicious," Nell continued. "My mother found out at her father's funeral and she never forgave him. I can see why my mother was so upset, but my father was in a bad position. He really should have told her the truth; they were her parents, after all."

"Oh, I see." Felicity nodded her head slowly. "That is tricky. What a terrible situation."

"I was so upset, I ran out of the restaurant," Nell said. "There's no chance they'll both attend my wedding. I'm so miserable, I don't know what to do."

"What will happen when they see each other at the fashion show?" Felicity wondered.

"The fashion show!" Nell panicked. "I've been so focused on keeping them apart, I completely forgot they'd see each other at the fashion show." She took out her phone. "I'll call my father and tell him not to come. I'll say it's overbooked and we have to save the seats for some big fashion editor."

"Don't call him yet," Felicity said, stopping her.

"Why not?" Nell looked up from her phone.

"I have an idea. How fast can Eliot get to St. Moritz?" Felicity asked.

"Eliot?" Nell repeated. "He's covering the ball drop on New Year's Eve."

"He must be able to get someone to cover for him in an emergency," Felicity said excitedly. "Call him and tell him to get on the first flight. I have to go see Raj."

"Will you tell me what's going on?" Nell asked.

"Not till I figure it out." Felicity walked to the door and turned around. "You're welcome to stay in the suite. The bottle of brandy is under the minibar."

Nell opened the door to her room and walked to the window. How could her father have lied to her mother for all those years, and why couldn't her mother forgive him?

The bells chimed eleven o'clock, and she picked up her phone. She'd promised Felicity she would call Eliot, and then she had a final fitting. Tomorrow was the fashion show, and she would glide down the runway in an organza gown with diamond buttons. Her job as a model was to make everyone believe she had a perfect life. She took a deep breath and wished they were right.

Sixteen

The Day of the Fashion Show
6:30 p.m.

Felicity

IT WAS THIRTY MINUTES BEFORE the fashion show, and the models were milling around in lace bustiers and silk garters. Raj was darting back and forth, making sure curling irons were unplugged, and the noise in the dressing room was so loud, Felicity could hardly think. But she glanced at the chiffon-and-lace gown with illusion sleeves, and the ivory off-the-shoulder dress with a tiered circle skirt, and there was nowhere she would rather be.

The last twenty four hours had been a blur of stockings that suddenly got runs, hairspray that wouldn't hold, and Felicity's biggest fear of all: a lipstick smudge on a strapless deep V-neck ball gown with a bowed skirt. But she gave the model a new pair of stockings, the beauty salon lent them a bottle of hairspray, and Raj whisked the gown to the laundry and returned it pressed and without any marks.

The dress rehearsal went off perfectly, and even Raj was pleased.

Katie looked stunning in the sheath with white satin panels, and the amethysts on Emily's ball gown twinkled under the lights. And Nell! When Felicity saw her in the organza gown with diamond buttons shaped like snowflakes, she thought she was a Disney princess come to life.

She and Raj worked furiously to put her plan in motion. Adam had been so supportive, massaging her shoulders and bringing her endless cups of coffee. When he finally went back to his room to change, he texted that he was so proud of all she had accomplished.

And she had finally finished a second design for Camilla! It had come to her all at once, and she couldn't sketch it fast enough: a see-through bodice stitched with silver thread, and an A-line skirt made of the sheerest tulle. Underneath the bride would wear a silver bodysuit, and her accessories would be chunky bangles and a silver-and-gold choker. Felicity studied the final design before she emailed it to Camilla, and it reminded her of a dress fit for Cleopatra. She had been so excited she was tempted to show Raj, but she stopped herself just in time. Camilla would reply soon, and she didn't want Raj to be anxious just before the fashion show.

She felt bad that she hadn't told Gabriel that she and Adam were back together. He'd done so much to help her, and she hadn't seen him since before she and Adam had dinner. She would try to stop by his office tomorrow before the plane left for New York.

There really wasn't time to think about anything except the journalists and celebrities who were waiting expectantly on the other side of the curtains. Felicity had peeked out earlier and couldn't believe it. The editor-in-chief of *Martha Stewart Weddings* was there, and Princess Beatrice of England, and an editor from *Vogue Italia*. And Felicity was almost certain she'd spotted Charlize

Theron with a good-looking man. She couldn't tell Raj. He'd go right up to Charlize and make her promise to let Felicity design her gown when she got married.

The best part of the show would be the finale. Only Raj could have pulled it off within twenty-four hours. Felicity would have to give him a present: a pair of Italian loafers to replace the worn loafers he'd had for years, or a cashmere overcoat instead of the coat he'd been wearing since they were in college.

Felicity ducked through the hallway and knocked on the door of the anteroom. Nell was the star of the show, and had a dressing room to herself. A chenille gown was draped over a chair, and a tulle veil hung from the closet.

"There you are," Nell said to Felicity. "I straightened my hair, but I haven't started with my mascara or eyeliner. I look like a wet cat who just took a bath."

"You look stunning without any makeup," Felicity said, admiring Nell's dark hair and almond-shaped eyes. "Everyone is going to love you."

"I'm so nervous that my parents will see each other and get into a fistfight. I should have told my father not to come. The minute they spot each other it's going to get ugly."

"They're not going to see each other, because your father is with Raj being outfitted in a tuxedo," Felicity replied. "He'll wait behind the curtains until the grand finale, when he'll escort you down the runway."

"My father is going to be in the fashion show?" Nell put down her lipstick.

"I didn't want to tell you until the details were in place." Felicity perched on the dresser. "Yesterday you were afraid that your parents would see each other at the fashion show. I realized that all week they've been in St. Moritz at the same time."

"Of course they have," Nell interrupted. "That's why I've been running around like a mouse in a lab experiment trying to keep them apart."

"You don't want to keep them away from each other," Felicity continued. "You want them to be at your wedding."

"What are you getting at?" Nell asked, curious.

"If you can't get them to come to your wedding in Nantucket, why not have your wedding in St. Moritz?" Felicity asked impishly. "Eliot is at the hotel barber getting a haircut, and I even asked Katie to perform a song. She sings in the church choir in Kentucky, and has a lovely voice."

"Eliot is here!" Nell gasped. "I left him a message yesterday, but he never replied."

"He couldn't get a flight, and didn't want to respond until he was certain he could come," Felicity explained. "Raj called Swiss Air and said Eliot was an important news anchor, and the agent magically found him a seat. He's so excited—I thought he would burst when I told him our plan."

"I still don't understand." Nell frowned. "This is a fashion show, not a wedding. I want my parents to be there when we exchange our vows."

"It's going to be a real wedding," Felicity said triumphantly. "Raj bought the wedding rings and booked the minister and reserved the honeymoon suite for you and Eliot. I couldn't believe it when I saw the price. He said the suite was a write-off, and he wanted your wedding night to be perfect."

"Eliot and I are getting married?" Nell gasped.

"Only if you want to, of course! Before the finale, the runway will be transformed into a wedding aisle strewn with red and white rose petals. There will be an altar with urns of orchids, and the harpist will play the wedding march.

"Your father will walk you down the aisle, and Eliot will be waiting at the altar. After the ceremony there will be fireworks on the mountain, and waiters will serve champagne to the guests."

"It's ingenious," Nell said excitedly. "By the time my mother sees my father walking me down the aisle, it will be too late for her to leave. I can't thank you enough." Her eyes grew watery. "It's a miracle! Both my parents will be at my wedding."

"Don't start crying or you'll ruin your slip, and I don't have a spare." Felicity hugged Nell. "Friends have to help each other. And it's Christmas—it's the time for miracles."

"I can't believe how everything worked out." Nell opened the tube of mascara. "You and Adam are back together, and Eliot and I are getting married. If only my parents could get along, everything would be perfect."

"That would be two Christmas miracles," Felicity said, laughing, and glanced at the clock. "I have to go. I'm supposed to be out front mingling with the audience."

"Where's Gabriel?" Nell asked.

"Gabriel?" Felicity turned around.

"The hotel doctor," Nell prodded. "I saw him in the lobby earlier."

"He must have been visiting a patient; I didn't see him." Felicity gave Nell a quick smile. "I'll see you on the runway."

Felicity crossed the hallway and wondered why Gabriel hadn't stopped and said hello. It was her fault; she should have invited him to the fashion show. But it would have been awkward with Adam sitting in the audience, and she didn't think Gabriel was interested in watching models parade down the runway in princess ball gowns and illusion veils.

Her phone buzzed and she recognized the New York phone number. She pressed Accept and put the phone to her ear.

"Felicity, it's Delilah." Adam's mother's voice came over the line. "I hope I'm not interrupting. I just wanted to say good luck. Adam told me all about the fashion show."

"Thank you," Felicity said. "It was a surprise when Adam arrived, but I'm glad he's here."

"He came for dinner, and we had a long talk," Delilah replied. "I knew he'd come to his senses."

"Come to his senses?" Felicity said guardedly.

"I'm not blind; I saw your naked ring finger at Christmas, and the way you left brunch so abruptly," Delilah explained. "Remember our conversation at Thanksgiving? Sometimes you have to give men a little push."

"A push?" Felicity repeated.

"I made Adam's favorite lasagna and mentioned that Adam's father freed up some investment money and was interested in helping Adam's business under the right circumstances. Most parents give their children a down payment on a house when they get married; it's not terribly different."

"You said you'd invest in the firm if we got engaged?" Felicity asked, horrified.

"Something like that," Delilah agreed. "I'm sure Adam will propose soon. I suggested he use my mother's ring; I have to get the stones tightened."

"He didn't say anything about getting engaged," Felicity answered. "He just said he wanted to be together."

"He'd hardly tell you when he was going to propose; that would spoil the surprise." Delilah laughed. "He's just like his father; all he needed was a little prompting. We're all so happy. John is excited about Adam opening a branch in Los Angeles; he loves visiting the coast."

"I have to go," Felicity said urgently. "The fashion show is about to start."

"Of course, I just wanted to wish you luck," Delilah replied. "After all, you're practically my daughter-in-law."

Felicity pressed End and leaned against the wall. Had Adam really come to St. Moritz because his parents were going to invest in his company? All he talked about was his firm, and he was so anxious to get ahead. Maybe his father had made an offer that was too good to refuse. She felt slightly dizzy, and hoped she wasn't going to be sick.

There was a rustling sound, and Felicity realized the fashion show was starting. She couldn't think about Adam now. Magazine editors and members of the jet set were waiting to see the debut of Felicity Grant's winter collection. She smoothed her skirt and hurried to the catwalk. Raj had put so much effort into the show, and she couldn't disappoint him.

Felicity stood in the back of the catwalk and glowed with excitement. The dresses had been warmly received, and the energy of the audience was intoxicating. Women wearing fur jackets scribbled down notes, and fashion editors tapped at their phones. Every time a model appeared everyone oohed and ahhed. Her designs really were gorgeous. The hand-embroidered tulle ball gown complemented Katie's creamy complexion, and Emily looked perfect in the pewter-colored dress with a silver muff.

The grand finale was about to start. Felicity held her breath. Nell appeared from behind the curtain, and she had never looked more beautiful. The tiara glittered against her dark hair, and diamond teardrop earrings sparkled in her ears. She wore a ruby pendant borrowed from Harry Winston. She glided down the runway on her father's arm, and everyone gasped.

Nell and her father made such a handsome couple. Todd looked every bit the movie star in black tie and tails, and Nell resembled a young Elizabeth Taylor. Todd delivered Nell to Eliot, and Felicity heard a strangled sound from the front row.

Nell's mother stood up, and her cheeks were the color of chalk. For a moment, Felicity thought Patty might faint, and wondered what she had done. But then Patty sat down, and Felicity noticed happy tears in her eyes. Patty took out a handkerchief and turned her attention to Nell and Eliot.

"Friends and family," the minister began. "Nothing gives me more pleasure than meeting a couple who are deeply in love. When I saw Nell and Eliot's eyes meet a moment ago, I knew that God had brought together two young people who will never part. Call it a minister's intuition, or just the knowledge from many years on the job, but I'll bet anyone a thousand Swiss francs that Nell and Eliot will go on to celebrate their fiftieth anniversary." The minister smiled. "No one will take me up on my bet? I guess I'll have to continue with the ceremony."

Everyone laughed, and Felicity wondered whether Raj had written the minister's speech. Eliot recited his vows, and Nell had tears streaming down her cheeks. Felicity had never witnessed anything so moving. When the minister pronounced them man and wife, the kiss lasted so long, there was nervous tittering in the audience. Suddenly the Grand Hall seemed too hot, and Felicity turned and ran until she reached the balcony.

The glass doors closed behind her, and Felicity rested against the railing. She gulped in the freezing air, and all she could think about were Adam's mother's comments.

Did she want to marry someone who had to be coerced into proposing? And how could Adam have suggested taking a break if he really loved her? The point of marriage wasn't finding the person you wanted to spend the rest of your life with; it was being with the person you couldn't live without.

She remembered when she'd modeled the ivory sheath on her first night in St. Moritz, when she was certain she would wear it to her wedding. But how would she feel when she walked down the aisle and wasn't sure why Adam was waiting at the altar?

The doors opened and Adam strode toward her. He carried two champagne flutes and there was a look of concern on his face.

"What are you doing out here?" he asked. "Everyone is waiting to congratulate you, and you disappeared."

"I needed some air," Felicity said, and suddenly wondered if she was just overwrought. She should get a good night's sleep; everything would be better tomorrow.

"It was an incredible success." He handed her a champagne flute. "The finale was spectacular. I've never seen two people so happy."

Felicity remembered the way Eliot had gazed at Nell when she recited her vows, and her eyes filled with tears. She wanted Adam to look at her exactly the same way: as if he'd found the greatest treasure, and never wanted to lose it.

"Are you all right?" Adam asked anxiously. "You're shaking, and your lips are blue."

"Your mother called to wish me luck. Then she said the strangest thing," Felicity answered. "She said your father offered to invest in your company if we got engaged."

"She told you that? It wasn't like that exactly," Adam said nervously. "We were just making dinner conversation."

"Dinner conversation that included tightening your grandmother's engagement ring and your father's eagerness to set up an office in Los Angeles! When you said you wanted to be together forever, I thought it was because you loved me. Not because it would help the firm become bicoastal."

"You're being ridiculous!" Adam replied. "I'd never marry you to get investment money. I worked so hard getting Doug to sign while you were running around with some Swiss doctor. Then I spent twenty hours on an airplane to come see you, and I got a greeting as frigid as a snowball. We finally had one great night together, and now we're arguing again."

The fireworks lit up the mountain, and Felicity inhaled the cold air. She looked at Adam, and suddenly everything was as clear as the icicles hanging from the pine trees.

"You're right." She nodded. "It's not going to work."

"What are you talking about?" he said, taken aback.

"I don't want to be disappointed that you didn't give me an engagement ring, and I don't want to wonder if you're going to suggest taking another break," she offered. "I want to be with someone who thinks about me when he wakes up in the morning, and can't sleep without me beside him."

"Felicity, we're both overwrought." He touched her arm. "Let's go to bed and talk about it in the morning."

"I don't think so." She shook her head firmly. "I'm sorry, Adam, but this is goodbye."

"You can't be serious," he tried again. "We love each other. We know everything about each other, and we want the same things."

"That's what I thought when you said we should take a break, but it's not enough," she answered. "Wanting the same things isn't the same as being in love. Love is a feeling so strong, an avalanche couldn't shake it. I'm sorry, Adam; we both tried. It's better that we stop now, so we both have a chance at something new."

Adam stuffed his hands in his pockets and looked up at the mountain.

"Fine. But if this is about that Swiss doctor, you could have told me and saved me the trip," he said angrily. "I'm going back to my hotel. I'll see you in New York."

Adam strode inside and Felicity gazed across the snow-covered valley. The lights twinkled in the village, and the forests were thick with fir trees. Her heart beat faster, but at the same time she felt a stillness, like when she stood at the top of the mountain and looked out over the magic carpet.

More fireworks lit up the sky, and Felicity noticed four stars shaped like a diamond. It was the same group of stars she'd seen on her first night in St. Moritz, when she wished for a miracle. The whole week came back to her: Gabriel rescuing her when she twisted her ankle, seeing Adam in the lobby of Badrutt's Palace, kissing Gabriel on the dance floor at the King's Club. She pictured the roses Adam sent, and making love in her hotel suite, and the odd feeling that something was missing.

A thought came to her and she hurried inside. The lobby was filled with guests milling around the runway, and Felicity tried to squeeze toward the elevator.

"There you are," Raj said as he stopped her. "I've been looking for you everywhere. Have you read the reviews? We're a smashing success." He took out his phone and read out loud:

"The debut of Felicity Grant's winter bridal collection took place on the famous catwalk of Badrutt's Palace, and was the best event of the season. Designers like Valentino and Carolina Herrera should take notes on Felicity's choice of models, fresh new faces who carried off the dresses with incredible polish; the gowns themselves left the crowd breathless. Felicity has a way of combining elegant fabrics and fanciful details to create a collection that is intelligent and whimsical at the same time. Her classic sheath was cleverly matched with a cathedral-length train, and her ball gown with an ermine-trimmed cape was so enticing, orders came in before the model completed her turn on the runway. The icing on the fashion show was the grand finale. The gown was a sumptuous organza creation with diamond snowflake buttons. In a burst of inspiration rivaling anything seen at Vera Wang, model Nell Mason married her fiancé, TV newscaster Eliot Hayes, in front of the astounded gathering.

"Three cheers to Felicity and her business partner, Raj Patel, for creating such a fantastic event. Our spies on the ground were happy to spot Felicity's boyfriend, sports manager Adam Burton, sitting proudly in the front row. We're thrilled that Felicity and Adam have resolved their romantic issues, and we can't wait to see what our favorite New York wedding dress designer has planned for her summer collection."

"That's wonderful, I'm thrilled. I'm afraid Adam left." She leaned against the paneling. "We broke up, and he's going back to New York."

"I don't believe it!" Raj exclaimed. "No one flies across the globe to break up with his girlfriend on New Year's Eve. The last time I saw Adam he was clapping and sipping champagne at the fashion show."

"I broke up with him," Felicity said, correcting him.

"Does this have something to do with that Swiss doctor?" Raj demanded. "I knew you've been acting differently."

"No, it's about love." She shook her head. "Adam and I might have the same goals, but I've learned that that's different from loving each other."

"Are you sure?" Raj looked at her intently.

"Very sure." Felicity smiled. "It will be good for business. Think about how much more time I'll spend in the workroom. The summer collection will be finished by March."

Raj studied her dark hair and wide eyes. She was wearing the simple black dress they had chosen together so it wouldn't overshadow the models.

"No one works harder than you. I'm lucky to have you as a partner," he said soberly. "And you're right. You deserve to be with someone who knows that when he met you, he hit the jackpot."

"I'd kiss you, but someone might post it online and make something of it." Felicity laughed. "Do you mind if I go upstairs? I'm exhausted, and I'd like to relax."

"Go, you've earned it." Raj waved his hand. "The press are so infatuated with Nell and Eliot that they can't stop taking photos of the happy couple. And Katie is a hit; I heard whispers that she could be the new face of Ralph Lauren."

"Thank you for everything." Felicity stepped into the elevator. "It's been the most magical week, even if it didn't turn out like I hoped."

The lights in the living room of her suite were on low, and the maids had closed the drapes. There was a tray of profiteroles with a card from the concierge wishing her a happy New Year.

She noticed a scarf on the side table and realized it was Gabriel's. He'd left it days ago and she'd never returned it. Fireworks exploded over the lake, and Felicity remembered it was New Year's Eve. The email with the designs for Bergdorf Goodman's bridal salon had been sent to Camilla and the winter fashion show was a success. Tomorrow she was going back to New York.

She felt like she was leaving something important in St. Moritz, but she was too exhausted to figure out what it was. There was a pot of hot cocoa on the coffee table, and she poured a cup. She'd worry about it tomorrow; now, all she wanted was to have a warm drink and go to bed.

Seventeen

The Day After the Fashion Show
12:00 p.m.

Felicity

IT WAS NEW YEAR'S DAY, and the village was completely quiet. Felicity stood on the balcony of her suite and gazed at the snow-capped mountains. The air was fresh and cold, and it was one of the prettiest places she had ever seen.

An email from Camilla Barnes had popped up an hour ago. At first she was afraid to open it; it would be better to bask in the praise of the fashion show and check it when she got back to New York. But she couldn't help herself, and clicked on the subject. The whole email was just two lines, and Felicity was certain it was a polite rejection. She had to read it three times before she believed what it said. Camilla had written:

ABSOLUTELY DIVINE AND COMPLETELY ORIGINAL!
Bergdorf Goodman's Bridal Salon would be honored to

include Felicity Grant in their Spring Bridal Event. Be in touch with details soon.

Best,

Camilla

Felicity had immediately texted Raj that she had to see him, but he'd texted back and said he was saying goodbye to Greta. It was the most wonderful news, so why didn't she feel happier? It was probably the letdown after the fashion show, coupled with the end of her relationship with Adam.

She sipped a white coffee and pictured all the things she would miss about St. Moritz: the ski slopes with their deep powder and wide vistas, the mountain huts where you could eat sausages and warm your face in the sun, and the boutiques filled with soft sweaters and bright ski gear.

Last night she hadn't been able to sleep, and when she finally drifted off, she had the strangest dream. She dreamed she was a princess in a castle, and there was a man on a white horse galloping toward the drawbridge. She woke suddenly and tried to return to the dream. But no matter how many sheep she counted or how much warm milk she sipped, she couldn't go back to sleep.

Adam had texted a curt goodbye from the airport, and she wondered if she'd made a mistake. But she studied the squirrels darting through the forest and felt lighter. You couldn't make someone love you, or it didn't mean anything at all.

New York would be lonely without their Sunday brunches of eggs benedict, and nights curled up with Chinese takeout and movies on Netflix. There would be no one to ask if a three-quarter veil worked with a tea-length dress, or if a rose-tinted bodice should be embroidered with pearls.

There was a knock at the door, and she wondered who it could be. Their flight didn't leave until this evening, and Raj had given everyone the day off.

"Nell!" Felicity said when she opened the door. "What are you doing here? I thought you'd be soaking in the bathtub in the honeymoon suite and enjoying the complimentary breakfast of scrambled eggs and fresh scones."

"The honeymoon suite is fantastic, and Eliot almost ate everything on the tray before I woke up." She smiled and entered the living room. "But I was worried about you. Raj said you went up to your suite after the fashion show."

"I broke up with Adam," Felicity said. "He's on his way back to New York."

"You did what?" Nell gasped.

"You can't force someone to love you. It's as impossible as predicting whether spring fashions will have bold colors or pastels." She traced the rim of her coffee cup. "When I saw the way Eliot looked at you when you recited your vows, I wanted the same thing for myself. Someone who loves me completely, and never has any doubts."

"Are you sure?" Nell asked. "Adam flew all the way to St. Moritz to see you."

"I'm completely sure." Felicity nodded. "I'm tired of hoping Adam will feel the same way about our future as I do. I want someone who can't live without me."

"You'll find that guy," Nell said firmly. "You are one of the warmest and loveliest people I know."

"I have too much to do to think about love anyway," Felicity assured her. "I just got some exciting news, and I have to work on the summer collection."

"You should have come to the Dracula Club," Nell said. "Everyone was gushing about Felicity Grant Bridal. I don't know how to thank you and Raj—it was the wedding of my dreams." She looked at Felicity. "My parents are taking Eliot and me to a late lunch at the Panorama Restaurant. It's at the top of the Piste Naire, and all the dishes are homemade. I came to ask you to join us—my parents would love to spend time with you."

"I'd love to come. I didn't know your parents are together—tell me everything!" Felicity exclaimed. She had been so caught up with her own problems, she'd forgotten to ask what had happened after the show.

"Not together, exactly, but they are talking to each other," Nell laughed. "They didn't seem happy after the fashion show, and I was worried they'd never speak to me. But then Eliot and I told them we were so grateful they were at our wedding, it meant the world to us. They ran into each other at the Dracula Club and I saw them dancing at midnight. This morning, my mother texted and asked if we'd meet them for lunch."

"Do you think they'll get back together?" Felicity asked.

"I'll be happy if they sit at the table without threatening each other with the bread knife." Nell twisted her wedding band. "But who knows, there could be another Christmas miracle. I better go—Eliot and I are going to take a horse and carriage ride before lunch. I'm going to miss St. Moritz; there really is something magical about the Alps."

———

Nell left and Felicity poured another cup of coffee. There was a knock at the door, and she wondered if Nell had forgotten something. She opened the door and saw a bellboy holding a huge bouquet of flowers.

"Can I help you?" she asked.

"Apparently you had two bouquets sent the other day but the second one was never delivered." The bellboy entered the living room. "The concierge said it was quite odd. After I delivered the first bouquet, a different gentleman ordered exactly the same flowers. The concierge discovered they were never sent so I was instructed to bring you these this morning. The hotel apologizes for the delay."

"A second bouquet of flowers?" Felicity asked, wondering who they were from.

"That doesn't happen often, even to our most beautiful guests," the bellboy offered. "The florist prepared a new bouquet but I have the original card."

"The card?" Felicity asked.

"The card that came with the bouquet." He handed it to Felicity. "I'm supposed to wait for a reply."

Felicity ripped open the card and her stomach did little flips. She scanned it quickly and read it again.

Dear Felicity,

I have to admit I was nervous when we met and you asked my advice about love. It's nothing like medicine, where you make a diagnosis and prescribe a cure. There are no medical journals to consult or previous cases to consider; love makes as much sense as the holiday people in St. Moritz who attempt to ski Diavolezza their first time on skis.

I know that now, because I'm falling in love with you and it's impossible to explain. We've only known each other a few days, but I've enjoyed every minute together. When you ran out of the King's Club after we kissed, I wanted to tell you how I felt. Then I saw you shivering in the moonlight, and I became as tongue-tied as a preteen boy playing spin the bottle. Instead, I wrote this note. If there is any chance you feel the same, please respond. If I'm completely off base, crumple up the card and enjoy the flowers.

Yours,
Gabriel

Felicity stopped reading and the bellboy looked at her expectantly. "What's your answer?"

"My answer?" she repeated.

"I'm supposed to wait for your reply."

Why hadn't she seen Gabriel's feelings for her before? The way Gabriel had carried her to her suite after she fell off the sled, and was genuinely worried about her. He'd gotten so flustered when she said she'd promised Raj she wouldn't see him anymore. And when she asked if he would behave like Adam if he loved someone, he'd answered that if he were in love, he would wrap his arms around her and say, no matter how hard it was, they would work things out.

How did she feel about him? Nell was right; he was terribly handsome, with his dark hair and brown eyes. Whenever she was with him she felt protected, like one of the pearls in the bodice of Emily's princess ball gown. And the kiss had been unexpected, but his lips were soft and warm.

They had only known each other for a week, but when they were together everything seemed brighter. She remembered sharing nut tortes at Hotel Hauser and visiting the Olympic Stadium and watching the snow polo matches. And she loved hearing his folktales: there was something in his voice when he repeated them that made her feel warm and alive.

The bellboy coughed impatiently, and Felicity started. What if she had been wishing for the wrong Christmas miracle all along? What if the real miracle was waiting for her at the doctor's office above the village?

"I'll tell him myself." Felicity jumped up and threw on a sweater. "Here—this is for you." She handed him some Euro notes.

"You don't have to do that," he said, but slipped them in his pocket.

"I want to." She beamed. "You've just given me the best news I could imagine."

Felicity hurried through the village and wished she'd worn a pair of boots. But she'd been in such a rush to see Gabriel, she'd run out of the hotel in a coat and pumps.

She knocked on his office door, but there was no answer. It was almost lunchtime; Gabriel was probably in the village having a plate of schnitzel. She was about to leave when the door opened.

"Felicity, what are you doing here?" Gabriel asked. "Come inside. You're not wearing boots; you must be freezing."

"I'm a little cold, but I had to see you." She stepped into the waiting room. "It's New Year's Day, and I was afraid you wouldn't be here."

"The office was busy all morning," Gabriel grunted. "I've had more cases of twisted ankles from dancing in high heels than a sports doctor has caring for a basketball team." He looked at Felicity. "Where's Adam? I would have thought you'd be enjoying your last day in St. Moritz together."

"I broke up with Adam." She sat on the sofa. "He left for New York."

"What happened?" he asked. "The last time I saw you, he sent roses and you were meeting for a fancy dinner."

"Adam and I may have wanted the same things, but we didn't love each other enough," Felicity said pensively.

"I didn't realize there were gradients of love." Gabriel grinned. "Like diamond ratings on a ski run."

"I want to be willing to sacrifice anything for the man I love, and I want him to feel the same." She paused. "It might be hard to find, but it's worth waiting for."

"I'm glad you know what you want. But why are you here?" he wondered.

Felicity fiddled with a cushion and adrenaline rushed through her. "This morning the bellboy delivered a bouquet of flowers and a card from you."

"From me?" Gabriel leaned down and straightened magazines on the coffee table.

"The flowers were supposed to be delivered two days ago, but they went to the wrong suite," she continued. "I read your card and told him I'd give you an answer myself."

"It was a silly thing to write." Gabriel paced around the room. "I got carried away."

"My answer is yes," Felicity said.

"What did you say?" Gabriel turned around.

"I've never felt quite like this before. I enjoy being with you, and you make me feel happy and alive," she began. "I'm not sure what will happen, but I'd like to give us a chance. You could come to New York, or I could spend time in Switzerland."

"My father is getting better every day, and I've always wanted to go to New York." Gabriel sat beside her. "Are you sure? I don't have much experience with love. I might not be a good bet."

"I haven't been successful in love either," she reminded him. "I'm willing to risk it if you are."

Gabriel gathered her in his arms and kissed her. His mouth was warm and she kissed him back.

"Nell and Eliot invited me to lunch. Would you like to come?" she asked. "It would be wonderful to spend some time together before I leave."

"My afternoon patient wants a cure for his hangover, but he'll survive if I'm gone for a few hours," he said, and nodded. "I'll get my jacket and put a note on the door."

"Would you do one thing for me before we go?" she asked. "Will you tell me a story?"

"A story?"

"So when I'm in New York I can close my eyes and remember the best part about being in St. Moritz," she said dreamily. "Snow falling on the pavement and Christmas lights twinkling in chalet windows, and you telling me a story."

"I know an excellent Swiss fairy tale. It's about a kind-hearted doctor who meets a beautiful maiden. They face many obstacles, but nothing can diminish their feelings for each other." He leaned forward and his lips touched hers. "It's a long story, and first I'd like to kiss you."

Eighteen

One Day After the Fashion Show
12:00 p.m.

FELICITY SAT ACROSS FROM GABRIEL on the deck of the Panorama Restaurant and tipped her face up to the sun. The sky was bluer than she had seen it, and icicles dangled from the roof. Waiters carried carafes of champagne and orange juice, and the terrace bustled with activity.

At first she worried that the restaurant was too high up the mountain, and there wouldn't be time to pack the wedding gowns before her flight. But Nell's father insisted it was worth it, and she was glad she came. Skis lined the walls, and the table was set with platters of homemade pasta and güggeli, which Gabriel said was Swiss-German for chicken, and was the best thing she'd ever tasted.

Nell looked every inch the radiant bride with her sparkling eyes, and Eliot beamed and whispered in Nell's ear. Nell's parents were warm and effusive and kept complimenting Felicity on the collection. The best thing was sitting across from Gabriel. He looked so handsome in a green ski sweater, and whenever their eyes met a thrill ran down her spine.

"It's a pity your friend Raj couldn't join us," Patty said to

Felicity. She was wearing a red parka and ski pants, and Felicity thought she could almost pass for Nell's sister. "You said he was a marketing genius. I'd love to pick his brain on how to increase foot traffic in the bookstore."

"He's saying goodbye to Greta." Felicity grinned. "Raj isn't known for long relationships, and this one lasted a whole week. I'm sure he'd love to talk to you. If you come to New York, stop by the atelier and Raj and I will take you to lunch."

"I'd love to, but I'm afraid I won't be in New York for a while." Patty looked at Todd conspiratorially. "Todd and I are going to be busy planning Nell and Eliot's reception."

"You're doing what?" Nell put down her soupspoon. She was wearing a white sweater and the emerald earrings her father had given her for Christmas.

"The ceremony was beautiful, but your mother and I decided you need a proper reception," Todd piped up. He seemed confident and relaxed in a leather jacket and dark sunglasses. "The house in Beverly Hills needs a new roof, and we wouldn't fit everyone into my place in Malibu." He ate a bite of chicken and rösti potatoes. "So we're considering the Beverly Hills Hotel."

"You're planning our reception together?" Nell glanced at her parents and thought there was something new between them. They kept glancing fondly at each other, and her father couldn't stop smiling.

"It's going to be fun. We haven't planned a proper party in years." Patty turned to Nell. "We'll start right after we get back from Sundance. Your father invited me, and I've always wanted to go. I'll have a chance to wear the lovely skiwear I bought in St. Moritz."

"How exciting!" Felicity commented. "I'm afraid I'm going to spend January and February stuck in the showroom. Raj said orders are already coming in from the fashion show, and I have some thrilling news. Felicity Grant is going to be featured in Bergdorf Goodman's Spring Bridal Fashion Show. It's very prestigious, and I'm going to have to work awfully hard." She beamed at Gabriel. "The only days I'll leave before evening are when Gabriel comes to New York."

"Felicity, that's wonderful news! You deserve it. I didn't know Gabriel was coming to New York." Nell looked from Gabriel to Felicity. Ever since Felicity and Gabriel had stepped off the chairlift, she could sense they were an item. Gabriel was sweet and attentive, and Felicity's cheeks glowed.

"Columbia Medical Center is making advances in pediatric asthma," Gabriel said. "And Felicity promised to show me Manhattan. We're going to visit the Museum of Natural History and the Guggenheim."

Everyone kept talking, and Felicity traced the rim of her wine glass. When she was a girl she believed a Christmas miracle would be hearing reindeer hooves on the roof and spotting Santa Claus sliding down the chimney. But that wasn't the only kind of Christmas miracle. The best Christmas miracle was being with people she cared about and seeing them all happy.

"I convinced Felicity to come back to Europe in the summer," Gabriel was saying. "We'll see the fjords in Denmark and spend some time in Copenhagen."

"Why Copenhagen?" Nell inquired.

"It's the birthplace of Hans Christian Andersen." Gabriel took a large bite of gnocchi. "Felicity loves to hear fairy tales, and I've told her almost all the ones I know. We'll visit the Hans Christian Andersen Museum and read everything he's written."

"That's a wonderful idea." Felicity gazed at the skiers in their bright parkas hopping off the chairlift. She turned to Gabriel and wondered how she could be so happy. "I don't ever want to run out of fairy tales."

Acknowledgments

It is always a pleasure and a privilege to work with my agent, Melissa Flashman, and my editor, Lauren Jablonski. Thank you to the whole team at St. Martin's Press: Karen Masnica, Brittani Hilles, Brant Janeway, Jennifer Enderlin, and Jennifer Weis.

Thank you to Traci Whitney, Sara Sullivan, Laura Narbutas, and Andrea Katz for always being there. And thank you to my children: Alex, Andrew, Heather, Madeleine, and Thomas for creating the magic in my life.

Discussion Questions

1. Felicity and Adam get into a fight on Christmas because she is expecting an engagement ring and Adam isn't ready because he is putting all his energy into his business. Who do you think is correct and why?

2. Nell doesn't tell her father and mother about the other being in St. Moritz. Would you have kept it a secret? Could Nell have chosen another way to resolve the issues between her parents?

3. How do you feel about Gabriel's relationship with Felicity in the beginning? Do you think they started as friends, or were there romantic sparks when they met?

4. St. Moritz is a magical location and Felicity is hoping for a Christmas miracle. Have you ever been anywhere that felt magical, and if so, where?

5. Being a wedding dress designer seems like a dream career, but it actually involves long days and very hard work. Are you living your dream occupation, and if so, has it lived up to your expectations?

6. Give your thoughts on Todd. Do you think he was right in the way he protected Alistair or would you have done something different in his situation?

7. What are your observations on Gabriel and Felicity's relationship at the end of the book? Do you think their romance will last, and why or why not?

8. Where do you see Todd and Patty a year from now? Do you think they will get back together permanently?

9. Can you imagine Gabriel living in New York or Felicity living in Europe? Where do you see them in five years?

10. Name something in your life that you wanted more than anything. Did it actually happen, and if it did, did it make you as happy as you thought it would?

HANDBOOK

DISCARD

COMBAT TERRORISM

FOREIGN AND DOMESTIC

STEPS AND PROCEDURES TO PROTECT YOURSELF